THE TRIDENT SERIES

ACE

Book 1

_____

By: Jaime Lewis

The Trident Series - ACE
Copyright © 2020 by Jaime Lewis

ISBN: 978-1-952734-01-4

Table of Contents

PROLOGUE

Afghanistan – Two Years Ago

Inhaling, she was overcome with the thick smoke that filled her nostrils. It was thick and made it hard to breathe. A light caress of a large hand swept across her forehead before a familiar voice echoed in the distance.

"Alex, can you hear me? Come on Alex!"

It was a voice she would recognize anywhere, and she was confused as the voice brought her back to reality. In her scattered thoughts, she searched for an explanation for Bert's presence. He hadn't been on the op; he was supposed to be manning the office back in Washington.

"Open your damn eyes, Alex!"

Her head was hurting so badly she wished he would stop shouting. The pain was so intense, and she couldn't understand what was wrong with her. Why was everything in her vision black?

"Sir, we need to get her on the chopper now."

She wondered who was with Bert and why she would need a helicopter. Was she and the team leaving to go home? Again, confusion wracked her brain as the throbbing pain continued to wreak havoc in her head.

"What's wrong with her? Why isn't she responding?"

"I don't know, sir. We'll know more once she's been evaluated. This burn near her hip requires treatment ASAP. Not knowing how close she was to the blast zone there's no telling if there's any major head trauma or internal injuries. I've got the IV-line in, but we have to move her now!"

1

She could hear the two men as they spoke about burns and head trauma. If she could just speak with her team, they could explain what was happening. Her body was jostled, and the movement caused her stomach to revolt. She felt like she was going to be sick. Her eyelids stuck together as if they were glued shut, but little by little she managed to pry them open.

"Stop! Look, she's trying to open her eyes! Oh god, Alex. Look at me, look at me!"

"Bert…" Her voice came out raspy and her throat had felt as if she had swallowed shards of glass.

"Stay with me. Keep talking, Alex. You're safe now. We're getting you to a hospital."

"Bert…the others…where are the others?" She was in so much pain that even speaking was an agonizing feat.

"There was an explosion, I'm so sorry Alex. They're gone."

She didn't understand. What explosion was Bert talking about? She was just with the team. They were playing cards while dinner was cooking. They were making plans for when they returned home. The last thing she remembered was getting a phone call and walking out the back door. What was she missing? Suddenly pieces started coming together. She wasn't far from the door when a bright flash of light blinded her. The next second, she was being thrown in the air. Her breath caught in her throat when the realization hit her. Someone had blown up the house.

CHAPTER ONE

The violent jerk of the plane jolted Alex from the painful nightmare. Her heart pounded in her chest as she desperately gasped for air. Leaning forward in her seat, she sucked in a few deep breaths as she tried to fill her lungs with oxygen and calm her breathing before a full panic attack travelled through her body. She lifted her hand to her throat, feeling it constrict. *No, no, no. Not now and not here.*

She dropped her head between her knees, then closed her eyes as she tried to control her breathing using the techniques she found useful in the past when these attacks made their ugly appearance. The problem was they weren't always effective depending on the severity.

After a couple of tense and eerily quiet minutes, her anxiety symptoms started to diminish and ever so slowly she sat up, making sure to keep her eyes closed. She wasn't ready to face the eyes of those on the small plane with her who had seen her at her worst. Gulping down her last shred of pride, she took a small peek and was surprised she hadn't alerted the three men sitting near the front of the plane. From her vantage point, she could see they had their heads buried in the massive piles of papers in their laps.

Going by the heat in her cheeks, she knew her face was probably a few shades of red. This had been a concern of hers ever since she answered that damn phone call. Having to come back to the place that left her with nightmares and scars was bound to cause those memories to resurface. It had been months since her last episode. At least then she had been at home and not in the presence of others.

She thought two years would've been enough time to get her head on straight after that shit show of a mission. But now she wondered if there would ever be a day she wasn't reminded of that ill-fated evening when she and her team were hunted down and attacked.

She reached for the bottle of water from the drink holder and took a few sips, wetting her parched mouth. She thought about how close she came to telling her boss no when he asked her about this assignment. Now she wished she had "accidentally" misplaced her phone. Especially considering she was only a day and a half into her dream vacation. She shook her head remembering she had just sat down on the lounge chair to soak up some sun when she heard that ringtone that only meant one thing. She was needed for a job.

She couldn't really complain since it was her job. Being an Intel analyst had its pros and cons. Unfortunately for her, because of her background and fluency in multiple languages including dialects in the Middle East, she was called upon regularly.

She had resigned her position with the NSA after what the government called a botched mission two years ago. It had been the best decision, because after returning home, she soon realized that those individuals she thought had her back didn't, including her former boss. Not too long after her resignation she had been offered a job with her current employer, Mason Whittemore, and she took it without a backward glance. She still lived in Annapolis, Maryland, just a couple of hours from her hometown, Virginia Beach, and worked out of her house; well, that was when she was actually home. Mason's company did a lot of work under the radar which meant most of her assignments took her out of the country. At first, she tried keeping a low profile and focused on analytical work, but that didn't last long. Mason was a former Special Forces soldier and wasn't stupid. Having worked along-side him on prior assignments while she was still with the government, he knew her talents and capabilities. She was fluent in multiple languages and was sought after in the intelligence community. She was constantly turning

4

down job offers from other government agencies as well as competing private firms. She was content working for Mason. He was a good boss and friend as long as you worked hard. This was why she couldn't say no to him when he called her, even though he explained to her he would understand if she wanted to decline.

Now she was in a plane heading back to the one country she swore she would never step foot in again, and along for the ride sitting just feet from her was the man she hoped she never had to associate herself with again. Unfortunately, she wasn't given the choice to cherry-pick who the government sent as their representative. Bert McMahon was a callous man who positioned himself before his team. She had worked under Bert for a few years, and even though he had some minor faults in his character, she had been blindsided when he turned his back on her the moment she needed his support the most. After the shit show, she went through, upon her return stateside after that mission, she had learned the hard way that Bert truly was a one-man show and didn't know the definition of the word team even if it was imprinted in his brain. Her respect for him diminished when he aligned himself with what the government thought happened when they decided she and her team were derelict in their duties. She knew then she wouldn't work for someone or an agency who wasn't honest or loyal to their employees. Not to mention throughout their working relationship he had made it known he wanted her in his bed. He went so far to even claim it was the norm in the world they operated in. He even had the audacity to ask her out on a date, after she resigned. *Creep!*

She didn't miss the subtle glances he'd been sneaking when he thought she wasn't paying attention. She knew that her silence was driving him crazy, considering the last time she had spoken to him was when she gave her notice. Thankfully, his colleagues with him had kept him confined to his seat.

Even though she couldn't choose who the government sent, she could certainly control her contact with him. When she brought up her concerns, Mason was adamant that Bert and his team were only there to provide support and act as a communication liaison for the government. As Mason put it, he was sort of working for her. She couldn't wait for the first opportunity to get a little payback. She wouldn't stoop to his level; she would, of course, be professional about it, but as the saying goes, karma is a bitch.

She had a lot riding on this assignment and not to mention the lives of five men were at stake. She didn't want to disappoint, nor did she want Bert getting his panties in a twist and causing issues for her. In her mindset, this was also a chance to redeem herself in the eyes of the government and prove to them they had made a huge mistake in letting her walk away.

A couple of days ago, five US security contractors were believed to be kidnapped in the middle of the night. They were part of a team hired to secure a weapons facility for Afghani security forces. The group responsible had also walked away with millions of dollars' worth of weapons—weapons that were paid for by the American government. She was sought out by the government because of her extensive knowledge and background of the suspected leader of the terrorist organization believed to be responsible.

The main suspect happened to be the same man that made her life hell for the past two years. The same man who claimed responsibility for the deaths of her five colleagues. Nobody else inside the government had the knowledge she possessed on Ashraf Fayed. After her team's failed attempt to bring him in, he dropped off the radar, until now. Her one goal in life after she had been released from the hospital was that if she was ever given the opportunity to face Ashraf again, she wanted to be the one who would end him.

She looked down at her watch; they still had a few more hours before they landed. She might as well try and get some more sleep. God only knows how much sleep she'd get once they got started. She reclined the seat and made herself comfortable, letting the hum of the plane's engines lull her into sleep with hopes of no more nightmares.

CHAPTER TWO

As the plane's tires bounced down the runway Alex released the large breath she had been holding. She didn't mind flying per se, it was the takeoffs and landings that jumbled her nerves. Once the plane came to a stop, she powered on her phone and scrolled through a couple of new messages. One was from Mason's office, so she listened to it and smiled when she heard her friend's voice.

"Hey Alex, its Bowman. By the time you get this, you'll have landed. But I wanted to give you a heads up that the team assigned to your operation is en route and should be meeting up with you at Bagram. Should be interesting. Anyways if you need anything give me a shout. Take care."

Dang, it had completely slipped her mind about the specialized team being brought in to assist. She wondered what Bowman meant when he said, "it should be interesting." She didn't miss the slight humor in his voice either.

Shaking her head, she reached for her backpack by her feet then pulled her boots and socks out. She took off her flip flops and placed them in her bag. She'd wear flip-flops twenty-four-seven if she could, but the flip-flops weren't the best choice of footwear with the terrain in this part of the world. After slipping her socks and boots on, she pulled up her left pant leg and strapped a knife to her ankle.

"I see you haven't changed when it comes to your safety. You were always prepared. My imagination can only wonder what other surprises you're hiding under there."

When she looked up she saw Bert standing there, his eyes raking over her body like some sex addict waiting to get his next fix. *What a sicko!* Thankfully, the jeans she wore covered her legs. The only skin showing was her shoulders and arms in the tank top, but she'd rectify that once she slipped on her button-up shirt.

She dropped her gaze back to the knife, entertaining thoughts of sticking the sharp object into his back just as he had done to her. She didn't feel the need to respond to his nasty comments, but sometimes she just couldn't hold her tongue. "It's fun to leave people guessing what I'm carrying and where." She glanced back up and couldn't help the slight grin when he narrowed his eyes at her. He looked like he wanted to say something but the gentlemen traveling with Bert interrupted their reunion.

"Excuse me, but someone from the base commander's office is outside. He said he wanted to speak with you."

"Tell him I'll be there in just a minute," Bert replied arrogantly never taking his cold eyes off her.

"Umm…He asked for Ms. Hardesty, sir."

She reigned in her smile at the shocked expression on Bert's face. Ignoring the angry man next to her, she adjusted the knife and slid her pant leg into place, before standing and gathering her belongings.

As soon as she stepped off the plane the hot dry air hit her skin sending a tremor through her body. She forced her rigid muscles to move even though they begged her to walk no further. Reality had set in and a funny sensation swirled around in her belly, and not in a good kind of way. Not wanting to cause a scene or look weak, she pretended she was looking through her backpack for her sunglasses while she talked herself off the ledge. Finding her sunglasses, she pulled them from the bag and put them on. The wind at that precise moment whipped around, blowing the fine dust this part of the world was known for everywhere. That was another thing she hadn't missed about this place; the mess the dust created. Those damn tiny granules found their way into everything.

She shook hands and introduced herself to the Sgt. He informed her that her "team" had already arrived and were anxiously waiting to meet her. Since Bagram was just a stop-over, he pointed out the area where she was to meet up with the convoy she would be hitching a ride with. The forward operating base, Camp Sunshine was about a two-hour drive from Bagram on some of the most treacherous roads within the region. In the last few weeks alone there had an uptick in convoys being ambushed as they traveled through.

With no further questions, she excused herself and took her bags over to the pick-up corral. She glanced at her watch and saw she had a little time to kill so she headed toward the mess hall to get a small bite to eat to tide her over until dinner. Bert and his two shadows decided to go in the opposite direction looking for a colleague of theirs. The last thing she needed was for him to be breathing down her neck the entire trip. Just that thought gave her the shivers.

As she made her way into the building, she came to a halt just inside the doors. Damn, they must either be serving something really good or people were just hungry because it was wall to wall people. She strategically moved about the room bustling with activity, weaving in-between tables and people.

She passed by a table of Special Ops guys and nodded her head in greeting. The one guy on the end looked up and nodded back before returning to his conversation. If you didn't know the traits of Special Forces soldiers most people would think they were just ordinary soldiers. But, thanks to her upbringing, she could spot them a mile away.

Her dad was a Navy SEAL. Tragically, he was killed in action when she was only six years old, leaving her with no immediate family. Her mother was no longer in the picture after having walked out on both her dad and her when she was just a baby. Unselfishly, her dad's best friend and teammate stepped in and claimed guardianship of her. Derek was still active duty, serving as a commander of his own SEAL team in Little Creek, Virginia.

As she moved deeper into the building it became even more crowded, to the point it made her uncomfortable. She was borderline claustrophobic and being only five-foot-three and finding herself in a crowd of people that towered over her kicked up her anxiety. Looking around for a path she finally gave up. By the time she made it to where the food was, she wouldn't have time to eat.

She had seen a side door earlier and knew that was her best bet in getting out of the chaos. In her quest to exit the building she made an abrupt one-eighty but wasn't prepared for the person who had been standing right behind her. As she bounced off the rather extra-large person she stumbled backward and lost her balance. Her arms windmilled around, and she tried to reach for something to grab onto so she wouldn't fall on her ass and make a fool of herself in front of everyone. When she thought nothing was going to save her, two muscled arms wrapped around her waist and hoisted her back up.

She gasped when her chest met his firm body. She tilted her head back and her breath caught in her throat when her eyes locked onto one very gorgeous man staring down at her. He stood over six feet with broad shoulders, jet black hair that was a little longer than military regulation and had a pair of blue eyes that drew her in immediately. He screamed sexy in a rugged way and she couldn't help the smile she gave him,

"Hi."

He smiled back, his eyes crinkling at the corners, "Hi." He replied in a low raspy voice.

She stood perfectly still as she couldn't pull her gaze from his eyes. She was captivated by the blue orbs. His thick black eyelashes made the blue irises pop. He shifted on his feet making her realize she was still wrapped up in his arms, and she was holding onto his arms. She started to feel awkward standing in the middle of the mess hall as if the two of them had just been named prom king and queen and were beginning their dance. But damn did it feel good to be held by those arms. She shook her head. *Oh, for heaven's sake, what is wrong with me?*

She tried untangling herself from him, but it seemed she only made matters worse because the crowd around them grew larger. Someone bumped into her from behind, forcing her closer to the man holding her up.

"Hang on." Was all he said and with no warning, her feet were off the ground and she clutched his shoulders as he moved them both out of the mosh pit to an area less crowded along the wall.

She gasped when her back hit the wall and he set her down. He grinned. "That was fun."

Fun? She wasn't sure about fun, but she knew her face probably showed how embarrassed she was, and she started rambling. Something she didn't do very often.

"I'm so sorry. I wasn't paying attention and didn't see you. I've never seen it so crowded in here before. Are you okay?"

He chuckled, appearing amused, but didn't release his hold on her. "It's all good, are *you* okay?"

No! "Yes, I'm fine." *As long as I don't look into your eyes or listen to your voice, I'll be fine.* He had one of those deep raspy voices that made her insides melt and gave her goosebumps.

Amusement twinkled in his eyes and the corners of his mouth twitched upward, "That was a pretty hard collision. Are you sure we don't need to exchange insurance information, phone numbers maybe?"

She could feel the redness creeping up her neck and into her face. But she also knew his type and that angered her knowing she fell for his charm. He chuckled, again, then released her and without another word turned and walked away, leaving her standing there staring at his back. She shook her head. *What in the hell just happened?*

She took a couple of breaths before starting towards the door she had been trying to get to. Just as she was about to push the door open, she picked up a weird vibe. Taking a quick glance over her shoulder her breath hitched as she met those familiar blue eyes staring back at her from across the room. Not wanting to further embarrass herself she quickly made a beeline for the exit as if her ass was on fire.

As she made her way back toward the convoy she tried to think about the upcoming assignment, but it was hard to when her subconscious kept throwing up images of the blue-eyed stranger. What bothered her was how flustered she felt. She could go toe-to-toe with some of the meanest sons of bitches on the planet and not blink an eye. But, one look into a particular set of blue eyes had her heart pumping double time.

She was checking her emails as she passed by a group of men and had to roll her eyes behind her sunglasses when one of them whistled. *Sorry, buddy, ain't that kind of woman.* Ignoring their teenage hormonal behavior, she trucked on until a familiar voice stopped her dead in her tracks.

"Are you seriously just going to walk right on by and ignore me?"

There was no way it could be him, she thought to herself. Although with their careers, it wouldn't have been a complete surprise if their paths had crossed. She turned toward the voice and there was no stopping the huge smile from spreading across her face.

"Oh my, gosh, Stitch!" She sprinted over toward him and when she was close enough and knew he would catch her she leaped into his open arms. She hugged him tightly. They'd been friends since they were both in diapers. There were four of them who grew up together and were still best friends to this day. But this guy was like a brother to her. Both him and Frost were SEALs, and ironically were assigned to the team under her uncle's command. It had been over a year, maybe close to two years since she had seen either one of them. Being constantly on the go with their jobs and living in separate states made it hard to get together often. Hell, she didn't get to spend enough time with her best friend Tenley, and she was a nurse. She suddenly felt a little emotional and blinked to dispel the moisture from her eyes.

He squeezed her tight then kissed the top of her head. "I have missed you so much."

She sniffled and knew she had to rein in her emotions before she became a blubbering mess. Normally she wasn't the mushy, easy to cry type of woman. But when it came to family that was her soft spot. "I've missed you too."

He set her down and took a step back as three other men walked up and stood beside him. Stitch introduced them as teammates of his.

"This is Dino, Skittles, and Diego. Guys, meet Alex. Derek's daughter."

She shook their hands. "Hello, it's nice to meet you."

"It's a pleasure to meet you as well, honey," Dino said and gave her a smile that would make women's panties fall right off.

"Damn, this just made my day. What brings you to this part of the world?" Stitch asked and she gave him a funny look before he chuckled. He knew she wouldn't divulge that type of information, but she would give him credit for trying.

"I should ask you the same thing." She grinned back at him.

He smiled. "Touché."

"Are you staying or just passing through?"

14

"Passing through. How about you?"

"The same." She looked at her watch and damned the time as she would love to stay and catch up with him, but she needed to get going. "I wish I had more time to stay and talk, but I need to get going or I'm liable to miss my ride." And she was confident that if given the chance Bert would leave her high and dry without a backward glance.

"Me too. Damn, Frost is going to be pissed that he missed you."

"Frost is here too?"

"Yeah, he and the rest of the team are here somewhere."

"Shoot. Will you tell him I said hi and I'm sorry I missed him?" She was disappointed as she would have loved to have seen Frost as well, even if it were just for a few minutes.

"I will, sweetie." He stepped forward and gave her another hug and she snuggled against him. She missed this. She missed her friends. Hell, she missed just having a life. "It was so good to see you. Maybe one of these days our schedules will mesh, and we can get together." He told her as he released her.

"I'd like that."

"Be safe."

"I always try."

She started to walk away, and she quickly put on her sunglasses because she felt the waterworks coming on. Seeing Stitch hit a nerve and made her realize how much she missed home. Once she was clear and around the backside of the building where she was supposed to meet her ride, only then did she let one tear escape. But she was quick to wipe away the evidence before anyone saw.

Lt. Commander Marcus "Ace" Chambers made his way through the crowd of people. He was in a foul mood after getting off the phone with his mom back in Oklahoma. His oldest sister, Mikayla

15

who was pregnant with her second child went into labor prematurely. From what his mom explained, the last two months for his sister had been difficult. The doctors had her on bed rest to try and alleviate the symptoms. Between the extremely high blood pressure and the fluid she was retaining, her doctors thought it was best to induce labor. Ace had hoped he would be stateside when she had the baby but because of unforeseen issues during the team's latest mission their deployment had been extended. And, now they were being reassigned to aid in the search and rescue of a group of security contractors who had been kidnapped. This was what he signed up for when he joined the Navy and he did love his job, but that didn't stop the guilt he felt at times. His family understood and always made it a point to remind him of monumental times like this when he couldn't be there.

The only positive from the call was that it led him to the mess hall wanting to grab a cup of coffee before he met up with the rest of the guys. If he wouldn't have, he never would've bumped into that woman. He rubbed his jaw as his thoughts kept going back to the green-eyed sprite who took his breath away. The moment his hands touched her body he felt a spark. It was like nothing else he had experienced before. He had to smile at the way her tanned cheeks turned a nice pink color. She looked so innocent and he was stunned at the instant attraction he had felt. She wasn't in uniform, so he wondered if she was a civilian contractor. The fact that she was carrying didn't go unnoticed either. He felt the small weapon tucked against her back in the waistband of her jeans which added to her appeal. A woman who was skilled in weaponry was a huge turn on.

Ace saw Frost and Potter hanging out by the door. He scratched his head before looking over his shoulder hoping to get one last glimpse of the sexy brunette who stirred something inside of him.

He couldn't get over how incredible the woman's eyes were. The deep green irises were the perfect color against her complexion and dark hair.

"Who are you looking for?" Frost asked as they walked outside.

"Nobody." It wasn't like he was going to see her again so why dwell on it.

Potter chuckled beside him and Ace gave him a sideways look wondering what was up with his best friend.

"I think the Lt. Commander just fell in love." Ace whipped his head around and stared at Potter who looked ready to burst at the seams.

"You saw her, too?"

Potter barked out a deep laugh. "Who didn't is the question you should be asking. I think she turned the heads of every male in that room."

"You met a woman? When? I didn't see anyone." Frost exclaimed trying to look back into the mess hall through the open door.

Ace waved them off. "It doesn't matter. I'll never see her again." That bothered him because he sure as hell wanted to see her again. He wanted to ask her name, where she lived, and why on earth she was here.

"Maybe you will, maybe you won't. Maybe it was fate."

"Since when did you become fucking Cupid?" Ace said turning to Potter.

Potter threw his hands up in the air in mock defense. "Hey, I'm just saying. You never know."

They walked through the base until they met up with others.

"Damn Ace, you look flustered. What's wrong? Did the mess hall run out of coffee?" Irish teased and Frost chuckled.

"Ace met a woman."

"You met a woman?" Stitch asked as if he was now surprised.

"Jesus, you fuckers make it sound like I don't date."

"Well, you really don't."

"Hey, speaking of women, Frost, you'll never guess who you just missed."

"Who?"

"Alex."

"Our Alex?" Frost replied and Stitch nodded. "What in the hell is she doing here?"

"Don't know and she didn't say. According to her, she's just passing through. She said to tell you hi."

Ace didn't miss the concerned look that passed between Stitch and Frost.

"Who's Alex?"

Stitch smiled. "A friend we grew up with."

"No shit. What branch of the service is she in?"

Stitch laughed. "None. She's freelance for a private firm."

Ace nodded his head. He'd heard Stitch and Frost talk about their friend. Then it dawned on him.

"Is that the commander's daughter?" He asked and Stitch nodded his head. Ace had never seen a picture of her, but the commander talked highly about her. She must be good at what she does to be over this way.

"Where did she go?" Frost asked looking around as if he was going to spot her.

"Don't know. She was running late and needed to go."

Ace glanced at his watch. "Well, we better get a move on it or we're going to miss our ride."

As they rounded the corner of a building, Ace heard Frost say something before he took off into a sprint. When he looked in the direction of where Frost ran off to, Ace came to an abrupt halt when he spotted a woman leaning against one of the vehicles. His chest tightened when he realized it was her, the brunette from earlier. She appeared deep in thought as she typed away on her phone until Frost called out to her and she looked up and smiled. Jesus, she was breathtaking.

Potter's voice pulled him out of his head. "You okay, man?"

He glanced over at Potter then nodded his head toward the woman. "It's her."

When they looked back Frost had the woman lifted into the air hugging her. Then it hit him. His mystery woman he had a hard-on for was his commander's daughter. *Fuck me!*

Alex couldn't stop smiling as she hugged Frost. He lifted her off her feet and twirled her around. Her brain was still trying to process the fact that Stitch and Frost were both here in Afghanistan at the same time she was. Now that she got to see Frost it brightened up her day.

"Damn, woman you look really good." He told her as he set her back down.

She couldn't stop grinning. "Thanks. I was upset when I had missed you earlier. I'm so glad I got to see you."

Being it had been a while since she'd spoken with him or Stitch, she was consumed with the conversation and didn't realize they had company until she sensed movement behind her. She turned to the left and her eyes widened in shock when it dawned on her that the guy standing next to her was the guy from the mess hall. He had removed his long sleeve shirt he was wearing earlier, leaving him in just a tan t-shirt that clung to his torso and well-defined biceps. He was broader than Stitch and Frost and her mouth started to water as she remembered how her body felt being held in those masculine arms.

"We meet again." He spoke in that raspy voice that turned her into a puddle of goo.

She smiled up at him and felt her heart skip a beat when he removed his sunglasses and her eyes met the blue of his.

"Seems so." She replied.

Reaching to shake her hand he smiled, "I'm Lt. Commander Marcus Chambers. The guys call me Ace."

As soon as his large hand enveloped hers, she felt a zing right to her core and holy hotcakes did her insides start to warm. That feeling stunned her for a brief moment and she looked up into those baby blue eyes again. She saw a flare in his gaze, but it passed just as quickly, and she wondered if she had just imagined it or if he had felt something too.

Remembering they weren't alone, she cleared her throat and reluctantly pulled her hand away. "I'm Alex. It's nice to meet you." She apologized again for running into him earlier. Not that she would mind bumping into him again. "I swear I'm not clumsy, it's just that sometimes the floor hates me, the tables and chairs are bullies, and in your case, people just get in my way." He let out a bark of laughter and she wanted to melt at the sound.

"Wait, you two met? When?" Stitch asked looking between her and Ace.

"Over at the mess hall. Right before I bumped into you," she said.

Stitch squinted his eyes as he looked at Ace. But then a slow smile crept upon his face. Alex sensed there was some sort of silent communication going on between the two men, but about what she hadn't a clue.

"Well, now that you two have been properly introduced, would you like to meet the rest of the team?" She pulled her gaze from the god next to her and looked over and saw the amusement on Stitch's face. Her best friend knew she was totally checking out his team leader. Oh hell, they all probably knew it.

Stitch made the introductions starting with Potter, the team's second in command. Just before she shook his hand, Potter smirked at Ace as if trying to hold back a laugh.

"What's so funny?" She asked on the defensive.

"Nothing, sweetheart. It is a pleasure to finally meet you. We've all only heard great things about you from the commander."

She eyed him over, knowing there was more to the story, but before she could respond, Stitch continued down the line. Some she had met earlier. Diego, she learned was an explosives expert. Irish, with blonde hair and blue eyes was the team's sniper, and seemed like the comedian of the group. Then there was Skittles, the team's intelligence specialist and tech guru. He looked a lot younger than the rest of the guys. And lastly was Dino who as Stitch put it, could kick anyone's ass in hand-to-hand combat.

They were all attractive men, but her focus kept zeroing in on one in particular. One she wouldn't mind getting wet and sandy with. She stole another glance in his direction and again locked eyes with him. *Dammit!* This was so out of character of her. She had been around and worked with plenty of good-looking men during her career, but never once had she felt the pull she got with this guy. Why now?

Pulling her gaze from his she glanced at the group. "It's nice to meet you all."

"The way you hauled ass earlier, I thought you'd be long gone by now," Stitch said.

"I'm still waiting on the others. They should be here any minute."

Stitch looked at Ace. "Do you know who we were supposed to meet?"

Ace pulled out his phone, "The POC says the guy's name is Alex."

Suddenly everyone got quiet and Alex found herself placed in the spotlight as she realized their point of contact was her. Holy shit! This was the team she was going to be working with. The funny part was Ace thought Alex was a guy. Surprise!

"I guess I've been waiting on you guys," she said grinning, but still partially shocked these guys were *the team*.

Ace looked at her. "I thought you worked for a private firm. This says there should be three agents from the agency."

She looked up at Ace and thankfully he had put the sunglasses back on. "I do work for a private firm. However, I'm the lead for this assignment. Those men you're referring to are on loan from the NSA. I was a last-minute addition you could say."

"Is that so?"

"Is that a problem for you, Lt. Commander?" She challenged and Ace grinned.

"No, ma'am."

"Good, then we should all get along just fine."

"This just keeps getting better and better," Potter laughingly said as he walked to one of the other vehicles.

Alex looked at Stitch. "What is he talking about?"

Stitch shook his head as he too snorted a laugh. "Nothing." He playfully bumped her shoulder. "I've been waiting for the day we got to work together."

Her smile slowly faded as his words sunk in. "Wait, if I'm working with you guys, then that means I'll also be working with Derek. Oh shit, I wonder if he knew." Even though Derek never expressed his opinion on her career choice, she knew he wasn't exactly excited when she informed him that she had been recruited by the NSA right after college. What he didn't know wouldn't bother him so that was how she kept it. But she knew he worried about her. If her uncle knew half the shit she found herself in over the years he'd probably lock her in a room and throw away the key.

She and Stitch both looked at Ace for an answer, but he shrugged his shoulders. "I doubt it, or I'm sure he would've let us know."

Ace was having a hard time digesting the news that the woman he'd been lusting after for the last thirty or so minutes was not only the commander's daughter, but also the Intel Analyst he was going to be working side-by-side with. Jesus, Potter was right, this was getting better and better. He just hoped he didn't fuck things up.

Knowing they needed to get on the road, Ace was about to start rounding up the troops when three men approached the vehicles, and right off the bat Ace got a bad vibe from the guy dressed in the neatly pressed khaki pants and button-up dress shirt with the sleeves rolled. He reminded Ace of some hoity-toity CEO that graced the covers of magazines. But when the guy walked over and put his hand on Alex's shoulder, his curiosity heightened.

Ace stepped closer just as he heard the guy ask her where she had been, and Ace wondered why it mattered. It wasn't like Alex was a child. He did however have to reign in his temper when the guy pulled off his sunglasses and blatantly raked his eyes up and down Alex's body, and he could tell from Alex's response she didn't appreciate the guy's show of admiration. Ace couldn't blame her. Yes, Alex was a beautiful woman, but damn, show the woman some respect. When she took a step back putting some distance between them, Ace used the opportunity to help her out.

"You must be the agents from the agency. I'm Lt. Commander Chambers," Ace interjected and held his hand out to the guy.

The guy shook his hand. "Bert McMahon. This is Mical and Roland, both are non-agents. At least for now. They are a part of a

23

new program the agency implemented and will be shadowing me."
Ace gave the two much younger guys a once over and swore the
kids looked like they just graduated high school.

"What team are you with?" Bert asked.

"Does it matter?" Ace replied with a bit of attitude. If his agency
didn't tell him specifics, then he sure as hell wasn't going to offer
any. When Bert's posture straightened and he clenched his jaw, Ace
knew he had hit a nerve with the guy. Anyone who studied body
language could sense this guy thought he was the shit. If he had to
guess, his eyes that were hiding behind the dark aviator sunglasses
were shooting daggers at him right this very second.

"I guess it doesn't, just as long as we all agree we're on the same
team." Ace narrowed his eyes. "For this mission at least. Isn't that
right, Alex?" Bert said trying to close the gap in-between him and
Alex. But it was clear by the look on Alex's face that she wasn't
comfortable around the guy, and suddenly Ace had a strange
protective feeling come over him and he stepped into Bert's path
before he could reach Alex. He didn't want to start anything, but he
also didn't want this guy bothering Alex when it was clear she was
uneasy around him. Once he got her alone, he would find out why.

"It's getting late and we're already behind schedule, so let's all
head to the vehicles and roll out," Ace said to the group but made it
clear to Bert that he wasn't getting access to Alex. At least not right
now.

Alex stepped up beside him. "I agree, Lt. Commander." She
looked up and threw a beautiful smile his way.

He smirked, then gestured to the awaiting vehicles. "After you,
boss." He couldn't help it and he loved the reaction he got from her.
The smile on her face and the sound of her soft laughter was
priceless. The precious look was short-lived as Bert approached
again and tried to convince Alex to move to his vehicle.

Jesus, he thought the agencies only hired smart people. Clearly, this guy wasn't getting the message.

Her quick and snappy reply had everyone's head turning. "You think it's best?" She reared back.

"Yeah, I do. You know, so we can talk."

She looked as if she were considering and Ace held his breath, hoping she wouldn't cave. Was it bad he was feeling selfish and wanted her with him?

"The only subject we need to discuss is this mission, and since I consider all of us here a team, I think it would be best to hold off on that *talk* until all team members can be present. That is unless you know of a bigger vehicle that all of us can squeeze into."

When Bert didn't respond, Stitch ushered Alex into the back of the vehicle, and Ace had to hide his laugh when he heard her mumble something about how she didn't have time for assholes with egos.

Bert started to say something but Stitch slammed the door in his face signaling that the conversation was over. Bert looked to Ace and Ace lowered his sunglasses, pinning Bert with a look that told him to back off. Receiving the silent message, Bert stormed off and got into one of the other vehicles. Ace took notice when Potter slipped inside the front passenger seat of the same vehicle as Bert. He smiled as he was quite sure Potter would get a read on the asshole and report back to him.

Ace slid into the front passenger seat and closed his eyes as he got a whiff of Alex's scent. Christ, two hours trapped in the vehicle with her coconut scented perfume or lotion was going to drive him crazy.

ॐ

Alex's patience was heading down a slippery slope as she climbed into the back seat and wedged herself in-between Stitch and

Frost. Bert just didn't know when to quit. She was trying to be professional, but she knew damn well that the mission was the last thing he wanted to talk to her about. He was acting as if he actually cared. But she wasn't stupid. Bert was only considerate when he wanted something. She instantly suspected he was up to something.

As Ace slid into the passenger seat, she pushed aside Bert's antics, at least for now. She owed Ace a huge thank you for intervening. Apparently, he had picked up on her agitation with her former boss.

Ace turned in the seat and pinned her with a look, and she was preparing herself for the onslaught of questions she knew was coming, but instead, she beat him to the punch.

"Thanks for your help back there."

She had surprised him as his frown turned into a small grin.

"What's the deal with your friend?"

Friend? Was he referring to Bert as her friend? *As if!*

She narrowed her eyes. "Bert is an old colleague, and nowhere near a friend."

She turned to look out the window but was met with Stitch's frown.

"What?"

"That's it? Just an old colleague? I call bullshit."

She sighed. "Stitch…" He arched his eyebrow and she knew she couldn't lie to him. But at the same time, she wasn't ready to go down memory lane. "Look, it's a long story and not one I want to get into now."

"But you will explain, later." He told her leaving no room for an argument.

"Yes."

When all three men seemed to be appeased with her answer, she pulled her iPod from her bag. With the sound of country music

26

filling her ears, she tried to focus on the road in front of their vehicle but instead, she ended up locking gazes with Ace. She felt the scrutiny from his eyes alone and knew Stitch and Frost weren't the only ones who would be asking questions later. With nowhere else to look she opted for the safe bet and closed her eyes as the music started to play, sending her into a relaxed state.

Alex felt her body being shifted and her eyes popped open.

"Have a nice nap," Frost said, smiling down at her. She must have moved in her sleep because her head was now resting against his side. Thank God she hadn't drooled or that would have been embarrassing. Although he'd seen her in much worse conditions, like the night they all snuck out and got drunk and the night ended with Stitch holding her hair back while she puked in the neighbor's bushes.

She sat up and was trying to adjust her shirt that had ridden up on the one side when Stitch peered down at her. His lips twitched.

"When did you get a tattoo?"

Damn, she hadn't realized the shirt had come up that far. He was referring to the quote she had inked on her skin to help conceal the scar from the injury she sustained during that last mission. The quote read, *"That which doesn't kill us, only makes us stronger."*

"Last year," She replied and then saw the base up ahead and changed the subject. Stitch and Frost knew she had been injured but they didn't know the specifics.

While they unloaded their gear from the vehicles, Colonel Johnson, the base commander, and his staff stopped by to greet them. She already knew she'd get along great with him. The longer they spoke with him, the more he reminded her of her uncle Derek. He went over some basic information and explained where certain areas were located on the base, such as the gym and mess hall.

"We've set up an area on the east side of the base that is more isolated. There are three buildings. Two larger ones have been converted into barracks. Lt., your team can choose whichever one you'd like, and then there is a smaller building like an efficiency apartment for you, Alex. I'll have Staff Sergeant Hill show you to the area. If you need anything, please don't hesitate to get a hold of myself or my staff."

"Excuse me, sir? How about the other gentlemen? Where will they be staying?" Alex asked, silently hoping Bert would be housed as far away as possible from her.

The Colonel squinted his eyes as if he knew what she was thinking. "I've already spoken to Mason and he filled me in on the history between you and Mr. McMahon. Mr. McMahon will be housed on the opposite side of the base." He nodded toward Bert and the other two who were still unloading their things. "I'll have one of the other staff members show them to their quarters."

She smirked. Mason was awesome. She would make sure to remember to repay the favor with a brand-new bottle of aged Glenfiddich. "Perfect."

"Well, I won't hold you up any longer. I'm sure you all would like to get settled. I've cleared a room for your team to use over at base command. It should be equipped with everything you need. If not, just let my staff know and we'll try our best to accommodate." He put his sunglasses on and turned on his heel, walking away.

Alex bent down to pick up her bag when she heard her name called. She looked around and saw the Colonel waving her over. Irish was next to her and took her bag. "Go ahead, we'll wait."

"Sir?" She asked once she was in front of him. The Colonel was a tall man with light brown hair that was silvering around his temples.

He removed his sunglasses and took a deep breath. "I didn't want to single you out in front of the others, but I want to be straight up with you. This is a somewhat small base and not frequented much by females. I want to assure you that I expect nothing but respect from my men when they are in your company. If at any time you have any concerns or problems, I want to know," he said, raising an eyebrow.

"Understood, sir."

"Good. Glad we got that out the way. Also, I received a message from Commander Connors. He would like for you to call him once you're settled. He said it didn't matter what time it was. You're welcome to use one of the phones over at base command."

She smiled. She would have loved to have seen her uncle's face when he found out she had been assigned to his team. "Thank you, sir. I'll be sure to give him a call. I have my phone I can use, but thank you for the offer."

He nodded his head. "Go ahead, your team is waiting on you."

She turned around and was shocked to see every single one of them standing there watching her with a careful eye. She had to remember these guys had trust issues, and examined everything and everyone. Either way, they looked fierce—not to mention they were all hot as hell.

She walked over, and Irish handed her bag and she slung it over her shoulder before lifting her other bag. Once she felt balanced, she looked at the guys.

"Ready?"

"Everything okay with the Colonel?" Stitch asked, and she really hoped they weren't going to question every little action. That was the last thing she needed; eight highly trained warriors up her ass and in her business every second of the day. Although she had a couple of girlfriends who would jump at the chance to be holed up with a team of SEALs. But for Alex, it was more like a nightmare. She was all too familiar with SEALs and their egos. Not to mention how bossy and demanding they were. However, there were some Special Forces guys who she had befriended over the years during her career that were pretty cool. So far, these guys seemed okay. Again, it helped to have Stitch and Frost around, but time would tell.

"Yeah, it's all good. I need to give Derek a call." She gave them a smile and her answer seemed to appease them as they started walking.

She kept a lookout as they made their way to their barracks, making mental notes on certain landmarks. The Col. wasn't lying when he said the area was isolated from the rest of the base. It was a small contained area surrounded by chain-link fencing topped with barbed wire. It reminded her of a prison yard, and in the center were three concrete buildings, arranged side-by-side with about thirty feet in-between each one.

They stopped in front of the buildings and she overheard the guys talking about heading over to the chow hall to grab dinner. She yawned, even with the sporadic naps on the plane, and in the truck, she still felt utterly exhausted. Tomorrow was going to be a big day. The first day of mission planning was always the worst and the longest, and she wanted to be on the top of her game. Her stomach seemed to disagree, because she felt it rumble.

"Alex, you want to grab some chow with us?" Stitch called out to her.

"Can I meet you there? I want to call Derek first."

"We can wait."

"You don't have to."

"Of course, we do." Skittles said. "You're part of the team." Even though all the others nodded in agreement, she found herself seeking out Ace's approval. With a grin, he winked at her and she couldn't help the smile that crept up knowing they were welcoming her into their inner circle.

"Thanks, I promise I'll make it quick."

As they went to their building, she entered the smaller structure that was going to be her home away from home. When she opened the door, she was hit by a burst of cool air and she breathed a sigh of relief.

She dropped her bags onto the floor, glancing around the place. The small cot made her laugh as she wondered if the guys had the same. There was no way with their sizes they would fit. Next to the bed was a small side table. Across the room sat a small table with a chair. It wasn't exactly homey, but it would do.

She sat in the chair and pulled her phone out of her bag, then dialed her uncle. It was already morning back in Virginia.

"Hi princess." Derek's loud burly voice came through the phone making her smile.

"Hey 'D'."

"I take it you made it to the base."

"Yeah, we're all here."

"Everything okay? No issues?"

"So far so good. The guys are waiting for me to head to dinner, but I wanted to call you first."

"Stitch and Frost must have been shocked when they saw you. I know I was floored when I got the paperwork early this morning and saw your name."

She chuckled. "I think we were all surprised."

"Everyone treating you okay?"

She rolled her eyes at his protectiveness. "Yes."

"Good…Do you know anything about the NSA agents?"

"Enough."

"What does that mean?"

"The one guy Bert wouldn't have been my first pick. The other two, I'm not sure about, but I do know the division head they work for, and she wouldn't have sent them if they weren't vetted. According to Bert, they are newbies and part of a new program the agency implemented."

"Tell me more about this guy Bert."

She rolled her eyes. What was it with these guys? "Remember my former boss I told you a little about?"

"Yeah."

"Well, it's him."

"Shit. And how does he feel about you being appointed the lead?"

"Eh, I can sense some animosity."

"Well, don't let him bully you. You're the boss, remember that."

She laughed. "I will, don't worry. If he doesn't want to cooperate, I'll sic my eight newly acquired brothers on him."

Derek laughed, but then he got serious. "Those men are some of the best and they have your back, so don't hesitate to use them how you see fit." Hmm…she without a doubt knew how she could use one of them. She slapped her palm against her forehead. *Don't even go there!*

"I won't. I gotta go now."

"Okay, honey. I'll talk to you tomorrow morning. Love you."

"Love you, too. Bye."

CHAPTER THREE

Alex was laughing so hard she was trying not to spew her half-eaten brownie all over the table. Dino had her rolling as he told her about a past mission in southern Africa that resulted in poor Irish being shit on by a rhinoceros.

Irish grimaced. "Dude, that animal didn't just take a shit. It was a projectile. To this day, I still have nightmares about it."

Alex wiped the tears from her eyes. "Oh my, gosh! I think I would've died. I couldn't imagine. What did you do?"

"Nothing I could do. I was in a position where I couldn't blow my cover."

Even Ace was laughing. "I think that was the only time our position was almost compromised."

"Compromised? How?" Alex asked.

Potter chuckled. "Because we couldn't stop laughing."

"How many showers did it take you to finally feel clean?" Diego asked trying not to laugh at the misfortune of his teammate. Although Alex knew they gave Irish plenty of shit about it. No pun intended.

Even with the stress from earlier, Alex found herself enjoying the moment. Hearing them joke with one another made her think of her uncles and all the times they sat around reminiscing.

"So, Alex. Tell us a little about yourself," Irish probed, trying to direct the attention away from him.

"What do you want to know?"

"Anything."

She hated talking about herself. "Let's see...my name is Alexandra. I was born and raised in Virginia Beach along with these two yahoos." She sent Stitch and Frost a grin. "Like them, I grew up living the SEAL family life."

33

"Well, you have one hell of a dad," Dino added.

"Actually, Derek isn't my biological dad," she admitted and could see from the shocked expressions they weren't aware of that little tidbit. Except for Stitch and Frost. When nobody said anything, she continued. "My real dad was a SEAL. He was assigned to the same team as Derek's. During a mission, they were ambushed, and my dad was killed as a result."

"Damn, I'm sorry to hear that," Potter voiced. "How old were you when that happened?"

"Six. My mom left my dad and me when I was just a baby. My dad came home from work one day to a note on the table. After my dad was killed, child services tried to find my mom, but they weren't successful. My dad's parents died before I was born, and when Child Services finally got a hold of my mom's parents, they told them they didn't want me. The only option was for me to enter the foster care system, but Derek stepped in and filed for guardianship immediately. Years later when I was older, he explained to me that it was my dad's wish that should anything ever happen to him and I was still a minor that Derek and the team take me under their wing. The state at first was hesitant to grant the guardianship because of his occupation and of course his single marital status, but with the help of some people in 'high places' and the support of the community, the guardianship was granted." She smiled remembering the day they had all celebrated.

"I lived with Derek but, I was raised by all my dad's teammates. They all hold a special place in my heart. They were always around teaching and guiding me through life." She smiled and laughed, "None of them knew anything about parenting. If it wasn't for Tenley's mom, they would've been so screwed."

"What did you do when they were deployed?" Ace asked, leaning forward and resting his arms on the table.

"Are you sure you guys want to hear about all of this?"

"Hell yeah. It's not often we get the scoop on the CO's personal life," Irish said and gave her that flirty smile of his she was sure drove the women nuts.

"I stayed with Tenley and her mom, Juliette. Juliette is my 'adopted' mom, per se. She helped me navigate through those rough couple of years when a young girl needed a female to talk to. As you can imagine a little girl living with a Navy SEAL—well really six of them—my childhood was not the typical fairy tale princess stuff that most little girls dream about." Alex smiled as she remembered every moment she spent with them. "I was somewhat of a tom-boy growing up. My uncles made sure I was able to take care of myself as I got older. By the time I reached high school, I was an excellent marksman. But in their eyes, I was their princess. Nobody ever messed with me. That's for sure. I wouldn't have changed a thing with how I was raised without my dad."

Alex told them the story of a time in her freshman year of high school, giving them an idea of just how out of touch the guys were when it came to female stuff. It was a couple of days before the fall homecoming pep rally at the school. She played soccer for the varsity women's team. All the girls were planning to wear their soccer uniforms to the pep rally, and for some added school spirit they were going to put bows that were the school's colors in their hair. Not giving him any explanation of why, she asked him if he could take her to the store to look at some bows. An hour later as they stood inside the Army/Navy surplus store looking at the newest models of hunting bows, she realized she should have clarified she needed hair bows. His facial expression had been priceless when she told him she needed *hair* bows, not hunting bows.

The guys laughed. Stitch was just starting a story of his own when the door opened and in walked her nemesis, Bert. He must have been looking for her because as soon as his eyes locked on her, he made a beeline towards their table. If she'd been fast enough, she would've ducked under the table and hid from him.

He stopped right next to her. She wished she could tattoo the word asshole across his forehead, especially the way he had his lips pursed. She caught her laugh before it came out.

"You're a hard person to track down. I thought you may have had second thoughts and headed back home."

He tried to make it sound like he was joking, but Alex knew there was no humor intended. Whether it was an intimidation tactic or whatever, it pissed her off.

"What, and leave the lives of those men in your hands? I don't think so. We all would know the outcome if that were to happen." She countered with a stare that showed she too wasn't joking or backing down.

With all eyes on Bert and her, he took a step back as if feeling uncomfortable. "Well, when you are finished up with social hour and have a minute, I'd like to speak with you, alone."

Like that was going to happen.

"Whatever you have to say, you can say in front of the team."

His eyes darted to the guys, then he leaned forward and spoke low so only she could hear. "You and I have some personal things to iron out. You cannot keep freezing me out. It's been two years for crying out loud."

She leaned back, putting much-needed distance between them and spoke slowly and loud enough that everyone could hear her. "As I said before, the only discussions I intend to have with you are those relating to this mission. Anything else you have to say doesn't matter, because I don't want to hear it."

He sucked in his lips and glared at her. "Why are you making this harder than it needs to be? Last time I checked we're on the same team."

"Is that so? Because the last time I checked leaders don't abandon their team in a time of need."

"Really? Is this what your attitude is all about? Bad shit happens, Alex. Yeah, it sucked but you need to get over it. It's been two fucking years."

She sucked in a breath. *Get over it?* How does someone ever get over losing five friends and knowing she came within seconds from succumbing to the same fate? Knowing she had an audience she needed to rein in her temper because she was seconds away from shoving her foot so hard into his manhood that his balls would be dangling from his mouth.

She stood up and was ready to go toe-to-toe with him, but before she could take a step in his direction she was pulled back and Frost stepped in front of her, getting into Bert's personal space.

"I think it's time for you to leave."

Bert surprisingly took a step back but pointed at her. "This discussion isn't over."

Her body shook with anger as she followed him with her eyes until he was gone. Frost put his arm around her shoulders.

"Are you okay?"

She looked up and knew he was pissed. But she didn't want him or anyone else for that matter fighting her battles. Not that she wasn't grateful for the back-up, because that little situation had the potential to turn very nasty and possibly violent.

She nodded. "Yeah, I'm good."

"What's the history between you two?"

She sighed and plopped herself down in the chair. *No better time than the present for story time,* she thought to herself.

37

"What details have you been given about this assignment?"

Ace leaned forward. "Pretty much just the basic. Like you, we were surprised when we got the call. Our orders were to get to the airstrip and a plane would be waiting. Derek said we'd be briefed when we arrived. The little we do know is that besides the hostages, we are also hunting down a suspected terrorist named Ashraf Fayad, who a couple of years ago, was suspected of using chemical weapons on hundreds of innocent civilians along with some other heinous crimes, including forming ties with ISIS. It was said he fell off the radar about two years ago after a botched op but has recently resurfaced with this latest attack."

Alex's body went rigid at the mention of the botched op. She hated hearing that term. Her actions didn't go unnoticed either by Frost sitting next to her. She knew it when he quickly glanced down at her and squinted his eyes. *Damn SEALs, they pick up on everything.*

Frost held up his hand and interrupted Ace as he kept a keen eye on her. "Were you involved in that operation? Is that what that altercation between you and Bert was about?"

There was complete silence from the group as they all waited for her answer. Eight sets of intense eyes were intimidating. She reached for her water and took a sip and swallowed hard. *Was I involved? Yep, and I have scars to prove it. Both physical and emotional.* If she said yes, she wondered if these guys would think she wasn't the right person for the job. Would they scrutinize everything she said and did from here on out? *Dammit!*

She slid her eyes back to the group and answered the only way she knew how.

"Yes."

Irish let out a low whistle at her response.

"How deep were you?" Ace questioned.

"Pretty deep." She answered and held Ace's gaze as he scrutinized her, waiting for her to continue. She took a long relaxing breath. She hated being under the microscope. When she returned to the states with injuries, she vowed she'd never step foot in that part of the world again. But duty calls, so here she was, sitting in the 'land of sand'. As strong and confident as she was, she would admit that having the SEAL team working alongside her provided her with an extra boost of confidence and a sense of security.

"As you all know, before I moved to the private sector, I worked at the NSA. Two years ago, I was the lead for a surveillance team sent to Afghanistan. It was supposed to be a simple couple of weeks doing reconnaissance and gaining new Intel on a potential new terrorist cell linked to ISIS that was being funded by a very well-known warlord in the region. The same individual who was suspected of using chemical weapons on innocent civilians."

She explained in detail all the surveillance she and the team had gathered—including how they had blended in with the villagers as they waited to see if Ashraf made an appearance. That man was smart and had always managed to evade being in the same area where they were, even though she and the team were told that he traveled through the villages quite often.

When she finished giving them the rundown, she noticed Ace's eyebrows were drawn inward, "I'm confused. If the government has all the Intel you've just described, then how was the operation botched? To me, it sounds like you and your team were very thorough."

She nodded her head at his questioning. "According to the government no Intel was received from that operation, and currently, I'm the only person who possesses all the detailed information about our target."

His eyes shot towards her and she felt as if they pierced right through her.

"How is that even possible? You had a full team. Surely you had to supply hard evidence. The government just doesn't lose something like that. Are you sure someone on the team didn't screw up and not send the file?" She could sense his agitation, and fully agreed with him, except for the part about not sending the file, but it didn't give him a right to have an attitude with her. It became clear he and his team were not briefed on how that op two years ago had ended.

With the tension growing thicker by the second, she took a deep breath and held Ace's glare, ignoring everyone else who was sitting idle watching their interaction. In a calm, professional tone, she rebutted, "Because, I'm the only one left who is still alive. All the Intel is in here now. At least what I can remember," she said tapping the side of her head. Soon they would see several journals she had in her backpack that held everything she could remember. She wasn't a fool; as soon as she was able to get a hold of a pen and notebook, she started writing everything down. And, it was a damn good thing she had an excellent memory.

Before he could react to the bombshell she'd just dropped she added, "And, just so we are clear Lt. Commander, our target for *this* op is the same asshole who was responsible for the explosion that killed five of my friends and colleagues along with destroying every single piece of *hard* evidence. Not to mention the server that our Intel was uploaded to was wiped clean. So that, *Sir,* is how it is possible."

She felt a little peeved at his line of questioning and before she said or did anything else she'd regret later, she excused herself.

Walking next door to base command she found a bathroom and locked herself inside. She turned toward the sink and turned the faucet on. She splashed some cold water on her face then used a paper towel to pat her face dry. Taking a deep cleansing breath, she hung her head. She understood where Ace's questioning was coming from. Hell, she'd have the same questions if she were in his shoes, but the audacity to speak to her in an accusatory tone was what upset her. He didn't intimidate her, and she sure as hell didn't answer to him either. If this was how it was going to be living and working side-by-side with this group, it was going to be a long couple of weeks for all of them because she was no push-over.

Ace sat at the table running his hand through his thick black hair. When Alex said she was involved, he hadn't expected her to be in that deep. He was still trying to come to terms that she was the lone survivor from the brutal massacre of her team. Damn, that had to have been tough to overcome. He'd lost friends to the war, but never a teammate, and he prayed that day never came. But he'd heard about survivors' guilt and the havoc it could wreak on someone emotionally. He had several questions he wanted answers to, specifically how Bert fit into all of this. She never went into detail about their relationship. He knew he needed to tread carefully and give her time to cool off. He pissed her off and that wasn't the wisest decision considering they were now working together. His main concern may come across to some people as being insensitive, however, he wouldn't be in the position he was if he didn't ask the right questions. Knowing a little more about her past, his concern was for her mental state and her qualifications given that her last mission wound up a clusterfuck.

"You were a little harsh on her, wouldn't ya say?" Ace knew his medic wasn't happy with him. Stitch had a soft spot, probably because of his medical background, but Alex was also his friend.

They all had soft spots for women and children unless they stood on the enemy's side.

"I wonder what happened to her team. We weren't told about any of that," Diego asked with a look of concern crossing his face.

Ace looked at Potter. "Were you able to get anything from Bert on the ride over here?"

"No, he pretty much stayed glued to his tablet and phone."

Ace took a bite from his brownie and swallowed. Shit, he wasn't even really all that hungry anymore.

"Whatever went down, there is a lot of bad blood between the two of them. Damn, I feel like an asshole with how I handled that."

"Maybe that's because you are an asshole." A snappy voice said from behind him.

Shit, he was so riled up he hadn't even noticed Alex had snuck up behind him. She was like a little ninja being all stealthy.

She sat back down and took a drink of water. She looked a little refreshed.

"Are you okay?" Skittles asked her and Ace could sense the guys were already acclimating to her, which was a good thing, but he still needed answers.

He shifted uncomfortably in his seat. He hated having to apologize. "Listen, Alex, I owe you an apology. Although I don't feel my line of questioning was wrong, I shouldn't have used the tone I did."

The nonchalant shrug of her shoulders surprised him, "It's cool. I don't wear my feelings on my sleeve. Plus, your concerns are valid. I get it, your team and this mission are your focus and priority. But you must understand, this is my mission as well and we do have to work as a team if we want to succeed. I don't mind you guys asking questions, I'd just appreciate a little more respect in how you ask."

He nodded his head. "I agree. Are you up to answering some questions and giving us a little background on what we may be up against?" Smiling at her he said, "I promise not to act like a dick. If I do, I'm sure that one of these clowns will kick my ass." He motioned to his team.

She chuckled while holding his gaze with those green orbs of hers, "Thanks, but I don't need anyone to fight my battles for me, Lieutenant Commander. I'll gladly kick your ass myself if you ever talk down to me like that again. I don't intimidate easily. I've never backed down from a battle and I don't ever intend to either. And yes, since you asked so nicely, I'll gladly answer your questions. I assumed you would have some." She smirked at him. "See, that was me being respectful."

Her spunk and sassiness was sexy as hell. He felt his dick twitch in his pants. As if knowing what she did to him, Potter held back a chuckle. "Damn, this mission is going to go down in the record books." He looked at Alex, "You're going to fit in great with us, sweetie." Ace couldn't help the glare he shot across the table at his best friend.

Ace peered over at Alex and caught her looking at him. "What more can you tell us?" She took a deep breath and he noticed her rubbing her right side above her hip. Whatever happened, the impression she gave it was a sore subject for her to talk about.

"It was two weeks before Thanksgiving. We were finishing up a six-week assignment. Our task over that time was to locate and investigate Ashraf Fayad. We spent days and nights traveling to various locations that he was known to frequent, interviewing many people. Some were more willing to give us viable information, while others avoided us at all costs out of fear that Ashraf's regime would retaliate.

43

The night of the attack we were just trying to bide our time until it was time to go home. We were playing cards while we waited for our dinner to cook. I received a phone call from headquarters, so I stepped outside to take it. I was surprised when I heard Derek's voice. He knew people, so I assume that's how he got the secured number to the phone. He was always concerned when I traveled, though he never knew exactly where I was. He had called to check-in." She paused for a moment and took another drink of water. "His phone call is the reason I'm sitting here today. We had spoken for about ten minutes before I turned to go back to the house. I was about forty or so feet from the house when it exploded, with my team inside." She took an unsteady breath and shivered as if she was reliving the moment.

"Shit...were you injured?" Potter asked.

She nodded her head, "The force of the blast threw me a couple of feet. I must have blacked out or something because I don't remember anything up until I was being loaded onto a helicopter. Bert was there with the medic. I was in so much pain that once they had me loaded and secured, I passed out again. I didn't regain consciousness until I was at the hospital. Besides a lot of bumps and bruises along my body, I had second degree burns just above my right hip."

"Was that why Derek had taken that week off and flew to Germany?"

"Yes. I was a total wreck. I had just lost my teammates, was in the hospital, and had the government demanding answers. Derek helped with some interference."

Ace grimaced, listening carefully as Alex recounted her ordeal, but there was something she said that nagged him.

"Alex, if you were unconscious, who called for help? How was the government notified?"

"I've been questioning that since I woke up in the hospital and could think straight. According to Bert, I'm the one who called it in, but I don't remember doing it. As I said, the last memory I can recall before being loaded into the helicopter was seeing the house explode."

"It's obvious your position was compromised, but by who, is the important question." The comment came from Dino.

"What happened next?" Ace asked. This story was getting more interesting as it went on.

"The first couple of weeks I spent recovering along with being questioned day in and day out by the agency, mainly about the missing Intel. All of the Intel we submitted was gone."

"That is what I don't understand, how does something like that happen? I thought the government has backups to the backups."

"You and me both. Every single night we uploaded our day's findings. But sometime between the explosion and when I got home, there was no trace of anything. The agency, of course, opened an investigation but it couldn't find anything wrong with the servers, and without the hard evidence the so-called failed mission was placed upon my team and me. Believe me, I was furious. Our country had lost five honorable people who were doing their jobs in trying to gain knowledge to protect our country from harm, and those desk jockeys at the agency just tossed the service records and memories of those individuals—my friends—out the window like a piece of trash. They didn't care about the lives that were lost. All they cared about was who they could blame because the outcome wasn't what they wanted."

Ace felt her anger and sympathized with her. He understood completely that a lot of government officials didn't give a shit about people getting hurt, they just wanted the job done. "What happened after that?"

"I resigned from my position and shortly thereafter I was offered a job with Mason, and now here I am."

Dino shook his head. "Damn, honey. That shit is messed up."

"Yeah, it is. But what can you do? Luckily, I had options, and I'm content where I am right now. Although I'll admit, I never saw myself coming back here again."

"So, why are you here then?" Ace found himself asking.

She looked him in the eye and what he saw excited him. There was a spark, a look of determination.

"To help bring those contractors home and to make sure that Ashraf can't hurt anyone else again. Although, I did have some stipulations the agency had to agree to before I accepted."

"Are you saying you bribed the NSA?" Ace asked her.

She shrugged her shoulders. "I wouldn't say bribed. I would prefer to say I gave them an option. Thankfully, they were smart and picked the correct one. Especially, considering I was two days into my vacation when I got the phone call telling me I had two hours to get packed and be at the airport."

"I'm curious to know what they gave you in return for your assistance," Stitch added.

"Full control. I only accepted the assignment if I was lead and Bert would be on an as-needed basis only."

"Damn, you must be Super Woman or something to have the agency giving in to your demands," Irish said with a slight chuckle.

She smiled. "They couldn't afford to not agree. I'm the only one with extensive knowledge of Ashraf and his regime."

"What about Bert? You mentioned he was present after the explosion." Ace now asked.

"I didn't realize Bert was even in the country. It was a surprise to me when I first heard his voice. When I worked under Bert, he was an okay boss. He had his pros and cons, but my view of him

46

changed the day he sat across the table from me and sided with the agency. He had no loyalty, didn't even try to state a case for me. He threw me under the bus just to save his own ass. To this day, I swear on my father's grave those Intel files were uploaded to the servers. I made sure each submission was successful. What happened to the information after it was received is a mystery, but something deep down in my gut says Bert knows the answer."

"What a dick," Irish said making her chuckle.

"Yeah, he is that, amongst other things. Ever since that day I haven't trusted him. Our paths have crossed a few times, but I've kept my distance."

Stitch scratched his head. "Is he the reason you resigned from the agency?"

"He wasn't the sole reason for my decision, but he had a lot to do with it. I can't work with someone who isn't going to have my back and fight for me when it's warranted."

"Well, he's a damn good actor, because he comes off acting as if you two were the greatest team."

"That's because he is trying to kiss my ass with hopes I'll go back to the agency. I've heard rumors the government let him, and a few others have a piece of their mind after the fiasco and how they treated me. They knew I was a good asset. He's being typical Bert and trying to put on a show in front of you guys hoping it gets him in my good graces and I'll change my mind. But that little outburst of his just a few minutes ago proves my point."

"Were you ever romantically involved with him?" She looked at Stitch and Ace waited, holding his breath.

"No, never. Although, that isn't saying he didn't try." She rolled her eyes. "There were many times he stepped over the line inappropriately."

Ace looked at her. "He sexually harassed you?"

"I always denied his advances but that didn't stop him from trying. He was relentless; even after I had left the agency, he tried calling me and asking me to meet him for drinks."

"What an asshole," Irish blurted out again Ace couldn't agree more. He would be keeping a close eye on Bert and he was sure the guys would too.

"You'll let us know if he continues to harass you," Stitch said pinning her with a look that left no room for argument, and Ace was pleased when she nodded her head.

Alex stood up and put her hand over her mouth covering a yawn. Ace was right there with her. After their last mission, it was going to be nice to get a decent night's sleep before they hit the ground running tomorrow.

"Thanks for letting me join you guys for dinner, but I'm exhausted. Does 7:00 am tomorrow work for you guys? Derek said he would skype in."

"Sounds good to us." Ace replied then added, "Remember you're the boss, you just tell us when and where and we'll be there."

She said goodnight to everyone and Stitch and Frost both hugged her. Ace actually felt a tad bit jealous which was ridiculous considering he just met the woman a few hours ago, but he knew what it felt like to hold her curvy body in his arms. She at least gave him one of her beautiful smiles before she left.

Ace waited until she was out of earshot then he looked at his team. He was even more curious about Bert after hearing what Alex had to say. He'd worked with a lot of intelligence guys over his career and most of them he wouldn't trust with his life. Just from his two interactions with Bert, and Ace knew Bert fell into that statistic. He wasn't too concerned about Alex, she seemed like she could handle anything thrown at her, but people like Bert were sneaky, and he wasn't about to let some psycho with a grudge throw a member of the team under the bus. Not on his watch.

"I'm not comfortable with this guy. He is pissed off and could be out for revenge against Alex. You all know me; I thrive on trust and loyalty. It pisses me off when someone is disloyal, especially to one of their own. From what Alex said he sold her and her team out on the last mission to save his ass, and that doesn't sit well with me."

"Well you heard what Alex said: he is on an as-need-to-know basis. We can only hope his interaction will be limited," Stitch said.

"Alex is lead, so that is the order we follow. If Bert says otherwise, he can take it up with the commander."

As soon as Alex returned to her barracks, she did a quick check of her emails. There wasn't anything pressing so she replied to a few of them. Tomorrow morning, she would start digging through some files to try and figure out where Ashraf was holding the hostages.

She made her bed before going into the bathroom to wash up. From the plane ride and the hot, gritty air she felt grimy.

As she made her way to bed, her and Bert's altercation was still fresh in her mind. He was up to something; she could feel it, and she just needed to find out exactly what his MO was. Until she could unravel his intentions, she would remember what her uncle said earlier on the phone. "The team has your back." Depending on what Bert had planned she just may need to call upon them to assist.

She crawled under the covers and closed her eyes. Tomorrow was going to be busy and most likely bring lots of questions, and lots of thinking. She needed to be on top of her game which meant she couldn't be distracted with the Lt. Commander's presence. But damn, he was hard not to look at. Just from the little time she'd spoken with him he seemed to have a great personality and demeanor. If she was in any other situation, she wouldn't mind taking the time and getting to know him better. But now was not the time to lust after a man. Not when the lives of five men were on the line and not when she had one terrorist to rein in. Nope, starting tomorrow it would be all business.

She hit the playlist on her iPod and turned the volume down low, and within minutes she was fast asleep.

CHAPTER FOUR

Alex stood, leaning over one of the tables in the war room Skyping with Derek. She had woken up around 3:00 am, and instead of just lying in bed she got up and headed over to base command to get a head start on the day's work.

"Are you positive that's him?" Derek asked her as she pulled up the photograph again on her computer. The photo was taken by a security camera at the compound the night the contractors were kidnapped. It also pretty much confirmed that Ashraf was indeed the mastermind behind the kidnappings.

"Unless he has a twin, I'm positive."

The photo was a little grainy, however as soon as she opened the file and the picture appeared, there was no mistaking the identity of the man staring back at her. The face of Ashraf's oldest son, Yaseen, was one she would never forget. Even after two years had passed, she could still feel those dark, cold eyes penetrating hers. She and her colleague had been posing as tourists at a market when she came face-to-face with him. Now that she thought about it, that slight arrogant smirk he gave her should have been a warning to her. From the stories she had heard about Yaseen, he was just as, if not even more dangerous than his father.

"So, how do you want to tackle this? We are at your disposal."

"I appreciate that. From the Intel I read over this morning, it's looking as if the kidnappers may have had some help on the inside. The government is trying to keep it under wraps. I'm surprised that they've been able to keep this away from the media. The truth always prevails."

"Yeah, well, I hope the truth comes sooner rather than later. We are up against the clock."

"Well, then, I suggest when the team gets here, we start pinpointing locations. I've also got my associate back home working on getting me a list of names of those who were working at the compound the night of the attack. There could be a connection."

She walked over to another table with several maps spread out on it. She studied the one map and quickly became frustrated. The number of possibilities as to where the hostages could be held were endless. With the mountains and valleys, there were so many different, not to mention creative hiding spots, though she did have a couple of spots to rule out.

Just as she was about to stick a few push pins into the map, the door behind her opened. Even after her little pep talk to herself last night about focusing on the real issue at hand and not her eye for the Lt. Commander, her eyes still gravitated to the sexy man as he led his team into the room. He looked calm and collected as he laughed at something Potter said to him. Then as if knowing she was staring, he looked directly at her and winked before addressing their commander and taking a seat.

She shook her head, Even if they were compatible, a relationship would never work between them—not with their careers.

With her mindset back on the task at hand, she slid right into her professional mode and got the meeting started.

Ace took a seat on a stool near where Alex stood. He noticed her as soon as he walked through the door. When he caught her looking at him, he was disappointed when he saw something pass within her eyes before she looked away. He sensed she was putting a wall up and was shutting him out before he even had a shot. He considered that a challenge, and boy did he love a challenge. He felt the attraction on their first run-in, and he knew she did too. He could see it in her body language. An attraction that strong between two people never comes often, especially how they met and the current environment they were in. She could try to run and hide behind the professional façade she was building but given enough time he'd break down the barrier. He smiled to himself, for now, he'd put the job first as he always did, but it didn't mean that in-between work there couldn't be some play.

He purposely chose the seat he did because she would have to walk past him as she made her way to the front of the room. When she did, he smiled and said good morning. She returned the gesture, again in a professional manner.

"If everyone is ready, we can get started," she said changing her tone and demeanor to all business.

"The floor is all yours." The commander stated.

After about forty-five minutes of what Ace could only describe as an exceptional overview by Alex, he felt more in the loop than he did yesterday. Alex was a very diligent presenter. She was open-minded and precise as she spoke. She also wasn't one to rush judgment, which was a good thing. It had happened several times in his career where someone overseeing the operation gets a "hunch" or "thinks" and they send the team in and it turns into a clusterfuck. But that didn't seem to be the way Alex operated. She had some pretty substantial evidence she presented but wasn't comfortable enough with it to send the team searching. She wanted some credibility and he totally respected her for that. It showed she cared about her work and those she was working with. Even Bert who was in attendance kept his mouth shut, though he didn't look happy sitting in the back with his arms crossed glaring at Alex the entire time.

"Okay, so based on the Intel, we know we're definitely on the hunt for this Ashraf character. Can you give us some additional background on him and what we could potentially be dealing with?" Ace asked Alex.

"Ashraf is a narcissist. He's all about showing the world he is unstoppable. He craves power and being in control. His hefty bank account doesn't help us. Again, he's the mastermind behind it all. But most importantly he is extremely dangerous and will stop at nothing to get what he wants."

She took a sip of water before pulling up some photographs on the screen.

"When the militants stormed that security compound, they were initially after the weapons. But, after reviewing the tapes and reading over some witness statements, I believe that the hostages were an afterthought."

"But they got the weapons. Why chance it all and take hostages?" Potter asked.

"As I mentioned before, it's a control thing. He thrives on it, gets off on the high, and what more says 'look at me, look at me' than taking five highly trained US security contractors hostage. I mean, three of those men are former Special Forces."

"Alex, when you say a significant number of weapons, is it known what type of weapons and the value?"

"The government hasn't given an exact number yet, but from the chatter, I'm hearing it consists of mostly small arms. However, there was also a large number of stinger missiles being stored there which as of this morning were still unaccounted for. If I had to guess, I would put a value somewhere around twenty million dollars."

"Jesus Christ." Ace said out loud and looked at Alex.

"Priority number one here is the hostages. Every day that passes drastically decreases the chances of those men making it out alive and we are already on what, day four?"

"If you had to go with your gut right here, right now, are there any places that come to mind that you would look?" Irish questioned.

"I have a couple I'd like to check out to rule them out. Our weakness will be the unfamiliarity of the area, while Ashraf knows the region like the back of his hand and can move around frequently and undetected."

Alex moved over to the table with the maps. When she bent over slightly to point at something Ace couldn't help the movement of his eyes to her ass. She had a mighty fine ass at that. Especially in the fitted tan capris pants she wore. When Potter cleared his throat and raised an eyebrow at him, he realized he was staring, and that Potter wasn't the only person who caught him because Stitch was grinning as well as Irish. *Fuckers...*

"Being that there are five hostages, and if Ashraf is making a move to take over a territory of ISIS within this region that leads me to believe he is in the vicinity. When I say vicinity, I'm talking within a 200-mile radius. From what I know based on past experiences Ashraf doesn't stray too far from his operations. However, he is good at concealing his identity. There are a few potential hot spots I know off the top of my head, although my gut tells me we won't locate him or the hostages there because it's just too obvious, but we wouldn't be doing our job thoroughly if we don't put them on the list."

For the next few hours, they studied maps, satellite videos, and discussed where a good starting point was. Without any credible leads or sightings of the hostages, it was merely a guessing game.

Alex's computer pinged with an incoming message. She excused herself and walked over to see what it was. She read whatever was on the screen then looked up.

"What is it?" Ace asked.

"It's a video. I'm pulling it up now."

Ace's gut tightened, wondering what type of video because nine times out of ten videos sent in this environment didn't end well.

Alex typed in something and the video appeared, showing five people, kneeling with cloth bags over their heads. Typical MO of terrorists. Since it was daylight, the area around them was visible giving a telling sign they were somewhere within the mountains. The base they were at was surrounded by mountains.

The guy standing in front speaking was covered from head to toe in black. The only visible feature was his eyes. Ace could tell those were eyes of a killer. He glanced over at Alex to see if he could gauge her reaction, but she was really studying the video as the man spoke. The problem for most in the room was that the guy spoke in a dialect specific to the region. Unfortunately, no one on the team was fluent. They all knew a couple of important words, but not enough to make out what was being spoken on the video.

The video ended without any type of bloodshed which was a huge blessing, but what he caught at the end of the dialogue certainly sounded like the guy mentioned Alex's name. Again, he glanced over at Alex who was chewing her lip but still staring at the now blank screen.

"Alex, correct me if I'm wrong, but wasn't your name mentioned there at the end?" Derek asked her, and when she turned to face the group, he knew by the look on her face that it wasn't good.

"They know I'm involved. He was taunting me."

"Was there any mention about your whereabouts?" Ace asked. This was a huge concern. If these people knew that Alex was in the country, Ace wouldn't put it past them to go beyond all means necessary to get to her.

"No, why?" She asked looking up at him.

Derek spoke up. "He's asking because we don't know if these people know where you are. They could be targeting you."

"I've only been here for twenty-four hours. The only people who knew I'd be here was Mason and whoever at the government level that put the request in."

Derek blew out a breath. "You know this changes things, right?"

"How so?" Alex asked, a little on the defensive.

"Because now I've got some sicko terrorist possibly wanting to put you in the middle of this situation."

"Whoa! Back up. First, you need to put the Alpha daddy brakes on. Second, I've dealt with a lot of other heavy shit in my career than someone just mentioning my name."

"What the hell is an Alpha daddy?" Derek fired back and Ace tried to cover the snort of laughter at her description of Derek's overprotectiveness. Luckily for him, his amusement went unnoticed.

"Derek, let me look into this a little more. I need to go over the video where I can study the frames. Give me a few hours and I'll give you a call with an update."

Ace glanced down at his watch and was surprised at the time already.

"Fine, but I want an update before you call it a night," Derek replied then signed off.

Alex ran a hand down her face. Derek was right, the video had changed the dynamics of the mission. Whether Alex wanted it or not, she was going to have an extra layer of security on her. Ace heard Stitch ask her if she wanted to join them for a quick lunch, but she politely declined saying she wanted to review the video and check-in with the division lead back in Washington. He was disappointed but understood that the job came first.

He wasn't complaining because in the last few hours he had gotten to meet Alex Hardesty, the career woman. He was intrigued by her professionalism as well as impressed with her knowledge and determination. She was a woman who seemed like she'd kick ass first and ask questions later. That just excited him even more. No wonder Mason Whittemore snatched her up. She was definitely a valued asset.

Before they left, he turned toward her, and she looked up at him with her bright green eyes. "Are you sure there isn't anything we can do to help?"

She gave him a warm smile. "No, but thanks for the offer."

Stitch walked up, "At least let us bring you something back to eat. I'm not sure what they're serving but we don't mind."

"I'm good, right now, Stitch, but thank you." She gave them both another smile and then the phone rang, bringing an end to the conversation.

As he and Stitch walked out the door, he stole another glance over his shoulder then looked back at Stitch. "Irish is going to hang around just to be safe."

Stitch smiled, "you must have been reading my mind. What she doesn't know, can't hurt her."

Stitch grinned then opened the door leading to the hallway that would take them outside. Ace followed, but not before taking one last look at the sexy brunette who stole the show today with her impeccable presentation.

Stitch slapped him on the back and chuckled. "Come on, Lt. Commander, I think you and I need to talk."

CHAPTER FIVE

Ace was blinded by the bright afternoon sun as he and Stitch stepped outside. Sliding his sunglasses on, Dino gave a chin lift, "What's on the agenda now, Lieutenant Commander?"

"How about some food and then you guys are free to do whatever? Alex said she'll let us know if anything pans out."

"She's not eating?" Skittles asked frowning.

Ace shook his head and had to hold back his smile. From the disappointed looks on the team's faces, it seemed they were hoping to spend time with her too.

After chow, Ace was walking with Stitch when Stitch glanced over with an amused look.

"What?" Ace asked, not breaking his stride.

"Alex is something else, isn't she?"

Ace wondered where this was going, so he took the bait and nodded. "Yeah, she seems to be, but again I just met her." That wasn't saying he hadn't liked what he'd seen so far. He already knew he wanted to talk to her more, although he would be crossing some boundaries considering she was related to his CO.

"Don't give me that shit, it's written all over your face. Since you two bumped into each other yesterday you can't keep your eyes off her." Stitch laughed, "You've been around the block with plenty of women Ace, but I've yet to see you look at any woman like the way you looked at Alex."

Ace's stride came to a halt as the others kept walking ahead. He glanced at Stitch. It wasn't like he was disrespectful towards women. "And what type of look is that?"

Stitch grinned, "You actually paid attention to her."

Ace rubbed his jaw and thought about it. Stitch was right. Although it had been almost a year since he had slept with a woman,

59

it was just two people in it for the sex. Who was he trying to fool? He felt the instant pull the moment the little powerhouse plowed into him. "Okay, I won't deny it, she's intrigued me. She doesn't seem to be like the women back home who throw themselves at us. That in itself is a positive."

"That's because she's not. She rarely dates." That was encouraging information to take in. "And forget about the 'man in uniform' routine. That doesn't affect her."

"What does that mean?"

They stopped next to a picnic table and Stitch sat rubbing his hand over his scruffy face. They all needed a shave.

"Alex grew up being a military brat. Being who she was raised by, she's seen it all and heard it all. Including the guys who thought the uniform could persuade her into their beds." Stitch chuckled, "She took total offense to it, and would tell them that too."

Ace grinned, "Smart girl. Although I do recall all of us doing the same a time or two. Especially when we were younger and had just graduated BUD/S." Stitch laughed but didn't deny it.

"Alex is hard to explain. She's different and special, and I'm not just saying that because she's my friend. She can light up the darkest room with her bright smile and fun personality. She's unbelievably smart and holy shit, can she kick ass." Ace gave him a sideways look and Stitch continued. "Seriously, you should see her in action. Put any weapon in her hand and she could disassemble it, reassemble it and fire it, hitting her target dead on 99.9% percent of the time." He shook his head and laughed as he kicked a rock across the ground. "Derek and those guys taught her everything she needed to know. She is an amazing person and friend."

Ace took a seat across from him and stretched his legs out.

"She sounds awesome."

"She is, but I worry about her. Frost does too, and even though the commander would never admit it to us, I know he feels the same."

"Why? With how you've described her she seems like she can hold her own."

"The amount of time she spends working; she never stops or even slows down for that matter. Shit, when she mentioned she was in Italy on vacation I almost didn't believe her. She's always on the go, bouncing from one country to the next assisting other operatives. I think she works more now being a freelancer than she did with the government. We are all just afraid that if she keeps going the way she is, she'll burn herself out."

"I'm surprised the commander hasn't talked with her."

"Oh, he's tried. Believe me. But she tells him she's fine and knows her limitations."

Ace wondered if there could be an underlying issue causing her to want to work more, maybe to keep her mind busy.

"What happened to Alex two years ago was awful. Did you all ever stop to think maybe she's putting all of those hours in to keep her mind busy, so she won't think about the past? PTSD can rear its ugly self in many ways. Maybe that's her way of dealing with it."

Stitch removed his sunglasses and started fidgeting with them. Ace took notice of the painful expression on his face.

"At the time, Frost and I didn't know all of the details. We only knew she had been injured during an assignment. I never put two and two together when Derek left for Germany. We weren't even told she was injured until a couple of months after it had happened." Stitch took a deep breath. "Her whole fucking team was killed right in front of her eyes. Knowing now it was a phone call that saved her life shakes me to my core."

Ace's chest tightened. Losing one team member was torture enough, but he couldn't imagine losing an entire team. He knew guys who endured and had witnessed what survivors' guilt could do to someone. It wasn't pretty.

"Do you think her being here could hinder our progress?" He felt like such a dick asking Stitch that, but he was responsible for the team. If she weren't mentally fit for the assignment it could cause issues.

"From what I hear, she's one of the best out there in the field she is in. I know Alex and she wouldn't have accepted the job if she felt she wasn't prepared. Alex has a toughness about her, along with a long streak of independence. Trust me when I tell you she won't be a hindrance."

That was all Ace needed to hear. Stitch was her best friend and would know her better than anyone besides her family of course, so with him saying all was good was music to his ears. They didn't need to add any more drama to the situation they were currently facing, nor the fact that he was attracted to her.

"What else do you want to know about her?" Stitch asked and Ace wondered where in the hell that question came from. He looked at Stitch and Stitch laughed.

"Oh, come on, man. It is so obvious you find her attractive. Potter and I both caught you looking at her ass."

"I don't know, the way you make it sound about her dating, it feels as if I don't stand a chance."

They were both quiet for a moment. Then Stitch spoke, "Damn, you really like her, don't you?"

Ace looked down at his hands and wondered how he could explain the feeling he got when he met Alex without sounding like a total dork. "You know how you hear about people meeting someone and knowing instantly that person is the one?" Stitch didn't say anything, but he nodded his head. "Well, I think it happened to me."

Stitch's eyes widened but Ace didn't miss the sly grin. "You think Alex could be the one?"

Ace held Stitch's eye. "Fucking crazy, isn't it?" Shit, he sounded ridiculous. He shook his head and went to stand but Stitch stopped him.

"Hold up. Look, if you're really interested in getting to know her, just be patient. Don't push her and don't be surprised when she tries to blow you off. One thing I've known about Alex is that she is exceptionally good at building walls."

"Well, I guess I have a challenge ahead of me."

Stitch chuckled. "Tread carefully and don't go pissing her off. Believe me when I say you don't want to go down that road. She could make a grown man cry." Ace cocked one of his eyebrows. "Remember she was raised by a slew of frogmen. Even though the commander was her legal guardian, each of her father's teammates treated that girl like their own daughter."

Stitched laughed along with him then got serious again, "You're a good guy and someone I have the utmost respect for. Knowing you both, I think you guys would be good for each other. All I ask is that you treat her right. She deserves that much. That is if you can make it past the commander." Stitch chuckled. "Good luck with that one."

He nodded his head in acknowledgment that he got the message loud and clear. Standing up, Ace stretched his arms and slapped Stitch on the back, "Come on let's go meet up with the others. I thought I heard Potter say he wanted to watch a movie. If that's the case, you and I both know we are in store for a *Harry Potter* marathon."

Walking along with Ace, Stitch put his sunglasses on and shook his head, laughing. "Too bad Potter can't learn some of the wizardry shit those kids use in those movies. It would sure as hell make our missions a lot easier."

Ace barked out a laugh. Potter's fetish with *Harry Potter* kept the team entertained.

CHAPTER SIX

Ashraf leaned back in his chair as he sat behind his desk looking out of the large window in his home. The backdrop of the Hindu Kush mountain range was breathtaking. The tranquil view of the snowcapped peaks that glistened in the rays of the sun normally brought a sense of calmness to him. But calmness was a far reach at the moment.

He spun his chair around, so he was now facing the man who sat across from him; Reynolds was his name. Ashraf had to hide his smirk at the look of fear on the American's face. Oh yeah, Reynolds knew exactly what would happen when he got angry. Normally it would lead to someone being severely injured, or worse, killed.

"Your 'simple plan' as you put it, has backfired. How in the hell did this turn into a train wreck? The last thing I need is your government on my ass again."

"Your son was caught on a security feed. Facial recognition traced him back to your organization. It also didn't help that your crew decided to take five contractors hostage."

Ashraf tapped his fingers on the wood desk. "But, I didn't."

"You didn't what?"

"I don't have any hostages."

"Well, our government says otherwise. That is a major reason why they brought that woman in."

Ashraf smirked. Reynolds didn't need to be privy of every single detail Ashraf had planned. Of course, they used real hostages in the video, they just weren't the hostages the government was claiming they had.

"That is another problem in itself. She came to close to ruining me the last time she was here. So, my question is what are you going to do about it?"

Reynolds swallowed hard. Drops of perspiration ran down his temples that he wiped away with the back of his hand. He could portray himself as a big shot, but when he was backed into a corner, he cowered.

"First, you have to know that I had no control over who the agency was going to contract. My initial thought was that they were going to keep it in house, but then one of the Directors mentioned her name, and now here we are. It's been over two years since that assignment, and all the evidence was destroyed before anyone had a chance to read it."

"Well, she must have something because why else would she be here? And, with a SEAL team at her disposal."

Alex had nearly brought down his entire organization. He gave Reynolds the evil eye. If things would have gone his way, she'd had been blown to smithereens just like the rest of her team. "Remind me again why she is still alive?"

"Ask your oldest son. I was ready to put a bullet in her head until he stopped me."

Ashraf leaned forward, resting his elbows on the desk.

"Yaseen sometimes thinks more with his dick instead of his brain. From the moment he saw her at that market, he has had some sort of infatuation with her. Although I can't say I blame him. Alex Hardesty is a beautiful woman and built to serve a man. However, beauty can be deadly, and in her case, she is as deadly as they come."

"I promise you she'll be taken care of. After I make her squirm a little."

"Well, she should be squirming now with that video my son put out there. Him calling her out personally should send her a message."

"Yeah, although, I can't say I approve of that."

"Like I said, my son thinks with his dick. Just see that you take care of her before she causes any other problems for me. Once she is out of the picture, I can start planning the takeover of the territory I'm acquiring," Ashraf warned then waved Reynolds out.

Ashraf opened the top drawer to his desk and removed a cigar. Taking a puff, he inhaled deeply, savoring the sweet, mild cedary taste. He thought about Reynolds. In the beginning, Reynolds was a great asset to his organization, and he was paid very well to run interference between the many government agencies who dared to investigate his dealings. But lately, he'd been a little sloppy and had gotten too comfortable. Now he was wondering if it might be time to sever ties with his American friend.

He propped his feet up on his desk and again stared off into the distance. His mind kept going round and round on the American woman. She was very good and thorough at her job. She had ways of getting information. If it weren't for the inside help, that he had to alert him of her and her team's presence in the area, she would have succeeded in ruining him, if not killing him. But thankfully money talks and he was able to avoid being brought down. In the end, her team got what they deserved, and, in his opinion, she should have suffered the same fate. Instead, she got a second chance at life, but damn if there would be a third. He would see to it that Alex Hardesty would never make it out of Afghanistan alive, even if his son didn't agree.

CHAPTER SEVEN

Alex stifled a yawn before rubbing her tired eyes. Glancing at the time, she gasped seeing how late it was. Thanks to the Red Bull she found in the mini-refrigerator she'd been going strong all day and apparently into the evening now. She sat up straight and stretched her arms over her head. Loosening her tense muscles felt amazing, although a proper massage would have felt even better.

She was feeling a little edgy since watching the hostage video a zillion times. She wasn't a hundred percent sure, but the guy speaking in the video she believed was Ashraf's son, Yaseen. She tried focusing on the eyes since that was the only feature she could see, and they mimicked those same eyes she remembered from two years ago. They were dark, cold, and gave the vibe of a killer.

The downside was that she couldn't get a read on the area the video was shot in. Unfortunately, she was going to need to bring Bert in and see if any of his people at the agency could take a look. She tried contacting him a few minutes ago, but had been informed by Mical that he was tied up in another meeting. She had spoken with Derek and gave him an update, and although he was trying to hold back on the protective mode, she knew he worried about her. Tomorrow when she went to see Bert, she planned on taking someone from the team with her just as a precaution because something in her gut told her that Bert wasn't about playing fair.

She shut her computer down and started to pack up when her stomach growled, reminding her that she hadn't eaten. Knowing the mess hall wouldn't have any food at this hour, she would have to settle for one of the protein bars she kept in her bag. She had learned long ago to always have some sort of snack on hand.

She snatched her bag from the table and took one last look around the room, making sure she wasn't leaving anything behind that could potentially fall into the wrong hands.

On the way out she waved to Staff Sergeant Hill who was still plugging away at his computer while talking on the phone. She thought she heard him talking in Dari. He was one of the more pleasant soldiers on base.

Strolling along, she noticed there wasn't much activity around the base. Probably because tonight was movie and poker night. Another reason to pass on seeing if there were any leftovers. Judging from what she overheard from a soldier today poker night was a place she wanted to avoid at all costs, as it tended to get a little rowdy.

As she got closer to the "prison yard" as she had dubbed her and the team's secluded corner of the base, she notice a couple of lights were burned out making the pathway darker than normal. A chill shot up her spine and the hairs on the back of her neck stood up, giving her an uneasy feeling. She glanced around but didn't see anything or anyone. The way the temporary structures were positioned around the solid foundations provided plenty of cover if someone wanted to hide from view. Picking up her pace, the three buildings nestled together came into view. The smell of smoke and the sound of a fire crackling followed by low laughter brought a small smile to her lips, knowing the guys were getting to enjoy a little downtime. Not wanting to intrude, she decided to circle around the back of the buildings and slip inside using the secondary entrance on the side.

CHAPTER EIGHT

The team had gathered around a makeshift fire pit, having a beer, and making small talk. The Colonel had invited them to the poker party, but they opted for the present and just chilled by the fire.

Ace was kicked back in the chair with his legs stretched out. He looked up at the sky. It was a gorgeous night. The air was crisp and cooling as the night went on. Clear skies made for the full moon to cast its light on the land below it.

While the others bullshitted about stuff back home, he went over in his head the particulars of the mission at hand. During dinner, the team had discussed how a group of insurgents had managed to abduct five highly trained ex-Special Forces soldiers. He ran back through his head all the details Alex had given them, and there were some parts he now questioned. None of the video feeds had captured any of the abductions nor did they reveal any shots of the contractors themselves, leading Ace to wonder where the contractors had been stationed during the time of the initial break-in. Being that he hadn't heard from Alex since they parted ways in the early afternoon, he took that as a sign she hadn't come across anything substantial.

Potter's voice broke his train of thought making him glance toward his second in command as he walked toward an open chair. Potter's presence brought some relief. Potter had been on Alex duty for the last two hours. So, if Potter was back that meant Alex was back in her barracks. What made Ace nervous was the shit-eating grin on his best friend's face. The two of them went through BUD/S training together. He knew from experience when Potter had that look it meant he was up to something, and nine times out of ten it didn't bode well for him.

They had formed a friendship from the start and Ace considered Potter the brother he never had. Growing up with three younger sisters he welcomed Potter as a male counterpart in the family.

Lowering himself in the chair, Potter popped open a beer. Ace watched and waited. When Potter swallowed half the beer in what seemed like one gulp, he glanced over and smirked.

"Your girl Alex is back safe and sound."

Ace felt a sensation in the pit of his belly just at the mention of her name. The jealousy he felt was high schoolish when the other guys stopped talking and glanced over at Potter. Stitch had a big grin on his face. Ace cocked one of his eyebrows.

"She isn't my girl."

Giving a quick snort, Potter said, "Yeah, keep telling yourself that Romeo. Dude, you were staring at her ass. Not to mention every hour you've asked at least one of us if we've heard from her yet. I can't say I blame you. She is a catch for sure. And, damn that little snappiness to her is a total turn-on if I say so myself."

"You'd be snappy too if your dream vacation was interrupted for something like this," Frost said to Potter.

"That sucks, but as we all know when duty calls you don't have a choice." Dino chimed in.

The talk about Alex and her vacation had Ace envisioning what she might look like in a bikini as the sun's warm rays penetrated her silky, smooth skin. He bet she filled out that swimsuit very nicely.

"What's your assessment of her Ace? And, not of her backside," Irish teased. Jesus, they were never going to let him live that down.

"She's definitely a wealth of knowledge. She's tough, but I get the feeling some of that toughness is an act to cover her nervousness of being back here after what she went through. We just need to keep an eye on her now with that video surfacing." He looked at Stitch and Stitch nodded.

71

"Speak of the devil," Dino said smiling, tipping his beer toward the direction of the barracks and several of the guys grinned.

Ace glanced over his shoulder as Alex strode towards them. She had changed. She had replaced her business casual look with black sweats and a fitted plain red t-shirt. Which if he had to choose, he thought she looked hot in the more comfortable set of clothing. Not to mention her t-shirt dipped low in the front, teasing him with a glimpse of her cleavage.

"I was starting to wonder if you were going to join us," Potter said to her and Ace gave Potter a questioning look.

"She and I ran into each other and I invited her to join us."

Ace looked at her. In the clothes she wore, and her long brown hair pulled up into a ponytail, she looked youthful, but still beautiful and all woman. He would thank Potter later. He noticed her fidgeting with her fingers and motioned to the empty chair beside him.

"Have a seat."

"You looked like you were talking. I don't want to interrupt."

"Nonsense. Sit down. We were just chitchatting," Irish said as he gave her body a once over. If Ace had to be worried about any of the guys hitting on Alex it would be Irish. Ace cleared his throat and Irish looked at him and grinned before shrugging his shoulders as if saying he couldn't help it.

As Alex sat down, he caught a whiff of coconut and found himself leaning closer as he handed a beer to her.

She thanked him then popped open the can and took a gigantic gulp. She then sighed before relaxing back into the chair. "God that tastes good."

"Have you been in that room all afternoon?" Stitch asked though they all knew she had.

"Yep. I tend to focus on work too much sometimes. Studying a video, frame by frame can be daunting and long. Not to mention my

72

reading list got longer after you guys left, but I got hungry and needed a break, so I came back to grab a protein bar."

"A protein bar? That was your dinner?" Frost asked.

She shrugged her shoulders. "And, lunch."

"You need to eat, Alex." Ace reprimanded her and right away he realized how much of an asshole he sounded like, especially when she narrowed her eyes at him.

Frost chuckled. "Watch it Ace, she doesn't pull any punches. She handed my ass to me numerous times over the years."

Ace watched as Alex's eyes took on more of an amused glare. Kind of like a mischievous look, and he grinned at her. "Good to know."

Alex wasn't sure the meaning behind Ace's words, and it sort of made her belly flutter. When Potter had spotted her trying to sneak into her building then invited her out to have a beer with them, she tried to think of any excuse to decline the invite. Even after she told him she'd be out after she changed, she debated on just locking the door and staying inside. Kind of like what she did today. She did have a lot of work to go over, but she could've taken a break to have lunch and dinner, but then again there was the possibility she'd run into Ace.

It was hard to ignore him each time she saw him. She found herself wanting to be around him, but at the same time he made her uncomfortable and she couldn't put her finger on why that was. There were a few times during the day while she was working and her mind wandered in the direction of him, and that bugged her because she didn't like distractions. And, he was a huge distraction. *Then why are you sitting here with him?* She wished at times she could just turn off her inner self.

Arguably, the reason could be that he was the first guy she'd been attracted to while on an assignment. He was your typical Alpha male that screamed dominance and authority, whereas with other men she'd dated she found herself more of the dominant in the relationship. *And, that is probably why none of them ever lasted.*

Thank goodness, Skittles spoke up, "Any news on the Intel front?"

"I think I identified the guy in the video." She looked at Ace. "I need to talk to Bert tomorrow." Ace narrowed his eyes at the mention of Bert's name. "I know, I don't like it either, but I need to ask him about an informant he's used in the past. As I've said before, I don't trust him as far as I can throw, but he's the one who was in contact with the guy. So, would it be okay to borrow one of your men to accompany me? Someone who has a good knack for reading people." She had a keen eye herself and was trained well, however, considering who she was dealing with she thought it would be good to have a second set of eyes. "The person would also act as my insurance policy so if something happened, which I hope doesn't, but if it does, I don't want Bert throwing me under the bus yet again."

Ace looked at Potter and Potter nodded. "Potter will go with you."

"Perfect, we'll go in the morning." She smiled at Potter and he winked. She took another sip of beer before she continued. "I did speak with Derek and I will explain more tomorrow, but be prepared to head out on a little side trip tomorrow night."

"Seriously?" Ace asked.

"Like I said, we'll see what Bert has to say. I remember the guy's name, and if my memory is correct this guy is a very credible source and has eyes and ears everywhere. He is someone we need to speak with."

Ace raised his beer. "Well then, let's all hope this information pans out and we can bring home those men quickly."

They spent the next hour or so just talking. The later it got, one by one, the guys started calling it a night until Ace and Alex were the only two left. The fire crackled breaking the silence. Alex downed the rest of her beer then shivered as the temperature in the air got cooler. She had meant to grab her sweatshirt before she came out but she hadn't expected to stay out this long.

"Here," Ace said removing his fleece pullover. Her eyes about popped out of her head when his t-shirt lifted revealing a set of delicious looking abs. Now would be a good time to call it a night.

"Actually, I think I'm going to head inside myself." She started to stand when Ace covered her thigh with his hand. She looked down but he didn't remove it, then their eyes met and in that moment the atmosphere between them changed instantly. It felt electrifying and Alex found herself wanting to lean into him, wondering how his lips would feel against hers.

"Don't go yet." He said to her in a low voice and gave her the saddest, yet convincing puppy dog look she'd ever seen. He didn't allow her to protest as he laid the pullover in her lap, basically telling her to put it on and that she was staying. "Tell me something about you."

Who was she to argue? Although she could argue with herself, but why try to fight the attraction they were both obviously feeling? Maybe talking with him would reveal something about him that would turn her off. She tugged his exceptionally large pullover over her head and immediately his scent engulfed her nostrils. She tried not to be obvious as she inhaled deeply. It was hard to describe other than it was just Ace's manly scent. Once she was settled she looked at him.

"What would you like to know?"

Smiling, he said, "Well, I already know you are a badass chick with a sense of humor." She laughed. "I want to know what Alex Hardesty is like in the real world. What do you like to do for fun? What don't you like? What is your favorite food? Those types of things."

She looked down at the case of beer sitting on the ground. "Any more of those left?"

He grinned before reaching down and pulling another can from the box. "A woman after my heart already." She couldn't help the giddy feeling in the pit of her stomach. She was so screwed.

As their conversation flowed, Ace was learning more than he imagined about Alex. He was finding out that under her job facade she was just a normal girl next door. She was funny, smart, cute, had a great personality, and was extremely passionate about the things she spoke about. What added to her awesomeness was that she was a huge sports enthusiast and loved attending live games. Football was her favorite, with baseball and hockey coming in a close second and third. Blue was her favorite color and she would eat almost anything smothered in buffalo sauce. She adored penguins and polar bears and had even adopted one of each through the Wildlife Foundation. She also didn't like it when people played on their cell phones at the dinner table. But what touched him the most was her family values. Listening to her speak about her family made him realize how important it was to her. When he asked her if she wanted a family one day, he was pleased when she said yes.

He was going to be thirty-five in November. He wasn't getting any younger and his mother had been pestering him even more lately about finding a woman to settle down with. He always imagined having a family of his own but knew that with his profession it would be difficult to find the right woman.

He hadn't done the dating game in quite a while. Not that he never tried, but it just never worked out. Either the woman couldn't handle the aspects of his job, or she was just in it to say her boyfriend was a SEAL. Sure, he had his fair share of hook-ups when the need for a release was evident. But sitting here with Alex he realized he wanted more than just casual sex with a woman he met at a bar. He had been waiting for the day he would meet a woman to share his life with. One who understood his career and loved him for him. The more he spoke with Alex, the more he was starting to wonder if maybe he had found his match in the most unexpected place.

It was getting late and the fire was burning down. He saw her yawn a few times and knew it was time to let her go for the night. "I should let you get to bed."

"I should, but I'm glad I decided to stay. I've enjoyed this." When she smiled at him it hit him in the chest. Damn, he wanted to take her into his arms right then and there and kiss the hell out of her. She removed his pullover and handed it back to him. He thought about telling her to keep it, but thought better of it. It had been an enjoyable evening so he didn't want to push it.

He stood and started to pour water on the smoldering embers when suddenly a loud crack echoed in the air. Knowing the distinct sound of a rifle firing, Ace went into defensive mode. His first reaction was Alex's safety. Grabbing her around the waist he threw both of them to the ground. He landed on top of her, using his body as a shield to protect her. His heart pounded and the adrenalin started to kick in, flowing through him like wild rapids. Reaching down to his ankle holster he retrieved the pistol he kept there.

"Alex, are you okay?" Ace murmured pushing aside a few loose strands of her hair. He held his breath for a response that never came and he began to panic. Stitch and Dino ran over and knelt down next to them with their own weapons drawn.

"What the hell? You guys okay?" Stitch asked.

Ace rolled off Alex and that was when he saw the blood trickling down the side of her head.

"Alex!" Stitch shouted as his eyes saw the trail of blood down the side of her face. He too was met by silence.

Stitch felt for her pulse. "She's got a steady pulse."

Together they rolled her over onto her back. Skittles joined them with Stitch's medic bag. Ace felt some relief when they found no other wounds on her body, but she did have a large gash on the side of her head near her temple.

"Let's get her moved inside. I don't like being out in the open like this," Ace said as he carefully lifted Alex into his arms. Once inside the team's barracks, he laid her on a cot.

Stitch started looking at her wound. "Damn, this is deep. She's going to need stitches. What in the hell did she hit?" He asked for some smelling salts.

Ace ran his hands through his hair. "My guess is one of the rocks around the fire pit. I heard the shot and just reacted, throwing us both to the ground."

Ace felt awful knowing it was probably his aggressiveness that caused her injury. He held her head steady between the palms of his hands while Dino ran the smelling salts under her nose. He whispered in her ear. "Come on honey, please wake up." When she started to stir, he let out a huge sigh.

Moments later Colonel Johnson burst into the room.

Alex fought the icky blackness impeding her vision. When she was finally able to push it aside, she sensed a state of confusion going on around her. She felt multiple sets of hands touching her body, not to mention the number of voices she could hear. The sound of heavy boots thumping on the concrete floor echoed in her ears.

But it was the deep resounding voice right next to her that had her blinking her eyes open and meeting the hardened expression of the Colonel.

"Is she okay?"

She wondered what he meant by that and went to sit up to ask when a blinding pain shot through her skull, forcing her to lie back down. "Ow!" She went to touch the spot that hurt but was stopped when a large hand grasped hers. When she looked up, she was met with Ace's concerned expression.

"What happened?"

"You don't remember?" He asked.

Fighting the cloudiness in her head, she tried thinking back.

"I remember hearing a gunshot and dropping to the ground."

"You hit your head," Ace said as he gently caressed her hair.

"Damn…" She tried to touch her head again but was met with a stern warning from Stitch. "Don't touch that. You're going to need a couple of stitches."

"Do we know who it was? Did anyone see anything?" She questioned as she tried to get her bearings.

The Colonel stood there with his arms across his chest looking mighty pissed off. "No, and we probably never will. My guess based on where you were standing is the shooter fired from an area west of the base. We've got patrols out there scouring the area, but it is doubtful we'll find anyone. Now and then we get local people from nearby villages who like to take target practice. It isn't uncommon to see a stray bullet venture onto the base, and normally it happens during the night. However, nobody has ever been injured." Alex could see the strain on the Colonel's face, and rightfully so, as every person on the base was his responsibility.

As they waited for one of the base medics to show up with a suture kit she thought about what the Colonel said, and as much as she wanted to believe it could have been an accident, something was telling her that the bullet was intended for her as a warning.

Once the medic arrived and stitched her up, he left with the Colonel but not before leaving her with strict instructions which she was none too thrilled about. She didn't balk at the acetaminophen he left for her or when he cautioned her to take it easy for the next few days. What caused a tizzy was his insistence that she not stay alone for the night. Hell, she was so wound up right now she couldn't sleep if she wanted to.

She was arguing with Stitch about needing a babysitter when he said, "You leave me no choice," and he grabbed her arm and stuck her with a needle.

"Ow!" She rubbed the red dot on her upper arm. "What did you just give me?" She demanded to know. She stood up ready to battle it out with him when suddenly she felt lightheaded and began to sway on her feet. She tried to hold steady, but her body had other plans. Ace caught her before she fell on her ass.

Stitch gave her a stern look. "I see your stubbornness hasn't changed any. I gave you something to help you sleep."

She went to say something but shut her mouth, remembering a phrase Derek used to say to her. *Pick your battles wisely*. So, why waste her energy fighting a battle she wasn't going to win.

"Fine," She said and relaxed, feeling the drugs start to take effect. She looked up at Ace. "I can walk next door, ya know?"

"I'm sure you can, but no need to have you falling on your face and making matters worse." And, with that, he started for the door.

Once back in her barracks Ace let her down. She was all dirty and decided a shower now would be good before she felt the full effect of whatever Stitch gave her. As she grabbed her PJs from her bag Stitch called out to her.

"Be a good patient and don't give Ace a hard time."

She gave him the middle finger over her shoulder as she walked to the bathroom and shut the door. She could hear Stitch laughing as he left.

Being that she was able to score some hot water, she took her time in the shower, being careful to avoid getting the stitches wet. Her brain was so jumbled with all that was happening. Could it have been just a stray bullet? Do they even know where the bullet hit? How close had it been to her or Ace?

And then there was Ace. God. She really had enjoyed spending time with him tonight, but she still had some reservations about pursuing anything with him. They both had to think about their careers. Careers that took the both of them all over the world at any given time. How could a relationship built on those foundations alone really thrive?

When the water started to run cold she turned it off and dried off before getting into her PJs. When she exited the bathroom, Ace was sitting in the chair. The look on his face was void of expression.

"Are you okay?" He asked.

She walked towards him and he stood up. His eyes kept going to the stitches.

"I'll be fine, Ace." She knew he was worried. It was written all over his face. "This little cut isn't enough to keep me down." She smiled.

He shook his head and looked away like he didn't believe her.

She placed her hand on his arm. "Ace, what's wrong?"

"After I had you on the ground and then you wouldn't answer me, and I saw the blood…I'm not gonna lie, I was scared."

She didn't know what to say, but something came over her and had her reaching for him. She wrapped her arms around his thick waist and hugged him. His body was tense, but seconds later she felt him relax and his strong muscular arms hugged her back. They stayed just like that for a few moments longer. Her cheek was pressed against the soft material of his t-shirt. Even though her heart was divided, they both needed this. Tomorrow when she could think straight she would process it all.

Ace ran his hand up her back just before he released her and she took a step back.

"You should get some sleep."

Just before she climbed into bed, she turned back toward him.

"Thank you, Ace."

With a nod of his head, she crawled into bed and she pulled her blanket up over her. Just as she snuggled into her pillow and got comfortable there was a knock at the door, and she groaned. Without opening her eyes, she told Ace, "Tell whoever that is, there's no more vacancy here." She couldn't help the small smile on her lips when she heard Ace chuckle. She heard the door open and managed to muster up a little bit of energy to open an eye wide enough to see Potter standing in the doorway. He and some of the others went along with the guys from the base to have a look around. As much as she was curious if they found anything out, her body and mind were just too tired. Whatever concoction Stitch stuck her with was pulling her under. She closed her eyes and drifted off to sleep.

Ace shut the door behind him, not wanting to disturb Alex. He knew by the time he got back inside she would be asleep. Stitch told him he gave her enough pain medicine to make her sleep for a few hours. She was practically asleep as soon as her head hit the pillow. He, on the other hand, was still amped up from the incident and he hoped Potter had news, but judging from the look on Potter's face it wasn't going to be good news.

"All we got was a description of a beat-up truck speeding away from the base perimeter."

Ace ran his fingers through his hair. "Fuck! That bullet could've been for anyone of us."

Potter agreed then asked how Alex was doing.

"She'll be okay, though probably a little sore when she wakes up. She was almost asleep when you showed up. Between the base medic and Stitch, they convinced her to have someone stay with her tonight."

Potter laughed. "Let me guess, you raised your hand first."

The amusement in Potter's eyes and tone of voice didn't escape him. Who in the hell was he trying to fool?

"Uh, huh…I'm sure you'll keep a real good eye on her, buddy."

Ace threw a punch at Potter's shoulder, knowing his friend was trying to rile him up. Potter chuckled again, "Hey man. Good for you."

Potter smiled, "There aren't many women out there who understand all the fundamentals of our job. The danger involved, not knowing where we go, and not asking questions. Most women can't deal with that shit, but she gets it all."

Ace didn't get to the position he was currently in by being stupid. He knew a good thing when he saw one. And, Alex Hardesty was better than just good. She was the whole kit and caboodle.

As soon as their conversation wrapped up, he made his way back inside. He walked over to where Alex lay sleeping and made sure she was okay before taking a seat at the desk. He closed his eyes and wondered how in the hell he was going to get through the night being in the same room as her and not touch her. He chuckled to himself. Stitch was right; he'd never taken an interest in a woman as he did with Alex—there was no denying the attraction. She was curled up into a little ball under her blanket and he was so tempted to scoot his cot right next to hers and curl himself around her just to hold her in his arms.

Even though it seemed like progress had been made tonight before all hell had broken loose, he had a suspicion come tomorrow morning she would slide back into the professional role and try to shrug off the connection they were building. But he was going to do his best to make her see they could be good for each other.

CHAPTER NINE

The next morning Alex and Ace found themselves rushed for time as they hurried into base command to meet up with the team. Alex was beyond frustrated and the day was just getting started.

They were running a little behind schedule which neither of them was happy about. They had gotten held up when Alex couldn't find one of her work binders she kept some notes in. They turned her entire room upside down looking for it, but it never surfaced. Then Ace had to help her change the bandage covering her stitches, leaving her feeling a little on guard and slightly aroused. He was both gentle and thorough, and it had her wondering if his hands would feel that good against the rest of her body. She got shivers now just thinking about it.

As soon as they entered into the room, she saw Derek was already on the video feed, and she cringed knowing punctuality was a pet peeve of his. But it was Irish's comment that set off her ability to change gears and put that professional wall in place.

"Nice of you two to join us," he said with a smirk.

Even though Alex knew he was kidding, the funny jab pissed her off making her mood even worse. Instead of giving him a comeback, she chose to take the high road and ignore him.

She looked at the screen as she got her computer and other materials from her bag. "Sorry we're late, but I seemed to have misplaced one of my binders and we were looking for it."

She heard a couple of snickers and mentally rolled her eyes, knowing they were probably thinking that her and Ace had some wild sexcapade last night. It was times like this that served as a reminder as to why she needed to keep her relationship with Ace strictly professional.

Someone cleared their throat and when she looked up Derek was looking at her. Well through the TV, it looked like he was looking directly at her. She didn't get the chance to talk to him after the incident last night, and with how flustered she felt right now she could use a big hug from him. Lately, it wasn't often she got to spend actual time in person with him but when she did, she always made sure she got her hugs in.

"How are you feeling?" Derek probed, and the last thing she wanted to do was show weakness here on the job.

"Fine," She replied as she powered up her computer hoping he would get the hint to move along the conversation. Apparently, he missed it.

"Just fine?" He pressed with an eyebrow raised, most likely because of her snappiness.

"What do you want me to say?"

Ace cleared his throat next to her, and when she looked up at him, he was giving her a look as if telling her to be nice.

She looked around the room and they were all staring at her now. She set down the cables she had in her hands. "Okay, let's address the elephant in the room. Despite a slight headache and a little tenderness, I'm good." She looked at each one, daring any of them to say something.

After giving her another once over, Derek continued, "Okay then. Let's get started."

And just like that she was once again back in her element and started with the information on the informant.

"A long-time and credible informant has come forward claiming to have a lead on our missing contractors." She pulled up a map then shined a laser pointer on a rocky area. "We believe they could be in this vicinity and that is interesting because the last time I was here this particular area had been a hotbed for activity. We had suspected

Ashraf would use this to his advantage. Various abandoned Taliban and ISIS hideouts are inconspicuous if you don't know where to look and would make a great makeshift armory, if not a place to stash a couple of hostages. The problem is that it is a very wide area containing a lot of hidey-holes."

"Is this informant the same one you wanted to speak to Bert about?" Ace asked and she nodded.

"The informant goes by the name Bashir. When I was here last, we had been introduced to several NSA-civilian informants who helped our population-integration specialists blend into the community and make the important connections that needed to happen. Unfortunately, Bashir prefers to stay out of the spotlight, so I don't have a rapport with him. But Bert does. This could be our first big lead."

"When can you talk to Bert?" Derek asked her.

"Right after we finish up here. Potter and I are going to go see him."

"Before we move on, I also wanted to mention that Intel also picked up some chatter regarding another man who goes by the name Reynolds. He travels around quite often and has been flagged as a person of interest in many terrorist activities, including recent incidents connected to Ashraf. Information collected says Reynolds is an explosives expert. But what troubles me even more, is that witnesses have described him as possibly as an American trying to mask his identity with the culture of the region."

"An American?" Derek asked looking shocked.

"Afraid so."

"Son of a bitch!"

Before she could go on there was a knock on the door and Staff Sergeant Hill stuck his head in.

"Excuse me ma'am, there is a gentleman by the name Bowman here to see you."

A wide smile spread across her face. Bowman was a colleague of hers from the agency and was also recruited by Mason the same time she was. But more so he was a really good friend. A friend who helped her tremendously maneuver through the turbulent times when she last returned home from Afghanistan. He had been her sounding board and saving grace at the times when it mattered.

"Thank you, you can send him in."

Ace stood by watching as the newcomer walked in, went straight to Alex, and pulled her into a hug. The body language between the two indicated Alex and this guy knew each other well and he couldn't help but wonder how well. He scolded himself. He wasn't dating her, so who gave a shit if they were an item. But it wasn't that easy to let go. In just the short time he'd known her she had gotten under his skin. He wanted her and he didn't like the jealous feeling inside him.

When the guy finally released her, she took a step back and introduced him to the group. Once the round of introductions were made, he turned his attention back onto Alex.

"How's Afghanistan?" Bowman asked her.

"It's okay," she replied taking a quick glance at Ace, who had moved closer to her.

"Really? So, the rumor I heard this morning about you running into some trouble last night is just that? A rumor?" He raised an eyebrow as he stared at the bandage on her head.

"News does travel fast, but I'm good. Being that you are here and not in North Carolina, something must be up. Not that I'm upset to see you. It's been a few weeks and it's nice to see a familiar face." She smiled at him and now Ace was biting the inside of his cheek.

"I was in the area for other reasons, but Mason contacted me the other night asking if I could do a little research, and, well, I got some info on those hostages you guys are looking for. Since I was in the area I thought I would deliver the news personally."

"Seriously?" She asked. "Where?"

Bowman frowned as he told her the location and Alex's jaw dropped.

"You've got to be freaking kidding me." Alex stared at Bowman as if waiting for him to say he was just joking.

"Wish I was sweetie. The informant lives on the outskirts of the village. He said he heard some rumblings from a few villagers who are known to favor terrorists because of the payouts. These men he overheard were talking about a group of men being held in a cave just above the village on the east side."

"Shit," Alex muttered and took a seat on the stool next to her. Her face which normally glowed with the suntan she had, suddenly had taken on a greenish looking tint and Ace found himself reaching out to her.

"Hey, are you okay?" He asked. When she looked up at him, her eyes gave him his answer. She took a few deep breaths, and before long the color started coming back to her cheeks.

"Alex?" Derek asked looking concerned just as the rest of the group was.

She reached for a cup of water and Ace could see her hands shaking.

"It's the same village where my team and I were housed."

Everyone in the room knew the outcome of that mission and now understood her jaw drop reaction. But, once again she surprised Ace when she stood and started developing a plan based on the information Bowman gave. He even supplied some satellite images of the area showing possible infiltration and extraction points, and they were immediately debating what their best plans of attack were. Every planned mission had an A, B, C, D, and sometimes even an E plan.

"Hey Bowman, this informant, his name isn't by chance Bashir, is it?" Alex called out as her fingers flew across on the keyboard.

Bowman looked surprised and nodded his head. "How'd you know?"

"His name popped up in some Intel last night. I was planning on talking to Bert about him since he's familiar with him."

Bowman frowned. "Mason mentioned that asshole was here." Ace's eyes widened and even a few of the other guys snickered. Interesting that Bert didn't have the best reputation amongst the intelligence community. "I hope you're not going by yourself."

"No. I learned my lesson." She nodded in Potter's direction. "Potter's coming along with me."

"Good."

Alex glanced at Ace. "Getting back to strategy. As long as Bashir is willing to meet up with you guys, I think it is best to plan the meet up after the sun goes down. I know the area well and some people live there who are always looking to make a buck, even if it means working for the enemy. If they saw you, it could spell trouble. At least you guys would be able to get the information you need and that would give you some time to plan for any unforeseen issues. I don't recommend dropping; in the area is too wide open. I think it would be best if you can snag a vehicle. There is a turn-off from the main road that will take you up the mountain. There are plenty of places to dump the vehicle further out and then you guys can go on foot the rest of the way."

Ace was getting ready to agree with her plan until Bowman spoke up with his comments directed at Alex.

"Well, I hope you brought along your gear and hiking boots because you'll be joining the team on this mission."

Alex's head snapped up and her mouth gaped open. "Excuse me? What do you mean I'll be joining them?"

Bowman turned toward the group. "Unless one of you guys are fluent in Pashto, then you are going to need a translator."

Ace could sense Alex's fear and knew she wasn't comfortable with this news at all.

Voices started to raise as everyone began to speak at once. Some were questioning Alex's presence on the mission, and even though it wasn't meant as a dig to her capabilities it annoyed Ace. If the mission needed her, then by damn she would be a part of the team.

Ace brought his fingers to his mouth and whistled loudly bringing the room to complete silence.

"How about instead of everyone trying to guess what would be best for Alex, that we let her decide? She knows what's best for herself and I think we can all trust her to make the right decision without jeopardizing the mission."

"I think that's fair," Derek said then looked at Alex. "Alex…go or no go? Before you answer, know now that nobody in that room or I will think any less of you or your capabilities if your answer is no." Even though he'd never say it out loud due to Derek's high respect for Alex and the job she held, Ace could see the battle his commander was undergoing. On one hand, he had to treat Alex as the true professional she was. But on the other hand, she was family, more so his "little girl".

"Thank you, Ace," she began and gave him a small smile. "While I appreciate all your concerns, I would never place myself or anyone else for that matter in danger. If I know I'm not cut out for something, I'll be the first to let you know and remove myself from the situation."

Irish the smartass cracked a smile. "I think we'd all be more than happy to watch your six, darling." Ace had to hide his smile when the guys laughed because they all knew that comment was more directed at him since he was the one caught staring at her ass yesterday.

Alex even laughed but then got serious. "I was called up for this assignment because of my knowledge and skills, and I intend to see it through to the end no matter what, so, I'm in."

The guys all gave a loud *Hooyah* and Ace put his arm around her shoulders and squeezed her. When she looked up, he grinned, "Let me be the first to welcome you, unofficially of course to Alpha Team."

She gave him a sassy smirk. "Why thank you Lt." She then turned her attention to the screen. "Derek, I promise I won't let you down."

"I have no doubt you won't."

CHAPTER TEN

Alex walked in tandem with the team as they descended a small hill leading them to the area that satellite images showed there were three cave entrances along the ridge. The issue at hand was they didn't know which entrance to breach, and there were a lot of caves in the area that had connecting tunnels. Besides the scarce shrubbery, the mountainside didn't offer a lot of cover for the team.

Bashir never showed at the meet-up spot, sparking some concerns about the status of the mission. When Alex and Potter met with Bert, he had been cooperative and hadn't balked, and even made a call right there to Bashir putting a plan together for him to meet the team a few miles outside of the village.

The moon was half-hidden behind a cluster of clouds supplying them minimal light. The guys had use of their night vision goggles. She on the other hand was going by her eyesight and what the guys were telling her. She was lucky to find body armor that fit her. The village below them was quiet except for the occasional sound of a goat bleating. Even though it was a cool night she still felt the beads of sweat rolling down her back.

She would be lying if she said she wasn't a little anxious. After all, she hadn't been part of a field unit in more than two years. She had become comfortable working behind the scenes. The positive was that they were on the opposite side of the village from where the house she had stayed in had once stood. She wasn't sure she could stomach seeing that site.

"How are our eyes in the sky?" She heard Ace ask Irish through his com unit. Irish and Dino were in an overwatch position at a high elevation, keeping a lookout on the area below.

"We are a go," Irish replied just as they approached the first cave entrance. Getting antsy, Alex took to step forward but was shoved back by Ace's large hand. He glared at her from behind his black face mask and she took heed of his warning. Seconds later he gave a hand signal indicating they were moving in.

Her heart raced as she raised her weapon preparing to breach. On Ace's signal, Potter threw a flash grenade inside. Once the device detonated, they all rushed in. Trying to see through the smoke was hard.

"Shit! They aren't here," Ace said lowering his weapon as they moved further into the cave. It was dark, but Alex heard Ace say the tunnel connected to one of the other entrances.

"Well, who in the hell is this, then?" Frost asked as he pulled a phone out and took a picture of the dead man lying on the floor.

Alex looked at Ace. Even though she could only see his eyes she could sense his disappointment and frustration. She felt the same.

She stood over the body as Skittles shined a light so she could see, and as gruesome as it was to look at, she did anyway. "Based on what is left of his face, I'm thinking it's our informant, Bashir."

"Son of a bitch!" Ace exclaimed and Alex looked at the chains that were still attached to the wall and she had to agree with him. The fact that Bashir's body was still warm to the touch, they most likely had just missed them.

"Someone tipped them off and knew Bashir was working with us," Ace said.

Unfortunately, this scenario occurred more often than people thought. Bad guys find out someone is working against them and they take out the informant and leave his body for the good guys to find. Classic intimidation tactic.

Ace, Frost, and Skittles scoured the tunnel looking for anything that could be taken for intel purposes. Stitch and Potter went to clear the next entrance. Alex stayed back to look around the opposite side of the tunnel. She noticed a blinking light coming from a crevice in the wall. Taking her flashlight, she directed the light to the area in question, and when her brain registered what she was seeing she screamed, "BOMB!"

She heard one of the guys curse, but she was too busy sprinting toward the exit to find out who. Just as she cleared the opening and spotted a large boulder, the mountain exploded. She tried to dive behind the boulder but ended up going too far and went over the ridge. The loose rocks made the ground unstable and she tumbled down the side of the mountain. Her body was out of control as she rolled toward the village below. Her body took a beating as she hit shrubs and rolled over sharp rocks. Her momentum was halted when she collided with another large boulder. The hard impact on her back took her breath away. Suddenly she was thrust into a flashback from that horrific November evening.

"Yes, Derek, I promise I'll be home in time for Thanksgiving."

"You better be, your uncle Tink is deep-frying that huge ass turkey just for you," he said with a chuckle.

"Tell him it better be extra crispy. Listen, I better go, dinner should be ready."

"Okay, honey. I love you."

"I love you, too."

Sliding her phone into the back pocket of her jeans, sudden movement by the edge of the house caught her eye. Someone was standing there, watching her. He was wearing a hat with some sort of emblem on the front. She met his eyes, but who was it? She blinked and he was gone, when suddenly she was blinded by a flash of bright light. The ground beneath her feet had disappeared as a scorching heat sensation rolled over her body. Something hard struck her head and she found herself floating into the darkness.

The sound of gunfire and people shouting jarred Alex back to the present. She looked around; she was still protected from view by the large boulders surrounding her location, but she was all alone. Her thoughts were scattered. Where was the team? Had they survived the blast? Were they hurt? She glanced up toward where the cave was and all she could see was smoke. Her throat began to tighten as if the devil himself had a hold of her. She desperately tried to draw in air to her depleted lungs. Dammit, this couldn't be happening. She needed to focus and try and locate the team. But first, she had to get herself away from the danger that was lurking just feet away. Any second and someone could stumble upon her.

She reached to use her comm unit and realized it was gone. *Shit!* Peering over the boulder she could see people starting to walk toward her location. There was no way she could just walk out into the middle of the melee, but she needed to move. She belly-crawled about thirty feet until she reached the back of a nearby house.

Once she was out of view, she painstakingly got to her feet. Stepping out into the open she began to jog down the dirt and rocky pathway until she came to another cluster of homes. Her sense of direction was all mixed up. The only positive was that she at least still had her weapon.

She had almost made it to the last house when a shot was fired and missed her head by mere inches. Taking a quick look over her shoulder she saw two men running toward her. Recognizing they were not friendlies, she took off in a sprint, zigzagging through the village streets. She turned to the left and quickly realized it was the wrong turn as it led her out into the open with no cover. Her only choices were to go back into the village maze which wasn't the best idea considering the blast had awoken everyone and they were now up and outside wondering if hell had just erupted from the mountain. Or she could just make a run for it and hope she could outrun them. As the voices grew louder, she made her decision.

She took the gamble and started sprinting. She ducked and weaved as bullets flew around her. Just ahead was another cluster of buildings and she pumped her legs faster. She came to a narrow alley on the right and turned down it. Then she made a sharp turn to the left and ran into a dead end. Her only escape was to climb a steep hill. If she attempted to scale it, she would be a sitting duck. Frantically she looked around for an alternative knowing the two men could come around that corner at any second. Spotting a hole dug out just below one of the houses she got onto her stomach and wiggled her body feet first into it. It was a tight fit and she prayed to god there were no living animals, insects, or reptiles inside. Her anxiety picked up as the walls of the hole began to close around her. She could hear her breathing echoing off the walls and tried to relax her breaths. She listened for any indication the men were close by.

Once the smoke cleared enough to see, Ace started to retrace his steps back toward the caves. They were all lucky to be alive. He and the rest of the team were able to take cover before the bomb had detonated. Thankfully they had been near the entrance and were able to make a quick exit. His focus immediately shifted to Alex. She had been on the other side and he had no idea if she had been able to make it out in time.

Now he was in a panic because he lost all communication with her. He didn't know what to think as different scenarios crossed his mind.

"Irish, do you have a visual on Alex? I've lost contact with her."

Seconds ticked by. "Negative."

"Fuck!"

A few moments later Irish spoke again, "Hang on, I've got some movement, stand-by."

"Copy"

His heart was racing, and it wasn't from running. It was fear.

"I got her." *Thank fucking god!* "Shit, somehow she got herself down in the middle of the village. She's about one hundred fifty yards due west of your current location. She's got company. Two men are on her tail."

Ace took off followed by Frost and Skittles. They made their way down the mountain making sure to stay out of view of the audience that had gathered to see what triggered the explosion. Once they were at the edge of the village, Ace listened as Irish guided him to her whereabouts.

"Shit! She ran into a dead-end. She's taking cover. If you take a left at the next alley, then a right and head straight, you'll run into her. I'll handle the two assailants."

They followed Irish's directions. Just as they made the right turn, he heard the two swoosh sounds and watched the two men ahead of him crumple to the ground.

He looked around for her. "Irish, where is she? I don't see her."

"Look to your eight o'clock. She crawled into a hole just below that house with the window facing you."

Frost spotted it and they made their way over. As he got closer, he wondered how in the hell she even got herself in there. It was tiny.

Knowing she was armed he didn't want to get his head blown off, so as they approached the hole Ace called out.

"Alex," he said and waited with bated breath.

"Ace? I'm here, but I think I'm stuck."

"I got Frost and Skittles with me. Do me a favor and turn on the safety of your weapon."

"How do I know it isn't a trap and someone has a gun to your head making you say things?"

Ace grinned. Smart woman. He looked over at Frost, asking for a little help, but Frost just chuckled.

"What can I say, she was taught well."

He and Frost both got down on their hands and knees while Skittles shined a light into the hole. When the light hit her face, he wasn't expecting for her to grin at him.

"Is everyone okay?" She asked first shocking him.

"All good, but let's get you out of there."

He and Frost each took a hand and pulled her out. Once she was on her feet, they both looked her over. Besides covered in dirt she looked to be okay.

He placed his hand on her shoulder. "You good?" She looked up at him and nodded. He spoke into his mic. "Alpha One, Three, Eight, and Nine heading to rendezvous."

"Copy that." Potter's voice came back.

Without saying a word, he took Alex's hand in a firm grip and led her up the steep incline. It was difficult to maneuver because of loose rocks and holes. She slipped a few times when the ground gave way under her feet, but he never let go. As they cleared the hill, a pick-up truck skidded to a stop, and Frost and Skittles jumped into the back. Ace flung open the passenger door gesturing for Alex to get in. Once she was in he slid in beside her. Being it was a tight fit for the three of them in the tiny truck cab, Ace ended up pulling Alex on his lap giving Potter room to shift gears.

"Go, go!" Ace shouted and Potter stepped on the gas guiding them away from the destruction.

Ace had so much equipment strapped to his body that Alex had to reposition herself, so she was sitting with her back against the door. Pulling off his face mask he closed his eyes for a few seconds. He felt as if he had an unlimited supply of pent up energy brought on by the adrenalin pumping through his body. It wasn't until he felt the small feminine hand cover his hand and give it a squeeze that made him pause. His eyes popped open and he was met with those green eyes that pierced his heart. Even though no words were exchanged, the emotion dispensing from her eyes told him everything he needed to know, whether she intended to or not. He made the decision right at that moment that she would belong to him, even if he had to knock down the imaginary shield she had erected around her heart piece-by-piece. He took her hand into his, not giving a fuck who saw it before turning his attention back to the road in front of him.

Alex found herself crashing hard as she laid in bed trying to fall asleep, however, the moment her eyes would close, thoughts of the mission invaded her sub-conscious, causing her to jerk awake, and leaving her in an exhausted state. Her body was sore all over and she knew come morning she would have bruising all over.

When they had arrived safely back at the base, she and the team had debriefed with the commander and Colonel Johnson, giving their firsthand account of how the night played out. After a lot of back and forth discussions everyone had their suspicions that the mission may have been compromised. There were too many coincidences to chalk up the theory of the events being just a fluke.

Bert had decided to grace the team with his presence and put his two cents in considering it had been his informant who was found murdered. He hadn't been all that upset, which wasn't a huge surprise considering Bert didn't have a conscience when it came to his own team so why would he care about someone who was your friend one day, and your enemy the next.

They weren't sure if the explosive device had been set on a timer or if it was manually detonated. Replaying the scene back in her mind several times had left her shaken. Bert on the other hand kept insinuating the bomb could've been a coincidence and the captors were trying to cover their tracks. Based on experience, Alex wasn't a big believer in coincidences. It also didn't explain Bashir's death or the fact that she had been chased by two men who clearly wanted her dead. She was thankful she kept herself in shape and was able to evade them. If Irish hadn't taken them out, she would've done it herself if it came down to it.

She couldn't describe the relief she felt when she heard Ace's voice as she lay squeezed in that damn hole. It wasn't until they were in the truck when she and Ace shared a moment that she knew he was worth taking a chance on. The look in his blue eyes said it all. It was hard to stay quiet for the hour drive back to base when all she wanted to do was tell him how she felt and hoped like hell she wasn't making a huge mistake.

A knock sounded at the door and she rolled off her rack. When she opened the door, she was shocked to see Ace standing there. She had anticipated him being tied up longer with Derek. His hair was wet, and he had changed into shorts and a t-shirt.

She stared at his lips and then he swallowed, and the way his throat moved looked sexy as hell. Looking back up and holding his gaze she asked, "Ace…is everything okay?"

He walked in, making her take a few steps back before kicking the door closed behind him.

The last couple of hours had been complete torture. For Ace, there had been maybe only a hand full of times in his entire career he ever felt panicked in the middle of a mission, and tonight was one of those. When Alex yelled bomb, he honestly thought they were all done for.

Prior to leaving the base, the decision to keep Alex behind had almost been made because he couldn't bear it if something had happened to her on his watch. It wasn't that he felt she wasn't capable. It all came down to him not wanting her placed in danger. Yes, it sounded sexist, but, looking back now, she had been an integral part of the mission and the reason they were all alive.

For the past two days, she has danced around him, but he wasn't going to stand for it anymore. When she held his hand in the truck and looked at him with those sultry and caring green orbs, he knew he was done for. The look she conveyed was a need that he couldn't quite understand at first, but then he got it. She was silently telling him she was ready. Now he just needed to see it through.

He would've been at her door sooner; however, he had gotten held up with paperwork that needed to be completed. Just seeing her brightened his foul mood. But now that she was eating him up with her eyes, he wanted to do nothing more than take her into his arms and show her just how he felt about her.

"Ace....is everything okay?"

"Yeah, everything's good, honey. I just wanted to come by and see how you were doing."

She walked over and sat on his rack that was still there. He followed suit, sitting next to her. He had so much he wanted to say to her but didn't know where to start.

When she turned her head to meet his eyes, the anger from earlier started to return seeing the bruise brandishing her skin along her cheek from the ordeal earlier in the night. As his eyes slid from her cheek to her temple and the stitches came into view, it made him angrier.

"I was going to come over after you guys got back. I can't find the ointment that the medic gave me, but I ended up laying down instead." She tried turning away as if she was ashamed of her injuries, but he wasn't going to stand for it. He clutched her chin and gently lifted her head until she was looking at him. She was so beautiful.

He gave her a soft smile. "I threw it in that little blue and pink bag in your bathroom."

He got up and retrieved it then made quick work dabbing a little of it around the stitches. Her skin felt so soft and smooth under his fingers that he couldn't stop his hands as they moved to her shoulders, then down her arms and followed the same path back up until her cheek rested in the palm of his hand. His thumb gently stroked the discolored mark. She was more than your average woman. She was a true badass on the battlefield. The way she jumped right into the action and meshed with the team professionally, anyone looking in from the outside would think she was an actual member of the team.

"Ace?" She questioned when all he could do was gaze into her eyes.

He moved his body closer and bent his head. His lips made contact with her shoulder and he smiled when he heard her breath hitch. From there he couldn't stop, she was too enticing. His lips left a trail of kisses up her slender neck to her jawline before hovering over her luscious pink lips that were just begging him to taste. He couldn't pull away, not now when he was this close, not when he could feel her warm puffs of breath against his lips.

Breathing hard himself he said to her, "I need to know, and now would be a good time tell me if you are involved with anyone."

Ace stared down at her. She looked so sexy, and her emerald green eyes drew him in further. She lifted her arms and looped them around his neck, scooting herself closer to him to where their mouths were just millimeters apart.

"So, I probably shouldn't mention my harem of men waiting for me back at home?" She playfully arched an eyebrow and he couldn't hold back the grin on his face right before he kissed her.

He didn't give her any leeway as he delved his tongue into her mouth and explored every mouthwatering inch of it. When she tried to pull him closer, he had a better idea. Breaking the kiss just briefly, he lifted her and placed her on his lap. He didn't care how intimate it felt with her on top of him, straddling his waist. He wrapped one of his arms around her and his other hand dove into her hair. With a slight tug on her silky brown locks, she gasped, and he used that opportunity to claim those delicious plump pink lips once more. The moan she let out intensified the desire that was flowing through him. All he kept repeating in his head was MINE, MINE, MINE....

Before things went from PG to R rated, he drew back. The two of them gazed at each other, both breathing heavily. With eyes still closed, he leaned forward and nipped her bottom lip, making her eyes pop open and she smiled. "Wow," She said pulling him in and kissing his jaw.

He barked out a laugh, "My thoughts exactly." He hugged her tight before kissing the side of her head. "Jesus, I can't get enough of you." He told her making her laugh and damn did he love the sound of her laugh. He bent his head and kissed her again. This time when he released her lips, he pressed his forehead against hers. They sat like that for several moments just staring into each other's eyes.

"I need to be honest with you, Alex." He finally said and she sat back but didn't remove her arms from around his neck.

"Honest about what?"

He took a deep breath. "Jesus, this is so out of character for me."

Now she looked concerned, and it wasn't what he intended. "Ace what is it?" She prodded and he reached up and tucked a loose strand of hair behind her ear. He admired her beauty both inside and out, and he knew his family would love her.

"Since that day you slammed into me, I haven't been able to get you out of my mind, and then how plans went to shit tonight.... well...I feel like it took a decade off my life. Sitting here with you in my arms, I...." He ran his fingers through his hair. "Shit... I'm very attracted to you and I know it seems impossible considering we just met a couple of days ago."

When she didn't say anything after a few long seconds and just gazed at him, he thought he may have gone too far, too fast. But then a smile slowly swept across her face as she stared down at him.

"Well, I'm glad to know that it wasn't just me who felt something. And, I must tell ya it scared the hell out of me. I've spent my entire adult life submerging myself into my work. I was constantly on the go traveling from one country to the next. I never had the time to meet much less get to know someone. But then you appeared out of nowhere and I wasn't sure what to think. My whole life has pretty much been spent living and breathing the military life. My assignments bring me in contact with a lot of military personnel. I see how guys and some women use their uniform and credentials to add a notch to their belt. I think deep down that is why I keep my distance and don't give in when I'm asked out by one." And, boy has she had a lot of offers. "I don't want to be on the other end of a one night stand. But something just clicked when we met and I couldn't shake it."

Ace cupped her face with his hands and looked into her eyes. "I won't lie. I've done exactly what you just described when I was younger. But I swear to you, the thought of you being an easy lay never crossed my mind. Hell, you turned me upside down when you looked up into my eyes the first time and smiled."

She smiled and took a big breath while placing her hand against his cheek. "So, what now? I don't know if I want people knowing we're—" she waved her hand in the air, "doing whatever we're doing. At least not yet."

He grinned. "What we are doing is getting to know each other. As far as the others are concerned, it's none of their business. I get you have a professional reputation to uphold, and the last thing I want is for you to feel uncomfortable."

"I can handle that," she replied and snuggled close to him.

"Hang on a minute." He stood and walked over to the main light switch and flipped it sending the room into darkness except for the soft glow of light from the small table lamp next to the bed. He scooted her cot closer to his, so they were touching. Then he took the two pillows and stacked them on top of each other. He laid down, then reached over, and guided her down next to him. He took a deep breath when she rested her head on his shoulder and placed her hand on his chest. Their connection felt so right. It brought a calmness over him. It was perfect.

"Ace...what are you doing?"

He closed his eyes and grinned. "What does it look like? I'm staying with you tonight." When she went to protest, he said, "I promise to be a total gentleman." He couldn't remember the last time he laid in bed with a woman and just held her.

"I'd like that." She whispered as she made herself more comfortable. Once she settled, he reached over and turned out the light.

As they lay there in the pitch dark with the silence surrounding them, he knew she hadn't fallen asleep. He had learned just in the short time that her mind never seemed to rest.

"What are you thinking about?" He asked.

"We've known each other for a good forty-eight hours but I feel like I've known you a lifetime."

"Me too, honey."

"Ace?"

"Yeah?"

"Thanks for coming by to check on me."

He didn't know what to say so he just squeezed her and kissed her forehead. In a matter of minutes her breathing evened out and she was fast asleep. He was a lucky man and he hoped like hell this worked out, because he was already in deep.

CHAPTER ELEVEN

"What in the hell do you mean she got away?" Ashraf shouted into the phone as he listened to Reynolds ramble on about how the Americans evaded the explosion he had set. It was the middle of the damn night and he had hoped to wake up in the morning with news that the deed was done and Alex Hardesty would no longer be a threat to him. This was very disconcerting. His face was red, and he could feel the pulse in his temple beating. He was beyond angry. He was full of rage.

"Those two idiots watching the place didn't detonate the explosive when they were supposed to. I had it all set. All they had to do was press the damn button. They followed her on foot, but she slipped away." Reynolds tried explaining, shifting the blame away from him. However, Ashraf didn't care who was at fault. They had a prime opportunity to eliminate her and they failed. It was unacceptable.

"Dammit! You said you would take care of her. I don't need this shit right now." Ashraf paced the length of his office.

"And I will. I can't help it if your men screwed up."

"Where are those two anyway?"

"Dead."

"Well, at least that saves me the hassle of having to eliminate them myself. What's the next move? I'm running out of time. The leaders of the coalition are expecting me to move the weapons within the week. And, what about the hostage situation? What is the latest on that?"

"Ms. Hardesty will be sent a clear message tomorrow that she needs to watch her back. As for the hostage situation, they think they were moved before they got to the location. Bashir is dead. He was getting too close to the truth and was a threat."

"You better damn well make sure you take care of this shit. I'm paying you enough money, so do your damn job. You've had two opportunities, and both were fucked up."

"Watch it, Ashraf. I don't take well to threats. I'll have you remember that I'm the one with the power to end you. All it will take is one phone call. We need to be careful. In case you don't remember, she is in the company of a team of Special Forces soldiers. We have our man on the inside, plus with me and my associate running interference back in Washington, everything will pan out in the end."

Ashraf blew out a breath. He was starting to hate Reynolds. He'd become a thorn in his side. But he was right; he knew too much and could bring him down quickly. He'd see that Reynolds completed the task of eliminating Alexandra Hardesty, and then he'd sever ties with the fucker making sure he was no longer a threat either.

"Just get the job done. I expect an update soon."

He disconnected and threw the phone across the room. It hit the wall and shattered. He was growing tired of the excuses. He had men that could've done the job when Alex had returned home after the last incident, but Reynolds had assured him she wouldn't be a threat again, that she had moved on. Look how that turned out. Now she was back, and he knew the real reason she was here, and that was to get revenge.

He plopped down into his desk chair and stared at a picture of Alex. Just because Reynolds said he'd take care of it didn't mean he couldn't have his own back-up plan in case Reynolds failed again. Smiling, he opened his desk drawer and pulled out another cell phone. Quickly dialing his oldest son, he got an answer on the second ring.

"Father, it's late, is everything okay?"

Ignoring his son's concern, he asked, "How bad do you want Alex Hardesty?"

Ashraf couldn't help the sly smile that had his lips curling upward as he explained his plan to his son. Maybe instead of killing her, she could be an asset to his organization. That is after Yaseen saw to the training process of her physical and emotional breakdown until she obeyed.

CHAPTER TWELVE

Alex awoke to a massive blanket of heat encasing her. At first, she tensed feeling the large arm against her hip, but then she felt the warm lips as they made their way along her shoulder followed by the deep, rough voice she knew too well.

"You're okay, it's just me," he spoke calmly and she relaxed back into Ace's embrace as he spooned her from behind. She gave her butt a slight wiggle against his front just in the right spot and heard him take in a deep breath, and she couldn't help but smile. *Damn, a girl could get used to waking up to this every morning!*

Carefully she rolled herself over to face him. She smiled and he flashed one back at her. "Morning beautiful." He placed a kiss on the tip of her nose. She wanted to melt at the sound of his voice. His normal raspy voice was a major turn on for her. But with the added extra morning rasp it was orgasmic.

"Morning," she said trying to snuggle closer to him. "What time is it?"

"Time for us to get up."

"Noooo," she whined and tried burrowing herself even more into his body. She had slept so well once she had fallen asleep. Knowing Ace was there and would watch over her probably helped her subconscious relax. "I'm comfortable and you're warm and snuggly." She whispered.

He snorted, "Well, that's a first. I don't think I've ever been called snuggly before. Come on, up you go." He tried sitting up, but she wasn't having any of it and latched onto him. She wrapped her arms and legs around him like a koala bear hugging a tree and laughed. They both got tangled up in the sheets and blankets causing them to lose their balance and they tumbled onto the floor.

Ace maneuvered himself, so he took the brunt of the fall landing on his back, with Alex sprawled out on top of him. Both were laughing hysterically when someone knocked on the door. Before they could blink an eye, the door swung open and the team came strolling in, clearly amused seeing the two of them on the floor.

Caught in a compromising situation, Alex buried her head in Ace's chest as a wave of embarrassment flooded her. So much for keeping things between the two of them. She could feel Ace's stomach shaking from his silent laughter.

She couldn't see him but she knew it was Irish that spoke, "Awe. Honey don't be embarrassed, at least we got here before the clothes started coming off because that would have been embarrassing. Well for you that is. As for us, I think we'd all enjoy the view."

At the sound of Ace's low growl, she turned her head so she could see the guys. Her lips lifted into a smile. "What if I tell you that I'm not embarrassed and that I'm just sexually frustrated that I forgot to put the chair under the doorknob so we wouldn't be interrupted."

He opened his mouth to say something but closed it again. Meanwhile, the entire room erupted in laughter. She had apparently shocked Irish into silence.

With Ace's help she was up on her feet even though her body protested, feeling a little stiff. She wished she could crawl back into bed with her new personal human heater.

Irish threw his arm around her shoulder. He stood around six feet, a tad bit shorter than Ace, and his blue eyes held a twinkle to them. "Are you sure you want him?" He asked pointing at Ace only for Ace to flip him off. "He can be pretty bossy you know?" She knew he was teasing so she played along and batted her eyelashes. "Maybe I like to be bossed around." She threw a wink his way and grinned. He dropped his arm and stomped away, muttering something about Ace being a lucky motherfucker. She laughed and looked over at Ace who was standing there watching her and Irish's playful banter trying to hide a grin. Oh, yes, he could boss her around all he wanted.

She looked him over, admiring his physique and handsome face. Although those weren't the attributes that drew him to her. She considered those delectable features a bonus. What she admired about Ace was his character. He was attentive, caring, comforting, fun, and surprisingly easy to talk to.

Breaking from her thoughts, Ace approached her and put a hand on her waist. His other hand caressed her cheek, "I'm going to go grab a shower."

She glanced over at the clock. It was a little after 8:00 a.m. *Damn, they had slept in.* "I need to get ready as well."

"I'll come back over when I'm finished, and then we'll walk over to base command."

She nodded her head. He gave her another kiss, this time a quick one on the cheek, then turned and moseyed out the door into the morning sunlight.

As she watched Ace saunter out the door with his team following behind him making comments about the two of them, she gathered her clothes and made her way to the bathroom to get ready for another day.

CHAPTER THIRTEEN

After a quick breakfast, Alex was in a rush to get over to base command. In the middle of breakfast, she had received an urgent text message from Bowman saying she needed to check her email. Right now, it was just her and Ace. The others weren't due to join them for another forty minutes.

She pulled up her email and found the one from Bowman. By the time she finished reading the report, she had goosebumps on every single part of her body. She kept repeating to herself that the report was incorrect—it had to be. Leaning back she kept re-reading the words on the screen thinking that maybe she was missing words or adding her own but that wasn't the case. It was Ace's touch to her arm that had her looking up.

"What's wrong?" He asked as if he could read her mind.

She went to speak, but out of the blue, she heard Derek's booming voice behind her. When both she and Ace turned, she was surprised to see him on the TV screen.

"Hey, what's up?" She asked, knowing they weren't due to connect with him until the team arrived.

"Mason called and said I needed to connect with you. I'm assuming you got the message from Bowman?"

She nodded her head. "I have."

"And?"

"And, what I read concerns me."

"Mason didn't know the specifics on the language in there. Bowman's still traveling, but when he got a hold of the document, he called Mason. The problem was that his reception was bad and they got disconnected. But before he lost contact with him, Bowman said it was important that you saw this and for Mason to call me to connect with you. What is this all about? I see there are locations highlighted in the report that mention possible sightings of the hostages."

As she tried to continue, she was interrupted by a knock on the door. Before she could stand, the door opened, and Colonel Johnson strode in. Glancing at Ace she saw that he was just as surprised as she was to see him. Ace stood and shook hands with him, then the Colonel turned to address Derek.

"Derek, good to see you again."

Derek? Why would the Colonel address him by his first name? Last night when they spoke on the phone it was all formal speak. But as the two men conversed, it became clear to Alex that the two higher-ranking gentlemen knew each other well. No wonder the Colonel had firsthand knowledge about her background.

"Alex, when Mason called, I thought it was best to include Colonel Johnson. I trust him completely, as you both should too."

Alex peered up at the Colonel who was standing behind them with his arms crossed over his chest leaning against the high-top table. She knew if Derek said to trust him then she needed to.

She looked back towards the screen as Derek continued, "Alex, why don't you fill us in on the details?"

She cleared her throat and began to speak. "Before we get into that, I want to follow up from our discussion last night. After the way last night's mission went down, I'm strongly convinced that the mission was compromised. With your permission, I'd like to create a list of individuals who have or had access to our files and information and start a process of elimination. That bomb was placed there intentionally and meant to kill us all. We were just lucky this time."

"Yeah, thanks to your keen eye," Ace said to her.

She smiled at him for the compliment. "Let's also not forget the lovely souvenir I got the other night," she said pointing to her stitches making all three men frown, so she kept going. "Now let's talk about this report. What Bowman sent me outlines the information that was said to be provided by first-hand accounts. However, I call bullshit. That is unless dead people can talk."

"What?" Derek asked looking even more curious.

She took a deep breath. "The information stated in the files could've only been divulged by someone from my previous team or myself. And, there are several reasons I know that didn't happen. One, our Intel mysteriously vanished. Two, the actual flash drives were destroyed in the explosion, and third, the only person alive and knows what was in those reports is me. So, I'm struggling as to how details from a past mission that the government swears they never got, ironically made its way into Intel on a case that I am working on." Now that she said all of that out loud, it sounded ridiculously crazy and she almost couldn't believe it herself.

Derek leaned forward and cautiously asked, "You're sure you didn't provide that information when you were debriefed once you got home? You were going through a lot at the time."

She shook her head. "I'm positive. I was so frustrated and angry that I stopped talking. They weren't listening to me anyway, so I didn't offer any further information. But I swear, Derek. This report mimics my accounts from two years ago. It is practically my words on there."

"Can you elaborate on the information provided in the report?"

She looked at the Colonel. "It references certain locations we monitored. The only difference is that this report links our hostages to the locations. It's like whoever sent the info in is teasing me."

"How many locations are we talking about?" Ace asked.

"There was a total of six, but only five of them are mentioned in the new report. However, our focus was on two of them more so than the others."

"What made those two more conspicuous?" Derek asked.

"The two locations were close to each other, northwest of Kabul. We had informants at both locations with access to the buildings. They provided times, even photos of certain individuals coming and going. According to both, they saw crates of weapons being loaded inside. Over three days, we blended ourselves into the crowds in local markets trying to get close enough." She explained how on the one day was when she came face-to-face with Yaseen, Ashraf's oldest son.

"Shit, what did you do?" Colonel Johnson asked.

"My job: I acted like nothing was out of the ordinary and was just a tourist on vacation doing some shopping. My colleague at the time was meeting up with one of the informants at the other end of the market. We constructed a plan to catch them off guard and get to the hiding spot to secure the weapons and any of Ashraf's men during their transport; however, the night of the raid our informant went missing. Not wanting to waste time, we carried out the plan anyway, but by the time we got there the weapons were gone. We realized that it had been a setup—the transporters suspected the informant was working with the government so they told him about the warehouse to see if we would show up. When we did, they killed him. His body was discovered a few days later."

She furrowed her eyebrows. "Now that I think about it, I'm curious as to why Ashraf didn't order us taken out right there. It was the perfect opportunity."

"Fuck…" Derek uttered and took a sip of water. "That doesn't matter because it didn't happen. Tell us about the sixth location. You said it wasn't mentioned in the current Intel."

"This one is complicated. Compared to the other locations, the building here was massive in size. Like a warehouse, set at the base of the mountains in a valley. It was near a village but far enough away from prying eyes. In my opinion, it was a perfect spot if you wanted to hide something. I've wanted access to this one ever since it popped up on our radar. Wouldn't mind still checking it out."

"Why couldn't you access it?" Derek asked.

"It sits just inside a green zone."

"You'd have to get clearance to go in since it's considered a non-combat zone," Colonel Johnson said tapping his index finger against his chin.

"Yes. Even with Intel flagging it, we got denied both times we requested. We were able to secure a spot from a nearby hillside and watch from a distance. People came and went moving bags and boxes into the building. Most nights someone stayed."

"Maybe a safe house." Ace stated.

Then Derek spoke up, "This is definitely noteworthy, and you're positive the valley location was not part of today's report?"

"Nope."

"My recommendation is that we push forward and begin to eliminate these locations one-by-one. If we're lucky, we can locate our guys and maybe nab us a few terrorists in the process."

While Ace and the Colonel were talking with Derek, Alex typed a few notes into her computer. The team would be arriving at any minute and she wanted to be ready so they could hit the ground running. Half listening to the conversation going on behind her, she heard Derek mention something about keeping a watchful eye and it caused her to remember the flashback she had last night. Her fingers slowed on the keyboard until they came to a stop and she closed her eyes. She started replaying the night through her mind. Slowly, the images started reappearing, the phone call, and the explosion. But those weren't the ones she was searching for. She suppressed her memory, searching hard for the stranger she saw.

A light breeze blew through, sending a slight shiver through her. She took a step towards the house when she saw movement to her right. There, by the corner of the house. He was looking right at her. Williams? He had a hat pulled down low obscuring his face so she couldn't positively identify him. She tried looking harder, but a noise distracted, her causing her to look away. When she looked back, he was gone, and then everything else was a blur. She couldn't breathe, her chest and throat constricted.

"Alex!"

Bert called her name. Wait...that wasn't Bert's voice. This voice was much deeper and rough.

"Alex!"

Ace! It was Ace's voice. He sounded so close, but still so far away. He would help her.

Ace was in the middle of discussing some strategy options when he noticed something was wrong with Alex. Her eyes were wide open, but it was like she was stuck in a fog. When he heard her gasp for breath, he knew she was in trouble.

Reaching for her he called out her name.

"Alex!"

He couldn't shake her from whatever had a hold of her. He picked her up and placed her on his lap. The Colonel handed him a cold towel and he placed it on her forehead.

"What the hell happened?" The Colonel asked.

"I don't know. When I looked over, she looked like she was in shock. Could've been a panic attack."

Ace glanced at the screen. "Commander, do you know if Alex has panic attacks?"

Derek shook his head. "Not that I'm aware of. Is she okay?"

Ace turned his attention back to Alex and saw her breathing begin to even out. He used the towel to blot her flushed cheeks. When he heard her curse, he knew she was back with them.

"I think she'll be okay."

꼭

"Shit!" She muttered when her brain finally caught up. The large hand pressed against her back reminded her she wasn't alone. She opened her eyes and was met with Ace's penetrating gaze. Feeling embarrassed, she tried to slide off his lap, but he held her still. Oh god, she couldn't believe this was happening. She had done so well to hide the attacks these last two years. Why now?

She heard Derek's voice calling her name. She didn't want to turn around and face him. She never wanted him to see her like this—to see what she had been dealing with.

"Alex, look at me, please." When she turned, she only saw concern.

"Are you okay?"

She nodded. "I'm sorry about that."

The Colonel handed her a bottle of water and she thanked him. He sat in the chair next to her. "Alex, you don't have to apologize. Trust me, sweetie, we've all gone through it. There's no need to be embarrassed, especially not around us."

She appreciated and respected his comment. "Thanks. Not many people do understand."

She looked up at Ace and could tell he was worried for her, but she needed to show him that she really was okay.

She tried once again to stand and this time he released her. But in all honesty, she didn't want to leave the confines of his hold, where she felt safe and protected.

She knew she owed them an explanation, so she decided now was as good a time as any. She took a few steps away before turning to face the three of them. When she started to speak, she was grateful they didn't try to interrupt with questions. Once she finished, Derek surprised her by thanking her for being open and honest, and told her how hard that must have been for her. They each asked a few questions, but it was two years ago and without a positive identification she couldn't very well just walk into the agency and say she saw a man.

Ace touched her elbow and turned her, so she was looking at him. "Alex, why didn't you ever mention to me that you've been having flashbacks, especially considering I've stayed with you for the last two nights?" Alex couldn't believe Ace's slipup and she knew he realized the mistake as well when he closed his eyes, probably wishing he could backpedal those words.

Ace wanted to kick himself for that mental slip. He opened his eyes and the Colonel arched an eyebrow in his direction. Derek's face was void of expression but was turning red, and Alex sat there hiding a grin behind her hand. *Shit.*

Thank god, someone's brain was firing on all cylinders as Alex jumped in to save the situation from going completely south to the point of no return. She turned her attention to the TV but not before a faint smirk crossed those lips of hers and she winked. Speaking quickly before Derek's head exploded, she explained how both Stitch and the base medic felt better if someone had stayed with her the first night, and then how he had stopped by to check on her last night and that she appreciated his concern, and that she asked him to stay last night because she was a little shaken up from the events.

The commander looked at Ace, "And, you just happened to be the one to volunteer your services?" His voice dripped with sarcasm. Ace swore that behind Derek's stoic look he could see him trying to conceal a smile. And, he wasn't sure if that was a good thing or a bad thing. What did he expect him to do? Nobody else volunteered, although it wouldn't have done any good because he would've overridden them.

Apparently, Derek's question was rhetorical because he followed up with a question directed at Alex.

"Are you sure you're good to continue?"

"Yes, I promise."

Derek sighed, "Alex, before you say anything, hear me out. Considering what we are dealing with and all the unknowns, please promise me that you'll take extra precautions. Try to stay with the team as much as possible. At least until we can get some clear information." Derek looked in the direction of Ace. "Since the Lt. seems to be generous with his *volunteer* hours, I'm entrusting him with your safety."

"What? Derek, you do realize that if I were involved in any other operation this conversation wouldn't be happening."

Derek gave his shoulders a shrug. "Maybe not, but this is my operation and my orders."

"You're serious? You're assigning a bodyguard to me?"

He grinned. "If that is what you want to call it. But think of it more along the lines of personal protection. Understood?"

She thought about it before she responded. There were bigger battles to be fought. "Do I have a choice?" She mumbled as she crossed her arms and looked over at Ace and judging by the grin on his face, he found it amusing. *Wasn't this just fucking dandy.*

"Alex, don't take it personally. My decision doesn't mean I don't respect your capabilities. I just don't trust the environment you've been placed in, and I'm not willing to take any chances, especially when I can provide you additional backup."

She thought about it and was surprised how easily she'd agree with him. Extra protection never hurt anyone. In fact, she had been in multiple operations where she could've used additional backup. She found the word rolling off her tongue with no hesitation. "Understood." The last thing she needed to be was uncooperative.

The look Derek gave her made her want to laugh. Knowing Derek, he had been prepared to argue his point because normally she wouldn't have given in so easily. She smiled when he just nodded his head, then glanced at his watch, "I need to take care of a few things before we brief the others. I'll talk to you all shortly." The screen went blank and the Colonel excused himself, leaving just her and Ace in the room.

Alex stood there as she nibbled on her lip, and even though she appeared so serious and deep in thought, Ace thought she looked damn adorable. "I hate it when he's right," she finally said, looking up at him.

He pulled her into his arms and rested his chin on the top of her head. "I know that was probably hard for you to do, but I agree with him. It never hurts to have a little reinforcement."

She hugged him around his waist and looked up at him, her mouth twitched up on one side, "Does that mean you'll be moving in with me for the duration?"

He raised one of his eyebrows. "You think I'd let any of the others stay with you?"

She ran her hands up his arms to his shoulders and couldn't help but egg him on. "I'm sure Irish would be more than happy to watch my six." She laughed when he growled low, drawing her in and hugging her tight. As he pulled away, he slipped his hand under her silky hair, palming the nape of her neck. She tilted her head back. He stared into her gorgeous green eyes.

She smiled and he saw the playfulness in her eyes. He moved closer to her lips. "I can already tell you're going to be a troublemaker. Just remember, I know many forms of torture techniques."

"Hmm…it could be worth the experience to break the rules."

God, how he wished he could take her somewhere and show her what he really wanted to do to her. Instead, he leaned forward and covered her mouth with his. He needed to breathe, but he couldn't get enough of her as he continued to explore her mouth until he was forced to pull away before he passed out from lack of oxygen. Her eyes were still closed as her chest rose and fell. He placed his forehead against hers, letting his heart settle down.

"Shit, baby, what are you doing to me? Keeping you a secret is going to be one hell of an order."

She opened her eyes and gave him that sexy little lopsided grin of hers. "Yeah, well, you almost let the cat out of the bag with Derek." She chuckled. "I don't think I've ever seen his face turn that red so fast. Not even when he and my Uncle Tink caught me making out with a guy in my junior year of high school."

"I think his expression was more intense than some of the combat missions I've been a part of." He shook his head then laughed. "Jesus, I can't believe I said that."

She was laughing with him. "Well, Derek is going to find out sooner or later."

He rubbed his hand along his jaw, "I know, but I'd prefer for us to at least be on the same continent when we tell him." His eyes widened at his next thought. "Jesus, I hope he doesn't think I slept with you."

He started pacing the room cussing himself out. When she started laughing at him, he stopped and stared at her.

"What is wrong with you? My commander is sitting at home probably thinking I had sex with his daughter and you're laughing."

She laughed harder as she walked over and hugged him. "Don't worry yourself to death. If Derek were truly upset, he wouldn't have assigned you as my *personal protection*." She giggled again as she used Derek's words, making him chuckle. "We just need to be careful in this room." He didn't understand and looked down at her, and then she grinned cheekily as she nodded toward the TV. "Remember Derek can pop in anytime he wants." He groaned causing her to laugh again.

Pressing his body against hers, he slowly backed her up against the table. He secured both of her hands behind her back. He could see how aroused she was. Her breathing picked up and her pulse could be seen beating on the side of her neck. She was getting pleasure from being at his mercy. He was in complete control. He bent and licked the shell of her ear causing her body to shiver. She closed her eyes and moaned, arching her upper body and causing her perky breasts to brush against his chest. "Are you sure you want me to keep my hands to myself? Not knowing if you're going to get caught is part of the fun," he teased, knowing damn well he would never put her in that type of position.

Ace's alpha male ways had all of Alex's senses on overload and she could feel her body coming alive. Her nipples pebbled beneath her bra, and when she didn't answer his question, he started torturing her neck with his lethal lips. Oh, dear God, she was going to explode. Not to mention anyone could walk in the room at any moment.

"Ace." She sighed.

"I love hearing my name fall from your lips." He kept up the assault, strategically leaving a trail of wet kisses against her skin, hitting certain erogenous zones. "You are too tempting to keep my hands off of you." He lightly bit down on the sensitive skin where her shoulder and neck connected.

"Oh god..." She uttered under her breath. She couldn't sense anything right now except for how good his soft and gentle lips felt against her delicate skin. Lord have mercy, did the man know how to play her strings. She tilted her head more to the side, giving him better access to her neck as he kissed, licked, and nibbled.

She was grateful she had enough of her senses to hear the approaching voices outside the door. Ace must have heard too as he nipped her shoulder one last time before releasing her wrists and backing away like nothing was happening.

She knew her cheeks looked flushed, hell her entire body felt on fire. When she looked up at Ace, his blue eyes had taken on a darker hue of blue. He took a seat at the table just as the team walked in and started claiming their seats around the larger table.

She couldn't hold back her laugh at Ace's expression when she took a seat at the other end of the table, right next to Irish. This should make for an interesting meeting.

If he could tease, so could she.

Once Colonel Johnson arrived and Derek re-joined on the TV, they began laying out their plan.

Three hours later, Alex's brain felt like mush. She was not only mentally exhausted, but she was also feeling a tad bit annoyed. After the first hour of explaining to the team what she discussed with Ace, Derek, and the Colonel earlier, they all agreed that since they had no other Intel to go on that they would work through eliminating the five sites. It wasn't until they brought Bert into the mix that things started to get a little intense. Since Bert was involved in the prior mission, Alex thought it would be a strategic move to get Bert's thoughts on her claims of the reports being very similar to hers.

The last two hours had been what Alex could only describe as blistering. As it seemed, Bert was up to his old tricks. He had been privy to some supplementary Intel from the agency to piggy-back on the reports received from Bowman this morning, however, it had been obvious he had no plans on sharing the new information until his colleague Mical spoke up and reminded him of it. Of course, Bert tried to bullshit his way around it saying he thought they had received the same information and didn't want to be redundant.

Bert's Intel included additional details about two of the sites mentioned in the reports. Because of their close proximity to one another, it was discovered that the hostages were being shuttled back and forth between the two using various routes.

It had been hard for Alex not to laugh when Derek tore into Bert's ass for not stepping forward with the said information immediately. That was then followed up by a scorching verbal beat-down from the Colonel, who threatened to notify Bert's superiors about his lack of transparency and leadership skills. Of course, Bert responded with his normal arrogance not seeming fazed by the reprimand. After a short break to let everyone cool off they reconvened and decided that the team would move out tonight to begin scouring the sites.

As the meeting winded down and the team discussed logistics with the Colonel's staff, Alex sat back in her chair and kicked off her shoes. She wished she had a pair of flip flops in her bag.

She picked up a stack of papers from the table and saw some mail that Staff Sergeant Hill had given her this morning when she arrived. She knew the two white envelopes were from Mason because he told her he was sending them to her. She pushed those to the side and picked up the larger manila envelope. She studied it noting it lacked a return address but was postmarked from Washington, D.C. She slid her finger under the flap breaking the seal. Before she could reach in to pull out the contents, some photographs spilled out onto the table. It had taken a couple of seconds to register what the pictures were and a sudden terrifying chill seeped through her body. She tried to speak, but fear had robbed her of her voice. She couldn't pull her eyes away from the picture closest to her. Black spots appeared in her vision and her body began to sway. She thought someone called her name, but she couldn't focus. Suddenly her stomach lurched, and she covered her mouth just before sprinting out the door.

Even as Derek spoke to him, Ace was keeping an eye on Alex in his peripheral vision. He knew something was amiss when she froze and looked as if she was in a state of shock while she stared at whatever was on the table. Others became aware when Ace called out to her. At first, he thought she was having another episode like earlier, and thinking she was going to pass out he called out to Frost who was the closest to her but it was too late as she switched gears and bolted for the door.

Ace was torn. He wanted to follow her to make sure she was okay, but he also wanted to know what in the hell caused that type of reaction from her. He quickly rounded the table just as Frost and Stitch each cursed. As soon as his eyes zeroed in on the photograph closest to where she had been sitting, he literally felt sick to his stomach. He almost didn't even recognize Alex as she lay sprawled out on the ground, her clothes tattered. She was bloody all over, and if he didn't know better, he would swear she was dead. Knowing this was what she overcame and had been dealing with for the last two years enraged him. Hearing about an incident was one thing, but to see actual visuals was disturbing. And judging from not only his reaction but the others in the room, it proved upsetting for all parties.

"Jesus, what is this shit?" Dino asked looking over his shoulder. There were other photos. Very graphic ones of burned body parts.

"Shit, these were taken on Alex's last mission here," Stitch spoke aloud.

"What did you say?" Bert asked as he too started looking over the photos. "These must have been taken before the rescue team arrived."

Ace suddenly got an awfully bad feeling in the pit of his stomach. Looking up from the photos he locked eyes with Derek and swallowed hard. This new development wasn't going to sit well with the commander, but this was a warning that all but confirmed that Alex had a target on her back.

Ace explained to Derek what was going on. He flipped through the photos, using a napkin so as not to disturb any possible fingerprint evidence. The more he saw, the worse his stomach felt. It was sickening, but unfortunately, the world was full of sick people. No wonder she was having flashbacks.

Frost was looking over Ace's shoulder as he flipped through the pictures. "How in the hell did she survive?" He stated angrily, and Ace had to agree.

"There are pictures of Alex specifically?" Derek demanded to know in-between a separate conversation he was having with someone else on his end.

"Yes, Sir." He told Derek there were pictures of her both before and after the explosion. All taken at different angles as if there possibly could be more than one person involved. "They're pretty graphic."

Irish held up a finger, interrupting Ace as he came around the table. "Did you say there are some of her on the ground *after* the explosion?"

"Yeah, why?"

"Let me see those," Irish said taking them from Ace. He watched as Irish carefully studied two of the photos that were taken of her at close range. "Bingo!" He exclaimed as he pointed at the pictures. "There's no phone in any of these pictures."

"What does a phone have to do with this?" Bert asked standing there with his arms over his chest.

Irish looked at Bert. "Alex mentioned you were there during the rescue."

"So, what does that have to do with a phone?"

"She told us that she was told by you that she was the person who called for support. However, she doesn't recall doing that."

"And your point is?" Bert questioned, clearly agitated by Irish's line of questioning. Ace found it rather interesting the defensive stance Bert was taking, and it was either his imagination, or Bert's face was actually turning redder by the second.

"My point is, where is the fucking phone? She would have had it in her possession if she were, in fact, the one who called."

Bert threw his hands in the air. "How should I know? I wasn't there. All I can tell you is what I was told."

Irish leveled his stare at Bert. "Unless she has some pretty mighty superpowers it seems mighty impossible considering she was unconscious. Is there someone who can validate that it was her who made the call?"

"Are you trying to insinuate something soldier?" Bert said revealing the ugly side of him.

"No, sir. I'm just stating the facts. Let's say she made the call before she blacked out, the phone should be on or near her." He pointed to the picture. "The point is that there is no fucking phone within her reach." When Bert didn't respond Irish continued his rant. "My theory is that if there is no phone, then she never made the call and someone else did. Possibly the person who took these pictures

130

and sent them to her, here. I'll be honest man; this smells awful fishy and I don't think we've been given all the factual details."

Ace hadn't seen Irish this fired up and opinionated in well, quite a long time. But the more he listened to Irish and his rational thoughts, Ace had to agree with his lead sniper. He felt the knot in his stomach grow. Coupled with the mysterious events that had occurred since they've arrived, along with the new revelations that Alex remembered from that night, Ace was feeling confident that someone was manipulating the situation to lure her back. A sudden surge of protectiveness rose within him.

Bert snorted a sarcastic laugh. "That is an insane theory. Why would someone go to all the trouble to eliminate her team but leave her there alive?"

Irish crossed his arms his chest and glared at Bert. "I don't know. But you're supposed to be the expert, so why don't you tell us? Why do you think she was left alive?"

"Jesus, I don't believe I'm standing here arguing with you over this. Look, there could be several reasons. Hell, maybe they thought she was dead. After all, she was supposed to be inside that house with her team."

"Enough!" Derek roared. "Mr. McMahon, while we all appreciate your expertise on this matter, your presence is no longer needed right now. So, if you don't mind, I'd like to speak with my team privately."

"What? But what about the missions being coordinated? We haven't finalized the details. I need to log everything."

"My team or the Colonel's staff will touch base with you regarding the mission when your assistance is required."

Ace saw the fire in Bert's eyes and knew the pompous man wasn't going to leave well alone. Ace could tell that Bert had it out for Alex from the moment he first met him. And, this little blow-up just added fuel to the fire. Alex was right, something was off with Bert, and his loyalty seemed elsewhere. From here on, they all needed to watch their backs.

Once Bert had stormed out of the room with his two associates at his heel, Derek asked where Alex was. This wasn't just the voice of a man who commanded a SEAL team, but of a man of compassion and love who was worried about his daughter's safety.

"Colonel Johnson, along with Potter and Stitch went to find her."

"I don't want her out of your sights for even a second! You got me? Not until we get some damn answers. This shit just got personal."

"Yes, Sir."

And in that instant, the mission went from just being a hostage situation to now protecting the person who was supposed to be finding the hostages.

Bracing herself on her knees, Alex heaved once more as she hovered over the toilet. She had made it to the bathroom just in time before her stomach erupted. Only when she felt settled did she try to stand and rinse her mouth out before she splashed some cold water on her face.

She grabbed a paper towel from the dispenser and patted her face dry. Taking a deep breath, she looked up into the mirror and the sight made her cringe slightly. She didn't look like the confident woman who everyone knew her to be. Instead, she saw a timid girl with tears in her eyes, ready to run home and hide under her blanket.

She shook her head and stared at her reflection. "I've got this." She said to herself, but deep down she felt the fear engulf her.

As much as she tried, she couldn't erase the images from her memory. Someone close to the situation was using this mission to scare her. But why? She placed her hands on the sink and hung her head as she closed her eyes.

A sudden knock on the door startled her, making her jump. "Alex?" The Colonel's voice came from the other side.

Drawing in one last deep breath, she discarded the paper towel in the trash before she opened the door. The Colonel stood there, blocking the doorway with his arms crossed over his chest looking just as dangerous as the other men. His firm jaw was tight, and she could feel the tension rolling off him. Just beyond the Colonel stood Potter and Stitch.

"I'm sorry." She took a breath. "It's just those pictures, on top of the flashback earlier," she paused, "it just brought back a lot of bad memories for me and well, I just needed a few minutes to compose myself."

He lowered his arms and placed his hands on her shoulders. "Alex, I've already told you. You don't have to apologize. Those pictures shook everyone including me. So, I can imagine the effect they had on you. Come on." He took her elbow and guided her back to the room. "Let's get you back before Derek starts calling in reinforcements. He needs to see for himself that you're okay."

Before they got to the room, she turned to face the Colonel, "If someone has a vendetta against me, I sure as hell don't want to bring any unnecessary trouble to your base."

"We'll get to the bottom of it. If I know Derek like I think I do, I'm sure he already has people working on it. And as for bringing trouble to the base. Look around, we're smack dab in the middle of a war. Trouble would have arrived here sooner or later. You wouldn't believe the threats we receive every day. We'll deal with whatever we're presented with. You have the entire base behind you." He gave her a reassuring smile and opened the door for her.

She walked into the room and all eyes went to her. *God, they probably think I'm some head case.* She glanced at the table and saw the photos had been stuffed into an evidence type baggie. She shivered at the sight.

She looked around the room meeting the eyes of every man, but it was Ace who she was seeking out. When their gazes met, she had to restrain herself so she wouldn't throw herself into his arms. Now was not the time to have a meltdown, and she knew if he touched her right now, she would completely fall apart. But that wasn't who she was. In all her twenty-nine soon to be thirty years of living and breathing, not once had she ever quit, and she wasn't about to start now. Clearing her throat, she straightened her shoulders showing the confidence she was known for.

"Are you okay, honey? I understand if you want -.

She cut Derek off as she shook her head, even though he looked angry and frustrated.

"I'm not quitting and definitely not about to run back home with my tail between my legs. I'm here, and as I've said before, I'm not coming home until I see this mission through and take down this bastard once and for all. Too many people have suffered because of him, not to mention the emotional toll that mission cost me. I lost colleagues and friends because of his violent acts. I'm not about to have five more American civilians added to that count. I need to do this." She pleaded with him, and meant every word. She wasn't leaving until she knew Ashraf couldn't harm another soul.

Derek's expression softened. "Emotional issues? Alex, how long has this been going on?"

Of course, that was the one thing he picked up on, but she waved him off. "We'll talk about that later. Right now, what's important is locating the hostages. Once we find them, I'm ninety-nine percent sure Ashraf won't be far. You have my word, Derek, I won't do anything stupid to put myself in harm's way. At least not on purpose."

"You already are."

"But, I'm in good hands. I'm with your team. The best of the best, right? Plus, you taught me well. I can do almost anything they can—admit it." She raised her eyebrows challenging him to deny it.

He let out a deep sigh. "Fine…" That was a little too easy in her opinion, as she thought for sure he would fight her decision. "I already have a call into other agencies to see if they're able to shed some light on the situation. Ace, gather your team and put a plan together to hit both locations that Mr. McMahon shared with us today. I know I don't have to say this, but be vigilant out there. Ashraf is a sneaky sonofabitch and could be trying to divert our attention. Alex, you'll man the mission from the base along with Colonel Johnson." She was perfectly fine with that plan.

"And, Alex, please be careful."

The Colonel stepped forward and put his hand on her shoulder. "She's in good hands, Derek."

She gave him a faint smile. "Thank you, sir, I appreciate it." She swallowed the lump in her throat. They needed to get to the bottom of this and fast before anyone got hurt.

"Thanks, Mike," Derek said.

The Colonel waved him off, "Just doing my duty here. I know if the roles were reversed you'd do the same for me."

"Damn straight."

"I better get going and get my guys updated on the particulars. Our assets here are at your disposal," The Colonel said making his exit from the room leaving Alex with the team alone in the room.

She looked toward the TV and took the open seat next to Ace. She needed to assure Derek she had this. "D, I know you're worried but—"

135

He cut her off. "Worried? Worried isn't the word that I'd use right now to describe how I'm feeling Alex. Do you have any idea how badly I want to get on a plane and come over there and bring your ass back here where I know you're safe?" He wiped his hand down his face and sighed in frustration. The only other time she'd seen him react like this was two years ago when he walked into her hospital room. "God, girl, even at thirty years old you still give me grey hairs. I swore to your father that I'd protect you and look; you've gotten yourself in the crosshairs of an extremely dangerous man, and, I'm sitting halfway around the world and can't do a damn thing about it."

She couldn't stand to see him exposing a side of him that most likely his team hadn't witnessed. Needing to put a stop to his nonsense she raised her voice, something she rarely did with any of her uncles but especially Derek. "Stop right there!" The shocked expression on his face made her want to laugh, but at least she had his full attention.

"First of all, knock the guilt shit off. Yes, you made a promise to my dad. And I'd have to say in these last twenty-four years you've done one hell of a job at keeping your word." She knew she had hit the spot when his hardened expression softened, and only then did she bring her tone down a notch. "Look at me, Derek. Take a really good look and tell me what you see?"

Resting his clasped hands on his chin, he smiled. "I see a beautiful, intelligent, loyal, decisive, and independent woman who I'm so damn proud of."

"You see, every quality you just described didn't just magically happen. I'm all of those and so much more because of you." She felt the tears burn the back of her eyes and quickly blinked to try and dispel them. "I love you so much, Derek, and I thank god every day for the wisdom you and the others infused in me, but you can't protect me from everything. You can try, but nothing is guaranteed whether I am halfway around the world or in my house."

She felt an arm go around her shoulder and knew it was Stitch. She leaned against him embracing his show of support and love. "Sir, you have our word, we'll watch over and protect her to the best of our ability," Stitch said resolute.

"Derek, you and I both know that I knew what I was getting myself into when I accepted this assignment. Hell, I knew when I took the job with the NSA right out of college that I was going to face danger, but that was the risk and choice I made. You of all people know how ops can go haywire at any given time. Plus, like you said I've got your team here." She reached over and squeezed Ace's hand, catching him by surprise.

"I know honey and I love you too. Look, I need to make a few phone calls so the team can roll out tonight. You guys keep me informed of any new information."

After Derek signed off, the room was silent, and Alex closed her eyes. With all the stress she was under, she felt a headache coming on and she rubbed her temples, being careful to avoid the stitches on the one side. Today had taken an emotional toll on her, but she knew she'd overcome it. She thought back to when she stepped off the plane a few days ago and she instantly had a gut feeling this assignment wasn't going to be an easy open and shut case. After being used as target practice, chased through a village by not one but two gun-wielding men, and not to forget the brush with death of being blown to smithereens, and now the threatening mail, she'd say her instincts were right on. She could only hope that the guys got lucky and recovered those hostages tonight. Knowing she had a long night ahead of her, she thought a nap and some aspirin may help ease the headache.

She was so unfocused right now she hadn't even heard Stitch calling her name until he placed his hand on her shoulder. She looked up at him and saw the worry in his eyes. She didn't want them to worry about her. They needed to be focused on the upcoming mission.

"Are you sure you'll be okay?"

She half wondered what they all would say if she told them no.

"I will be. I know you guys have some things to discuss for tonight. While you guys do your thing, I think I'm going to lie down for a bit. Maybe afterward I'll start digging around on the dark web and see if I can find some information on this Reynolds guy." She hadn't forgotten about that guy. Maybe he was the missing link. "If we can get a lead on him, he could possibly lead us to Ashraf."

"Let's focus on tonight's mission and hope we find the hostages, then we'll worry about Ashraf," Stitch said.

She looked at Stitch with a serious expression. "I won't rest until Ashraf has been caught. Dead or alive."

"Alex, I'm not saying we won't go after him. All I'm saying is let's get through tonight and see what cards we are dealt with. I know how important it is for you to get the closure you want. But you need to remember in our line of work we don't always get what we want. Our first priority is locating those hostages and bringing them home."

She felt a little taken back by his sudden attitude. Did Stitch seriously think that she was putting the cart before the horse?

"I'm sorry, I didn't realize I needed to be reminded of what our priorities are." Stitch raised his eyebrow and she glared right back at him.

Ace had enough and stepped in between the two of them. "Look, standing here bickering like children isn't going to help the

138

situation." He turned to Alex. "Don't get so defensive. We're all aware of what the priorities are."

Alex dropped her arms to her side. "Whatever, I'm out of here." She could feel the eyes on her as she snatched her bag off the table and started walking toward the door.

"Why don't you go with her? I'll brief you in a bit." She looked up and saw Ace was talking to Stitch. Out of the eight of them, he was the last one she wanted with her right now.

As Alex walked alongside Stitch in silence, she glanced over and could tell from his taut posture and serious expression that he wasn't happy with her.

"Stitch, why don't you go back and be with the team? You're needed there. I promise to lock the doors. It's in the middle of the afternoon." He just grunted and kept walking until they were just passing the chow hall and he stopped.

"How about we get you something to eat first? You haven't eaten since breakfast."

She shook her head. The last thing she wanted was food. Although she could go for a ginger ale to help settle her nauseous belly. "I'm not hungry."

His annoyed sigh told her that he was beyond frustrated with her. *Oh well.* She didn't ask for a babysitter. They made the rest of the short walk in silence. As soon as they got to her place, she quickly grabbed a change of clothes and headed for the bathroom to change.

When she emerged from the bathroom, she found Stitch sitting in the chair with his head resting on his hands. She felt a little bad for bickering with him. They were all at their wit's end but that didn't give them any right to jump down each other's throats.

Stitch lifted his head enabling her to get a good look at those brown eyes gazing up at her.

"I'm sorry," she said walking over and standing in front of him.

He shook his head. "You aren't the only guilty party. I'm sorry too." He stood up and pulled her into a hug. "I know you don't want to hear this right now, but I am so worried about you."

"Stitch…" She tried taking a step back, but Stitch held her against him.

"No, please just hear me out." She relaxed and rested her cheek against his chest. "I'm not the only one. Frost, Derek, your other uncles, they worry about you too." He chuckled. "You've always been a risk-taker even when we were kids. We all knew your career was dangerous, but knowing what you went through two years ago and now believing that this sick bastard could be targeting you doesn't sit well with me. I'm with Derek and would love to throw your ass on a plane, but I understand your need to be here. I know how important finding justice is to you." He pulled back and looked down into her eyes. "I promise you that I will do everything in my power to help you take down that son of a bitch when the time comes."

She smiled and hugged him. "I love you. You and Frost are the best big brothers I could ever ask for."

She released him and walked over to her and Ace's makeshift twin size bed. Climbing in, she pulled the covers up to her chin and laid her head on the pillow.

"Alex?" Stitch called her name in a whispered voice.

"Yeah?"

"What you said to Derek earlier, is it true?"

"What?"

"About you still struggling with what happened?"

She shrugged her shoulders, "Occasionally something will trigger a flashback, but I deal with it." She wasn't going to bring up the attack she had earlier in the morning.

"You know if you ever need someone to talk to myself and Frost are always here for you."

She smiled. "I know, and I appreciate it. Derek and the rest of my uncles have been trying to get me to open up a little more with them."

"Have you talked to anyone about what you went through?"

"No."

"Why not?"

"I just haven't wanted to. I think walking away from the agency and then getting that job with Mason's firm helped some. I know that probably sounds weird, but getting back to work kept my mind off it."

"Just promise me you'll call if you feel the need to?"

"I promise."

"Okay. Get some rest."

She smiled then burrowed herself further into the pillow. Her eyes soon got heavy and moments later she was drifting off to sleep.

Alex hadn't been asleep for too long when the sound of the door to her room opened, jarring her awake. She knew it was Ace who had entered because she could hear him talking to Stitch. They were talking low, and with the steady hum coming from the air conditioning unit she couldn't hear their exact words.

When she heard the snick of the door again, she rolled over and was met by Ace's warm smile.

"How ya doing, sweetheart?" He walked over and sat next to her. He ran his knuckles down her cheek.

"Okay."

He pointed to a covered plate sitting on the table next to the bed.

"I wasn't sure if you'd be hungry or not, so I fixed you a plate."

His thoughtfulness warmed her, and she smiled as she sat up. He pulled her into his side and she snuggled closer savoring the feel of being close to him until her stomach growled, and Ace laughed.

He unwrapped her plate and handed it to her.

"What time is it?" She asked him as she scooped up a forkful of the steaming chicken and veggies.

"A little after six."

"Wow! It felt like I wasn't asleep for that long. No wonder I'm starving."

She was surprised at how hungry she felt. It was common for her to lose her appetite while she worked. She never could understand why, but she did. She'd always chalked it up to her nerves. She ate until her stomach couldn't hold another piece of food and then set the plate aside before getting up to grab a bottle of water.

When she returned, Ace stopped her before she sat back down and pulled her between his legs holding her firmly. His hand moved under her shirt, touching the skin along her hip just above the waistband of her shorts. She knew the moment his fingers brushed over her tattoo and scar because he stilled and gave her a curious look.

"You guys aren't the only ones with battle scars." She ran her fingers through his hair, loving how it would stand up in different directions. He looked so sexy.

He lifted the hem of her tank and took a peek of the words tattooed on her hip. He surprised her when he leaned forward and gently brushed his soft lips against the puckered scar. In an instant, she was overcome with so much emotion of his affection and compassion.

His gaze lifted to hers, "That which doesn't kill us, only makes us stronger." He repeated the words inked on her skin. "That holds a deep meaning."

"It does. I wanted something to remind myself that I was a survivor, and that I will continue to fight no matter what obstacles are put in front of me."

He cupped her face, "It's perfect," he said then kissed her on the lips. "You are perfect."

She pulled back a little with a slight grin and blushed, knowing she wasn't perfect. She had plenty of hang-ups about herself. "I wouldn't go to that extreme. You just haven't noticed any of my flaws."

He grinned, "We all have flaws, baby, but you're perfect for me." He released her and stood up, taking her hand and helping her up. "We need to get going. We need to go over a few details before we head out."

As he turned his back to her it immediately registered that he had changed into his uniform for tonight's mission. She never understood why some women lusted over a man in uniform until now. She never really took the opportunity to stare at a man in uniform because it never appealed to her. But studying Ace as he stood before her dressed for battle, she could see why. It wasn't just about a sexy, macho guy dressed in battle fatigues, it was the man beneath the layers of fabric and armor and what he represented in a relationship: security, safety, stability, honor, and discipline. He looked over his shoulder and she was caught red-handed staring at his nice firm butt.

"Like what you see?" He asked sarcastically with a sexy grin.

She sucked her bottom lip in between her teeth and bobbed her head up and down enthusiastically. She wasn't going to lie. He was sculpted like a masterpiece from head to toe. When he laughed, she just shrugged her shoulders. "I guess we can call it even. You were caught staring at my ass the other day, and now I was just returning the favor." She winked.

"Come on, before you make us late," He chuckled again leading her out of the building.

"How would I make us late?"

"Because if you were still looking at me like you were going to eat me up, it would be your fault that I made good use of those cots inside," he stated before a slow smile spread across his face and she felt the blush grow across her cheeks. He just laughed then ushered her along.

Dammit, how in the hell was she going to get through the mission tonight after he says something like that?

CHAPTER FOURTEEN

Alex laid in bed wide awake just as she had done for the last six nights. She glanced at the clock; 3:56 a.m. Sleeping had become very problematic for her. She chalked it up to stress considering how things were unfolding. As the days passed, they all knew time was running out. Yesterday another video was intercepted, revealing the person speaking was indeed Yaseen Fayed, Ashraf's oldest son. Other than threats, nothing significant had been revealed. It was almost as if the video was sent just to taunt them. The only differentiating the second video from the first was the location. The more recent one was shot inside a rather large building.

When the team headed out six nights ago she honestly believed something positive would prevail. But night after night scouring hidden caves on treacherous hillsides and abandoned villages, all they were left with was more questions. On a couple of the nights the team had been met by enemy forces adding more mayhem to the situation.

Back at the base frustration was mounting because it seemed as if Ashraf was always one step ahead of them. With help from Mason's team back home she'd done a background check on everyone she had on the list to investigate, and everyone came up clean. That left her scratching her head, because somehow Ashraf was aware of their plans.

Each time the guys left the confines of the base her stomach would ache with worry until they returned. It didn't matter that she was in constant contact with them throughout the mission. The anxious feeling was almost too much to bear. In a short period, they had all come to mean a great deal to her, and it would devastate her if anything happened to anyone of them.

The only positive information she had gathered through intelligence was that some of the explosives the team had run into had been at the hands of the mysterious Reynolds character. It was mind-boggling, because with all the sophisticated technology and assets the government employed in their research, they couldn't seem to find anything on the guy. No pictures, no personal data, no nothing, except for what they had to go on from witnesses. It was as if the guy operated as a ghost; one who had extensive military and, or operative training. The guy definitely knew how to play the game, but so did she, and sooner or later she would expose him.

Bert, since getting his ass chewed out by Derek and the Colonel had stayed in the shadows and only offered his services when asked. According to the Colonel, the agency had Bert working on other assignments within the region that had taken him off base at times, which hadn't upset her in the least. His two colleagues had stayed behind and sat in on the mission meetings. They were both very intelligent and they seemed to be more personable and forthcoming without Bert hovering over them. They even offered suggestions. Although on a few occasions during the missions Mical looked nervous or anxious as if he wanted to say something. At one point during the latest mission when Potter and Diego disarmed the explosive device with just seconds to spare the poor kid looked like he was going to pass out, but when she asked him if he was all right he seemed to bounce right back.

Last night, Bert had made a rare appearance in the war room while the team had been conducting a raid. His presence had made it a little uncomfortable, although she was grateful for the Colonel's ability to run interference when it was needed, like when Bert tried to override her decision to have the team move back when enemy forces had been spotted about a mile in the direction they were heading. He had wanted them to continue with the plan, but it wasn't safe—not to mention it was a stupid idea. After waiting a few hours they were able to move ahead with no resistance. After that dust-up all Bert did was stare at her. It was a cold, hard stare, one that would've frightened others. She wasn't scared per se, just more creeped out by it, and the Colonel sensed it drawing Bert's attention away from her.

With a silent sigh, she turned onto her side, being careful to not wake Ace who was sound asleep if going by his low snores. She propped herself up on her elbow and watched him as he slept. He had one arm thrown across his ripped abdomen while the other was stretched out above his head. His chest rose and fell with every deep breath he took.

Her heart and feelings for him grew with each passing day. She wanted so bad to wake him so they could talk, but she knew he needed his rest. In his line of work, sleep was a hot commodity as those soldiers never knew when their time for rest would come.

In between mission planning, prep work, and executing, her and Ace took time to learn more about each other. She loved listening to him talk about his family and his childhood. Being an only child, she was excited to learn he had three younger sisters who she couldn't wait to meet, along with his mom Charlotte. Two of his sisters, Maxie and Mikayla were married with children of their own. The youngest of the Chambers clan at age twenty-seven was Mia, who currently was enrolled in veterinarian school in New York. She was surprised when Ace revealed to her that when his father had unexpectedly passed away a few years ago he had come very close to leaving the team to go back home to help take care of his family. Alex would have to thank his mom because if it weren't for her intervention and convincing him to keep his course in the SEALs, she wouldn't be lying here with him now.

Her past relationships held no comparison over Ace which was odd considering the little time they had known each other. The attraction was mutual and powerful. He made her feel complete. That sounded strange even to herself, but what she was experiencing with Ace was utterly unique. It was definitely uncharted territory for her. Was it love? She wasn't certain, but something in her gut told her it was pretty darn close.

Ace stirred next to her then surprised her, "How long are you going to lay there and stare at me?" He asked, never opening his eyes.

When she didn't answer, he opened his eyes and looked up at her, then frowned. "You okay? What time is it?"

She leaned over him a little to check the clock. "Almost a quarter to five."

"You've been tossing and turning all night. How long have you been awake?"

Great, now she felt bad for disturbing him when she knew he needed the rest. He must have realized what she was thinking because when she rolled over and left her back facing him, he curled his big body around hers, and kissed her bare shoulder.

"What are you thinking right now, babe?"

"I feel bad for keeping you up. You and the guys have been working your asses off. I should've been more aware."

He rolled her onto her back and maneuvered himself between her legs. Using his forearms, he kept most of his weight off her. He shifted again, and she widened her legs creating more room for him to nestle in. As soon as she felt his hard length press against her belly, she sucked in a breath as her libido came roaring to life.

He stared down into her eyes. "You've got a lot on your mind. Your restlessness didn't faze me, so don't think it did."

He kissed her forehead and she wrapped her arms around his torso. Dragging her nails ever so lightly over the skin of his back, she felt his muscles jump beneath her fingertips. She heard him suck in a deep breath before he dropped his head and kissed her neck. She tilted her head to the side giving him better access. His lips then moved down her neck, leaving a trail of wetness behind until he reached her collarbone and nipped the sensitive skin there, causing her to gasp and her pussy to clench. She felt his smile against her skin before he soothed the love bite with his tongue.

Her body felt so alive and on fire. She wanted him to take her now. All the nights and mornings they'd spent sleeping together never went beyond kissing and maybe an occasional touch here and there. But right now, her body was primed and ready.

She rocked her hips upwards into his cock and when he lifted his head, she saw the hunger in those magnificent blue eyes. Oh yeah, he wanted her just as much as she wanted him. He started to move his hips in sync with her movements. Both rubbing against one another but never breaking eye contact. The friction caused them both to moan. She yearned to feel his naked body pressed against hers. Her hands slid down his ribcage moving to the waistband of his shorts when suddenly Ace pulled back. *What the hell?*

She was ready to combust, and judging from Ace's exceptionally large and erect cock, he was all but ready for a game of Pole Position. And, she wasn't referring to the race car game. That wasn't even a close comparison. She was thinking of Ace's man pole as he positioned it to slide inside her wet heat and send her into a satiated burst of pleasure. So, what the hell was the problem?

Just as she was about to protest, he dropped his head against her shoulder and nuzzled his face in the crook of her neck. The warm puffs of air against her skin sent a warm sensation through her body adding to her already aroused state.

149

She wasn't sure what happened but obviously, his thoughts had drifted somewhere other than getting down and dirty. She gave him a moment as her body was trapped under his weight.

"Just give me a minute sweetheart, please." He uttered in a tone that sounded strained.

Gently, she caressed his arms up to his shoulders. "Ace, please talk to me."

Raising his head, he rested his forehead against hers then took a deep breath and exhaled.

"I can't believe I'm saying this, and trust me, baby, there is nothing more that I want right now than to bury myself so deep in you and make you mine, but damn if our first time together is going to be in a cold, dreary, concrete room in Afghanistan." He brushed a loose hair from her face. "You deserve so much better. This delectable, sweet body of yours should be laid out on a huge fluffy bed surrounded by candles and flowers." He softly kissed her lips. "I want our first time to be special and meaningful - for both of us. I want to take you out, let the desire build through dinner before I take you home, strip you bare, and make love to you all night with no distractions or interruptions." He dipped his head and gave her a passionate kiss that left her feeling like a limp noodle. As if he had nowhere else to be, he took his time as he made love to her mouth. She could feel the emotions he poured into the steamy kiss. It was as if the two tongues were dancing in a rhythm like no other, and when he ended the kiss, he gazed into her now watery eyes before he kissed the tip of her nose.

"Happy Birthday, baby."

Her heart felt like it was going to burst with joy. The uncertainties she thought she might have had just minutes ago were now thrown out the window, because she fell in love with him at that moment. Between his words of promise for the future and his acknowledgement of her birthday, she knew deep down this amazing man had captured her heart. She couldn't stop the big, fat, lone tear that leaked out the corner of her eye before plopping on the pillow.

With a sappy smile and a frustrated groan, she asked him, "Got any ideas on how we can fast forward this mission so we can go home and get to that date?"

His laughter bounced off the bare walls, sending a warmth of love through her. He rolled off her and she cuddled against his warm body, draping her arm over his chest. They laid there, nestled in one another's arms. She felt loved and protected.

"Ace?"

"Yeah, sweetheart?"

She smiled to herself, loving when he used that endearment. "How is it that a guy like you isn't in a committed relationship?"

He scrunched his eyebrows together. "What do you mean?" His voice was rough and raspy. She snuggled closer to him. She didn't want to imagine him with any other woman, but she was curious. Ace was a great guy.

"Kind, caring, smart, strong, confident, not to mention very handsome among other things. Any woman would be crazy to not try and snatch you up. I'm sure you have women dropping their panties at your feet all the time. Hell, that probably goes for your whole team as well. You know, now that I think about it, I've never heard any of them mention a girlfriend, wife or fiancé."

He laughed. "Nope, none of us are tied down. Wait, let me rephrase that. None of *them* are tied down. As of a week ago, I'm officially off the market." He placed a kiss on the top of her head. It warmed her to hear the happiness in his voice, and it made her wonder just how long it had been since his last serious relationship. "I tried the dating scene, but it never evolved."

She sympathized with him. She could relate and understood it was hard for a woman to commit not only to a man, but to his job as well. It took a unique woman to accept the challenges of being involved in a relationship with a SEAL. Her own mother walked away from her dad for the very same reasons. She was also familiar with the infamous frog hogs; the women who frequented SEAL hangouts looking to score a night in a team member's bed. Although she'd rather not think about Ace hooking up with one, she wasn't naïve either.

She ran her palm up and down his chest. "You know I'm not like others you've dated, right?"

"What do you mean?"

"I grew up in this life. I fully get the demands of your career. I know when to mind my own business, but if there's something you feel I need to know, then I trust that you'd talk to me, and if I do happen to step over the line, just tell me so. Just remember in my line of work I like to ask questions." She grinned at him. "I really won't take it personally. I also know there will be times when you just want some space. I watched for years as my uncles came back from missions and went through their issues. It was all explained to me at an early age and I get it. Again, I just ask that you be honest with me. I'm good at a lot of things, but a mind reader, I'm not. I can promise you that I'll always be there for you and support you. I learned growing up that open communication and support are the keys to a lasting relationship."

She took hold of his large hand and linked her fingers with his. "The only issue is going to be the distance between where we live and our jobs." She placed a kiss on his bare chest just above his heart.

જી

Ace laid there in awe. Listening to her talk about her home made him visualize in his mind what it could be like sharing one with her. She could be that someone who he had always dreamed of who would be waiting for him when he returned stateside from missions. A partner to talk to and lean on when needed. A real future to look forward to. Jesus, he was a lucky bastard, but like she mentioned, they needed to work out the long-distance issue. Four hours between them wasn't acceptable. He wanted to see her every chance he could.

He stroked her shoulder as she lay curled up next to him, running her little fingers along his chest. "Baby, I know I've probably said this a lot in the past week, but do you know how amazing you are?"

"I think I'm beginning to get the picture," she said laughing.

As the sun started to rise, Ace knew he only had minutes before Alex got up and would start getting ready for the day. But he wasn't ready for her to leave him just yet. He was content tangled up in the sheets with her. She sat up and started to make her way over him, but he placed his hands on her hips, stilling her as she straddled his waist. He had to hold back the groan that was threatening to escape his mouth as he looked up at her and imagined how she would look naked in this exact position, throwing her head back in pleasure while riding him. Tamping down his desire, he filed that thought away for the time being. Until then, he would take pleasure in waking up next to her with her rumpled hair and cute pajamas with the penguins and polar bears on them.

"Where are you going?" He asked her.

"To start getting ready. Mason sent me a file on another case he wanted me to look at for him."

"But it's your birthday."

"So, I still have work to do, and you have a mission to prepare for." He mentally sighed knowing she was right, but that didn't mean she couldn't celebrate her birthday.

He looked up into her green eyes. "We need to do something for your birthday."

She gave him a funny look. "And what in god's name do you recommend we do on a military base in the middle of a desert of all places?"

He grinned, and in a flash, had her flipped onto her back with his lips pressed against her neck. She started to giggle until he reached the lobe of her ear and sucked it into his mouth. "I can think of other things to keep you occupied."

Ace didn't want the moment to end. He wanted to keep her in bed and love on her. He knew he had gotten her aroused, and it just made him smile even more.

She put her hands on his chest and shoved him back and he looked at her, "What?"

"What were the words out of that impressive mouth of yours just a little while ago?"

The corners of his lips curled up and he gave her a mischievous look. "Oh, I can show you just how impressive my mouth can be."

She jumped up almost knocking him off the bed and darted towards the bathroom, grabbing her clothes on the way. When she got to the doorway she turned around and eyeballed him.

"What?" He said again, throwing his hands up dramatically, even though he knew exactly what she was talking about. He was trying to hold back his laughter as she set her hands on her hips. Hips that he would like nothing more than to hold onto while he slid his needy cock into her wet, hot pussy. Just imagining that almost had his eyeballs rolling back into his head.

"How can you say something like that to me and not expect me to want more?" She pointed her finger at him, "You are a very, very evil man Lieutenant."

"It's called patience," he said giving his shoulders a slight shrug. "Patience is key in my line of work." He was ready to explode in laughter from the shocked look on her face.

Thank god there was a knock on the door because he wasn't sure how much longer he could last in a room alone with her before he said fuck it and threw her over his shoulder and took her back to bed. Shaking his head he got up and answered the door. Stitch walked in and looked over toward the bathroom and saw Alex standing there in her pajamas with her arms crossed in front of her chest, glaring at Ace.

Stitch cracked a smile, "Happy Birthday Sunshine. Who pissed in your cornflakes this morning?"

She opened her mouth to say something but then pulled it back, but he didn't miss the eye-roll.

Ace couldn't hold it in anymore. He started laughing so hard he was bent over holding his stomach. Righting himself he walked over to Alex and hugged her.

"I'm sorry, I shouldn't have teased you. And, I have to tell you it took a lot of patience to restrain myself." He leaned back to look at her and he swore there was amusement dancing in her eyes, but she still gave him the stink eye.

"It's a damn good thing I like you," she said as she got up on her tiptoes and kissed him before closing the door to the bathroom in his face. He just chuckled.

He looked over at Stitch who was watching them, not having a clue as to what the hell was going on. Ace just shook his head, "Trust me you don't want to know, man."

Grabbing a t-shirt out of his duffle Ace pulled it over his head. "I have to head over to base command and make sure things are ready for Alex's surprise. Do you and the guys mind hanging out

155

with her for a while to keep her occupied? She mentioned she needed to get some work done."

Stitch smiled, "She doesn't have a clue, does she?"

"Nope," Ace said grinning.

"Nice. Just so you know, if you pull this off, it's going to go down in the record books. Nobody has ever been able to surprise Alex for her birthday. Trust me, we tried plenty of times back in the day."

"Well, I couldn't have done it without all of you guys. With keeping Alex away while trying to plan, and getting Tenley to help back home, I owe you guys. Not to mention we haven't had much downtime in the last few days."

Stitch jerked his head toward the bathroom where Alex was. "You know you've got yourself one hell of a woman? A woman like her is hard to come by in our world. The guys consider her one of us already."

Ace stood up, "I do, and I have no plans of letting her go."

Stitch's mouth morphed into a wide grin, "Holy shit! You're falling in love with her, aren't you?"

He wasn't going to lie or think it was less manly of him to admit it. "I think so. It's like I told you the other day. The moment we met something just clicked. Now, knowing even more about her just validates it."

Right at that moment, the bathroom door swung open, and he locked gazes with her. Yeah, there was no thinking about it. He was in love with her.

"Are you leaving?" She asked.

He walked over to her while she squatted to grab her socks and sneakers. She was going for comfort today, wearing her hot pink running shorts—that in Ace's opinion were too short—and a black tank top. When she stood back up, he tugged on her ponytail.

"I'll be tied up most of the morning with meetings regarding tonight's mission. Go with the guys, have some breakfast. Afterward, someone will go with you to base command so you can get whatever you need to do for Mason done." He gave her a quick kiss. "I'll come and get you for lunch around noon."

She smiled. "Sounds like a plan, Sir." She snapped to attention and saluted him.

He pointed at her. "Wise-ass."

Alex's eyes followed Ace as he walked out the door. Damn, she had it bad. Then her gaze fell on Stitch who stood there with a sly smile on his face.

"What's that look for? You're up to something."

"You love him, don't you?"

She blew a breath out, "That obvious, huh?"

"I'm happy for you."

"You don't think it seems crazy? I'll admit the first couple of days I tried to convince myself that it wasn't worth the trouble to get involved with him. But then every time I saw him I kept gravitating toward him. I can't explain it."

"Alex, I've known you your entire life. You don't just jump into situations without thinking it through, and you wouldn't have admitted it if you truly didn't feel that way. You two are good for each other. On the other hand, I can't wait until Derek finds out."

She laughed and slapped his arm, then hugged him. She looked up at Stitch and smiled. He touched her head where the stitches were.

"This is healing nicely. How about we stop by medical and see about getting the stitches removed?"

"Really?" They were starting to bother her with the itching. Well, that was at least a good birthday present.

Hours later, Alex found herself buried in work as if that were anything new. Come to find out Mason's "little" translation project wasn't exactly so little. They were trying to track down a Russian man, Yegor, who the Chinese alleged was a spy. The United States had credible evidence that the man was playing both sides. It was just a matter of who was willing to pay more money for information. The United States could care less about the riff between the two countries. What they *were* interested in was getting their hands on the blueprints of a new nuclear-powered attack submarine the Russians were rumored to be building, and the word on the street was that Yegor had a copy of the plans. However, judging from a surveillance recording she was currently listening to, Yegor wasn't fairing too well against his interrogators. It seemed the Chinese had uncovered Yegor's years of double-crossing them and weren't happy about it.

With her earbuds in, she couldn't help but wince and squirm in her seat each time she heard Yegor grunt or scream. Yegor was getting a beat down and then some. Finally, after what seemed like hours of torture, she heard one of the interrogators mention the word *blueprints*. Turning the volume up she waited.

Come on...give me the answer I need then I can turn this shit off.

Yegor's labored breathing could be heard clearly. She knew he wasn't going to last much longer. He started mumbling something about the ocean breeze. It wasn't making any sense to her so she searched the internet for businesses with the name ocean breeze, specifically places where someone could hide something, like banks or places with storage lockers. As she scrolled through a list her eyes zeroed in on a banking entity named Seabreeze Banco located in Switzerland. With a couple of clicks on her keyboard, she browsed through Yegor's background. When she read Yegor had a sister who lived in Switzerland, she wondered if ocean breeze could be related to Seabreeze. She was deep in thought when a shrilling scream erupted through her earbuds followed by a gargled noise she knew unfortunately all too well and was aware that Yegor had lost his battle.

She sent a quick email to Mason letting him know what she found out and what her opinion was on the situation. She smiled when she got an immediate reply. She swore the man never slept and worked non-stop. But that was most likely why his company was one of the most sought after. She pulled the earbuds from her ears and threw them onto the table. Leaning back in her chair she closed her eyes trying to scrub the last couple of hours of audio from her mind.

She found her thoughts drifting into a direction she hadn't seen coming. For the first time, she started to question her career choice. Was this the life she wanted to live for the next twenty or so years? One where she had to put her life on the line and constantly look over her shoulder? She was compensated very well for her services, but was the stress of the job worth it? Money wasn't an issue. Between her inheritance, savings and investment accounts she wasn't hurting financially.

The main question was could she just give it all up? She would have to consider what she wanted to do post "fieldwork". There was no way she could just sit around and do nothing. Maybe once she got back home, she'd take a few days and visit her uncles and run a couple of ideas by them and get their thoughts. She let out a long sigh.

"That bad, huh?" The deep voice from across the room echoed.

She opened her eyes and met Potter's dark eyes where he was sitting with his feet propped up on the mini-fridge. Being inundated at work, she had forgotten he was even there.

"Could be better. Having to listen to an interrogation isn't how I imagined I'd be spending my birthday. But then again, who thought I would be here? I should be on the beach enjoying my vacation with a cocktail in my hand." She ran a hand down her face.

Potter dropped his big feet to the floor with a thud and sauntered over to the table she was working at. Pulling out the stool next to her, he sat down. He studied her, and she knew his eyes were focused on the dark circles under her eyes. She noticed them this morning, but sleep hadn't been her friend lately.

"What's really bothering you?" He asked and she wondered how he could tell things were festering under the surface because in her mind she thought she was doing a good job at concealing it. She tried to deny it, but he held his hand up, "Don't tell me nothing. I thought you knew by now that you can talk to any of us."

She looked him over. Potter by a good two or three inches was the tallest man on the team and undoubtedly the meanest looking one. It was rare to catch him with a smile on his face. With his darker complexion, high cheekbones, firm jaw, and black hair, she wondered if he came from a Native American background. Like Ace, the feature that caught her eye the first time she met Potter was his eyes. Instead of the blue of Ace's, Potter's were a very dark blue, almost appearing black the majority of the time and they gave him a furtive look.

She recalled Ace telling her that Potter didn't have any living family. She felt sad for him but was glad Ace's family had welcomed him. Since meeting and interacting with Potter, she sensed he was an observer. He liked to watch from afar and analyze things taking place. Just like he was doing now with her.

"Would it sound awful if I said, all of the above?" When he didn't answer she continued. "This mission has got me all twisted up because all we are dealing with are setbacks. I feel like someone

160

is purposely toying with us. You know, dangling that carrot in our faces and then just as soon as we get close enough to get a nibble, they snatch it back. I'm missing something and it's pissing me off!" Her voice rose on the last sentence.

"Is that all that's bothering you?" He calmly asked, and she wondered how he could be calm now, considering he was part of the team that had to keep following up on all the somewhat bogus leads and each time coming back empty-handed.

She didn't say anything, and he just cocked his eyebrow as if telling her he was waiting for her to answer. Damn, he was good at reading people. She crossed her arms and huffed out an annoyed deep breath.

"I don't know if I want to continue with my career."

Potter sat there for a moment with a stoic expression staring at her, and after a few seconds of studying her he stood and held out his hand. When she took the offering, he gently helped her off the stool and pulled her into the biggest hug she had ever gotten. The impromptu gesture had totally shocked her because Potter didn't appear to be a person to give cuddles. She wasn't sure if she should hug him back, but she was a hugger herself and couldn't help it as she tried to wrap her arms around the guy's massive body.

"One thing that I've learned over the years in my line of work is to not hold shit in. In most cases, it will only do more harm than good. You hear me?" He said, half-lecturing her.

She nodded against his chest. "Yeah, I got you."

He nudged her chin up. "Good. First, as for your concerns about the situation here, there is definitely something suspicious about it, and hopefully, we'll get some answers soon. You have been working your ass off, so don't ever think we don't realize that. Second, the dilemma concerning your job. Let me ask you a question. Do you enjoy what you're doing?"

161

She chewed on her lower lip thinking about how to answer. She must have taken too long to answer because Potter said, "It's a simple yes or no, honey."

Do I really enjoy it? She asked herself and was pleased when her inner thoughts gave her a quick answer.

"I don't think I enjoy it. I like what I do because it gives me a sense of feeling I'm helping or contributing to something bigger than myself, but no, in all honesty, I can't say I enjoy it. I mean, come on, do you honestly think I enjoy hearing a man get the shit beat out of him before being executed?" She rubbed her forehead in frustration. "Does that even make sense?"

"If you told me you actually enjoyed listening in on an interrogation, I'd have asked Derek to order a psych evaluation for you." He made a grunting noise, "Nobody should enjoy that shit. Trust me, I run and oversee most of our team's interrogations, and I hate it with a passion. But I do it because I know I have to. And because I love being a SEAL, and I love my country and what we stand for."

"I get it, Potter, I love my country as well, but deep down I believe there are bigger adventures I'd enjoy even more while still doing good for others."

He graced her with one of his rare smiles, "Well, I believe you have your answer."

Throwing caution to the wind, she decided to hug Potter again and gave him a big squeeze. "Thank you."

"If my best friend wasn't crazy about you, I'd throw you over my shoulder right now and hide you away from the world." She giggled and smiled up at him. Potter was a good man and a great friend.

"Potter, why in the hell do you have your hands on my woman?"

They both turned to see Ace standing in the doorway with his hands on his hips and one of his eyebrows arched.

At the same time, Potter and Alex both started laughing. Potter bent down and kissed the top of her head, "You better get over there before he blows a gasket."

Alex walked—well more like skipped over to Ace and leaped into his arms giving him a big hug. She felt a little more relaxed now that she had her little pep talk with Potter.

Ace gave Potter a questioning look and Potter signaled to him he'd talk to him later. He gave her a quick kiss on her cheek before setting her feet back down on the floor.

"Did you get that project done for Mason?"

"Yes, actually just finished up a couple of minutes ago."

He grinned. "Good, because the Colonel needs to see us for a quick chat."

"Is everything okay?" She asked wondering if there was some news on the hostages.

"Yeah, it's about tonight's mission."

"Okay, let me just get my things."

Potter grabbed her bag for her while Ace took hold of her hand and laced his fingers with hers. Together the three of them walked down the hall to another room. When they arrived at the closed door Ace let go of her hand to let her enter first.

Alex sensed something was up. Ace was acting funny, but she couldn't put her finger on it. She shrugged it off, telling herself she would ask him later. All the scenarios she was drumming up were so off from the surprise that greeted her on the other side of the door.

"SURPRISE!"

Alex screamed and jumped backward almost knocking Ace over. She did a double-take as she stood there speechless, taking in the room that was decorated with red, white, and blue streamers and balloons. Not to mention the rest of the team and Colonel Johnson standing there grinning. Ace leaned down and whispered in her ear, "Happy Birthday, baby."

She spun around and looked at him as the tears leaked from her eyes. Yeah, there was no stopping them. She was so overcome with emotion she almost couldn't even speak. "You did this?"

He smiled and she could tell he was thrilled they had surprised her. "It was my idea, but everyone had a part in pulling it off."

She raised up on her toes and put her arms around his neck, "Thank you. You don't know how much this means to me," she whispered and kissed his cheek.

"I'd give you the world if I could," he admitted to her and kissed her back.

Hearing laughter coming from behind her she turned around and looked at everyone while wiping away the tears. "I don't know what to say. I was so not expecting this."

Stitch answered for all, "Ace came up with the idea but honestly I didn't think he could pull it off."

She laughed, "Well, you can say you finally succeeded because I honestly had no idea."

"We had an early dinner brought in," he said pointing to the table on the far side where there were a bunch of pizza boxes stacked up, and she wondered where in the hell they were able to get pizza. "And, we have a cake for dessert."

She walked over to the table and there sitting in the middle was a birthday cake along with a bunch of envelopes.

The Colonel stepped forward and hugged her. "We all wanted to do something special for you since you had to spend your birthday here."

She looked at all the men that stood before her. "Thank you all so much. You really don't know how much I appreciate this. I'll admit it sucked to think I had to celebrate it here, but what I don't regret is celebrating it with all of you."

After pizza and conversation, Ace lit all thirty candles on her birthday cake as everyone sang happy birthday.

While they enjoyed cake, Alex asked the Colonel where Staff Sergeant Hill had been since she hadn't seen his friendly face around the last couple of days.

The Colonel took on a grim look and her gut clenched. "He took a few days of leave to be with his family. His mom passed away. She'd been battling cancer for a few years."

She frowned. "I'm sorry to hear that."

"Me too. He's actually due back sometime this evening."

Alex made a mental note to reach out to Hill later and offer her condolences.

Once they were all finished with the cake, Ace handed Alex the envelopes from the table.

"These are for you. And, to give credit where it's due, Tenley had a hand in helping pull this off, along with Derek. Between the two of them, they got us the cake mix and frosting in record time, along with the pizza."

Alex couldn't believe the thought and effort that had gone into making her day as special as it was.

She took the envelopes and opened the first one which was from Ace. Inside was a photograph of a Jaguars football jersey autographed by the entire team. Confused, she looked at Ace who was sitting next to her smiling. "Umm...I don't understand the photo."

"The item in the photo is your present. The jersey is at Tenley's house. She took the picture and emailed it to me and then I printed it out here at the office."

She felt her face light up with surprise. "Oh my god…are you shitting me?" She shouted, bouncing up and down in her seat as one would do when they got such an awesome present. "You got me a jersey autographed by the entire team? I love it!" She leaped into his lap almost knocking them and the chair over. She looped her arms around Ace's neck and hugged him. "Thank you, thank you, thank you!"

Ace chuckled and secured her with his arms she wouldn't fall off. "You're welcome." Neither one missed the smirk that the Colonel gave them. So much for being discrete.

Not making any effort to remove herself from Ace's lap, she grabbed another envelope off the table. Each envelope was from a team member and inside held a picture of the gift they got her. Potter got her a gift card to buy books for her tablet, Dino gifted her with a spa package to an upscale spa in Virginia Beach, meaning she had to visit to use it. Diego got her a set of Navy Christmas ornaments she'd been wanting but never got around to ordering. She got tickets to the upcoming Country Music Festival from Frost. Stitch got her a wall display for her Challenge Coin collection she started when she was a kid. She received some new Photoshop software she'd been wanting from Skittles, and Irish gave her a gift only a sniper would give: a year membership to the local gun range.

After the last card was opened, the only thing that remained on the table was an actual present wrapped in brown craft paper with an envelope attached to it. She opened the envelope first and read the note inside:

Alex,

Hearing your uncle over the years speak so highly of you, I can't tell you how much it has been a pleasure to finally meet you and to serve alongside you, although, I wish we'd had been able to meet under more favorable circumstances. You are an incredibly special woman, one with many talents and a very bright future still ahead of you. If I had a daughter, I would hope she'd grow up to be a confident, intelligent, and beautiful woman as yourself. Please know that once your job here is complete, if you ever need anything, you have another 'uncle' you can call upon if needed or if you just want to talk.

Happy Birthday!

Col. Johnson

She took the wrapped gift and opened it. One look at the contents and she threw her head back and laughed. It was a picture of her and the Colonel. She was wearing an I Love Army t-shirt. On her third day at the base, she had lost a bet with the Colonel and had to wear the shirt around the base for an entire day. Noticing something folded under the picture frame, she picked it up and saw it was the actual t-shirt she wore in the picture. She unfolded the shirt and saw the front of it was covered in signatures.

Looking at the Colonel he told her, "I got as many guys as I could on the base to sign it, so you have a little souvenir to take home with you."

It may be Army, but this gift would hang proudly on her wall at home. She slid off Ace's lap and walked over to where the Colonel was sitting. He stood up and enveloped her in a hug. And, damn did she need that hug. She didn't have her uncles here, so this was the next best thing. She stepped back and looked up at him. She was trying desperately to keep her emotions in check by blinking back the tears.

"Your words mean so much to me. And, I already consider you a part of my extended family."

One-by-one she walked around the room and thanked each guy with a hug. She was so overcome with emotion she couldn't stop hugging them, even causing them to chuckle. Finally, she turned to face them all.

"I am so humbled by all your thoughtfulness. This birthday has been one of the most special ones I've ever celebrated. And, here I thought it was going to be the shittiest." She cracked a smile. "It doesn't surprise me though that a bunch of stealthy SEALs managed to pull off this surprise. Over the last week, all of you have come to mean so much to me and I just want you to know that even though we don't share the same blood, I consider each of you a part of my family."

She heard her voice cracking and knew she needed to wrap this up before she started crying. "So, thank you guys again for making my day special and one I'll never forget."

As soon as she finished talking someone from the Colonel's office came in letting him know he had a phone call from Washington.

After the Colonel left, Alex looked at Ace. "Well, I guess playtime is over. You guys ready to go over the plans for tonight?"

CHAPTER FIFTEEN

"Fuck! Get the hell out of there!" Ace yelled into his mic as explosions rocked the area around them.

Gunfire followed as the team ran to take cover. They were outnumbered, and Ace feared there was a good chance they wouldn't make it out alive unless the air support he called in for arrived within the next few minutes.

"There!" Dino pointed to a cluster of boulders and they took cover behind them.

"Where are Stitch and Diego?" Ace asked as he lifted his rifle and fired at two of the three men approaching. Potter fired off a round hitting the third guy and he dropped to the ground, a bloom of blood covering his chest.

"They're pinned down on the other side," Irish communicated as he too picked off incoming enemy forces.

"Fuck!" Ace reached for his radio. "Where in the hell is the air support?"

"One minute out," Skittles stated.

"Stitch, you and Diego need to move. Air support coming in hot. Less than one minute."

"Copy, we are approaching your location from the west over the hill at your three o'clock."

Ace looked up and saw the two figures making their way down the bare rocky slope. He lifted his weapon and started firing at another wave of angry forces coming their way.

Just as the enemy forces were gaining their position to strike again with heavy artillery, two attack helicopters crested the nearby ridge and rained down a hail of gunfire onto the approaching crowd. An orange glow rose above the smoke, lighting the sky up as explosion after explosion rocked the mountain.

169

Seconds later the world felt like it stood still. There was no movement, no sounds, there was no nothing. When the smoke eventually cleared, and Ace was able to get a visual on the intended target location, his stomach clenched, seeing the entire area decimated. Bodies were strewn across the ground, but what caught his eye were the two huge craters in the ground where the buildings once stood.

Potter looked over with a grim expression. "This just turned into a recovery mission."

"Afraid so." Nobody inside those buildings would've survived that blast. Hell, he wasn't even sure if they could find anything to pull DNA from.

"Is everyone good?"

"All team members accounted for and in one piece."

Thank god for that.

"What the fuck was that?" Frost asked joining them. The others gathered around as well, all glancing at the destruction.

Ace shook his head. He wasn't even sure what went wrong.

"I don't know. We were cleared to move in." Ace was already compiling a list of questions he wanted answers to. "Let's fan out and see if we can find anything."

They all rose to their feet, then a call came over the radio that added more mystery to the situation.

"Alpha One, this is Eagle One. Operation is aborted. Area is still considered hot and hostile. Extraction team incoming with coordinates…"

Ace had no words except, "Eagle One, copy. Team awaiting exfil."

❦

Alex looked like a raging bull in a china closet as she stormed across the base, moving people out of her path who dared to cross

170

it. Her expression alone should have warned those approaching her that now wasn't a good time. To say she was pissed off was a huge understatement. If she didn't tamp down her emotions she was liable to be charged with murder.

Bert McMahon had better have a damn good explanation for his actions involving the unmanned aerial vehicle that was being used to aid the team during the mission. The video feed from the UAV had been unexpectedly interrupted the exact moment the team was moving in over the ridge of the compound. Had the feed not been disrupted, anyone watching would have seen the large contingent of enemy forces that had been awaiting the team's arrival.

Once Alex had confirmation that the team had been safely extracted from the side of the mountain and she had time to take a breath, she started making phone calls trying to figure out what the hell had gone wrong. The agency had provided credible intelligence indicating the hostages were being held in one of the two structures within the compound. She had been so focused on getting answers that she hadn't realized that Bert had slipped out of the room. Normally when things turned ugly, he always made it a point to interject some sort of snide comment. Anything to get a dig in at her. But tonight he acted different, and after talking with the operator of the UAV along with a former colleague at the agency, she knew why he appeared uptight, and now she was looking for answers.

Only having listening capabilities and hearing the audio of the team being overrun by enemy forces had her on the edge of her seat. Even though the team had been outnumbered, it didn't stop them from giving everything they had until air support arrived and leveled the mountain side.

There had been times during the skirmish where she struggled to keep her tears at bay, but the tears now that were threatening to return were out of pure anger.

As she approached Bert's housing quarters, Mical and Roland stepped out the door, and when they spotted her, Alex swore they both seemed nervous.

"Is he in there?" She called out.

Both looked at each as if asking how they should answer. She wasn't up for a round of games so instead of waiting to hear what type of bullshit answer they were going to give her, she just barged in. Catching Bert off guard he swung around and eyed her telling the person on the other end of the line that he had to go.

"What in the hell are you doing here?" He asked her. He looked unhinged and wild. Something was off.

"I think you know exactly why I'm here, and I expect the truth, not some politically correct bullshit answer."

Bert took a slug from the bottle of whiskey and grimaced as the liquid burned on the way down. Tonight's mission hadn't gone as he had planned, and now, he waited for the phone to ring knowing Ashraf would be calling.

How in the hell those SEALs had survived on the side of that mountain had been a fucking miracle. The plan had been to take out two birds with one stone.

The compound that Alex and the team thought was to be holding the hostages was a rival terrorist group that Ashraf had been wanting to eliminate. *The Caucus* was what they called themselves. When Alex had chased Ashraf into hiding two years ago, the leader of the Caucus set his sights on Ashraf's territory.

With the help of some informants, the Caucus had been tipped off that the SEALs were planning a raid and had been ready to defend their land. The SEALs had no clue what they were walking into thanks to the video feed from the UAV being interrupted. That had been the genius work of another double-agent whose loyalty lay where the money was.

When the UAV's feed was cut, it had been too late for the team to abort the mission. They had already been made and never saw the enemy until it was too late. However, he underestimated Lt. Commander Chambers and his team. Even he had to admit, they were one badass team. The only good that came out of the fucked-up night was that the air support had taken out the majority of the Caucus, including its leader. The bad news was that the team would be returning which meant Alex would be under their watch once more making it difficult to lure her away.

He needed to come up with a plan and quickly because once he delivered the news to Ashraf, he would surely want to take matters into his own hands, and he couldn't let that happen because then he'd be out just shy of a million dollars. He already had made a lot of money over the last couple of years, however, this last payment would guarantee he'd be set for life. This would be his last mission before he would turn his resignation into the agency. From there he'd sneak away to his private hideaway he already had secured and live out the rest of his life relishing in the sand and sunshine.

He wondered where his two asshat associates of his had wandered off to. Those two had been a pain in his ass since his boss asked him to mentor them. He wasn't thrilled about having the two shadows, and he had to adjust his plans accordingly so they wouldn't suspect anything was up. They were nosey little fucks.

The ringing of his burner phone brought him out of his contemplation. Pressing the button to answer, he didn't even have a chance to speak before the angry voice spoke.

"What the fuck happened?"

He closed his eyes and sighed.

"It was a minor setback. At least Caucus isn't a worry to you any longer."

"I'd rather deal with the Caucus than having that bitch and those SEALs playing in my backyard."

Bert was starting to dislike Ashraf with each passing day. He was the most ungrateful bastard he'd ever met. And, that is saying a lot considering all the scumbags in the world he had come in contact with.

"Look, Ashraf, you'll have her."

"You have twenty-four hours to bring her to me or our deal is off, and we both know you don't want that."

Suddenly the door behind him burst open. When he turned and saw who had dared to barge into his private quarters a slow smile started to form. Maybe this wouldn't be as hard as he thought.

"I'll have to call you back." As he hung up he could hear Ashraf shouting.

"What in the hell are you doing here?"

"I think you know exactly why I'm here, and I expect the truth, not some politically correct bullshit answer."

Oh, you'll know the truth soon enough sweet angel.

Alex took two steps back with every step Bert took towards her until her back hit the wall. She glared at him as he stood in front of her with a blank expression. He placed his hands against the wall by her head, caging her in. That was when she smelled the alcohol on his breath. *Had he been drunk during the mission?*

"Why did the agency order the feed to be cut?"

He just stared at her for a few seconds before moving his hand and taking a strand of her hair and twirling it around his finger. His actions were creepy and had her on edge.

"Alex, come on now, I know you haven't forgotten everything you learned while at the agency."

"I'm not following."

He smirked. "Sometimes you have to make sacrifices for the overall mission to prevail."

She took in his inebriated state as an opportunity to put some distance between them. She shoved him backward, and when he stumbled she tried to skirt around him, but he snagged her wrist, squeezing it hard. He yanked on her arm pulling her in close. She tried to pull away, but his hold tightened.

Was he saying that the agency risked the lives of Ace and the guys for the mission? That didn't even make sense.

"Are you admitting that the agency was willing to stand by and witness the murder of an entire SEAL team? For what?" She shouted and tried to pull away but to no avail.

She stared him down, her jaw taut, and her teeth clenched. "Our men, the same men who fight for your freedom could've died up there. Why?"

"Come on Alex. You know how things work. Sometimes you have to give and take even if it means putting the good guys in the line of fire." He let out more of a cackle than a laugh, but all it did was piss Alex off.

"You are something else. It makes me wonder what else you've been hiding all these years. Maybe you were behind my team's murder."

"Back off Alex," Bert said in warning. Oh, had she hit a nerve, or was she uncovering the truth of what happened two years ago?

"You deliberately knew the team was heading into a death trap, and you didn't say a goddamn thing."

"But they survived, so what is the big fucking deal? Those SEALs know what they're getting into. They understand that every mission they go out on could potentially be their last."

"What about the hostages? That is the reason we are even here, and you and the agency killed them! That is blood on your hands!"

She had enough of this. "I am only going to ask you once. Release my arm and step back."

Instead, he pulled her closer. "Come on Alex, you know how it is in our world." He made a move to kiss her and she shoved all her weight into him, knocking him off balance. He didn't fall, but he did let go of her. She went for the door, but Bert tackled her sending them both onto the floor. She took the brunt of the fall and felt the pain in her side.

Bert tried sitting on her, but she bucked him off and when he went to advance again, she kicked him in the groin. He shouted and grabbed himself. While on his knees, she did something she had wanted to do for a long time. Drawing her fist back, she swung with all her might, hitting him square in the nose. She knew the moment she heard the crunch of bones and saw the blood splatter that she had broken his nose.

While he screamed and carried on about his nose, she made a run for it. Her first stop was the Colonel's office.

Four o'clock in the morning and Alex was still sitting in the base command building waiting for the team to return. She thought they would've been back by now, but knowing how screwed up things were, there was a good possibility they had gotten held up during their debriefing.

She had all intentions of going back to her building to get some rest, but after her altercation with Bert she wouldn't put it past him to come looking for her, so she opted to stay at base command where people were around. The Colonel had sent two MPs to Bert's quarters, but he wasn't there, and after searching the base it was as if he disappeared. She tried calling Derek, but he had been on another call.

God, she felt so tired. She crossed her arms and laid her head on the table. She had just closed her eyes when her computer pinged with an incoming message via the instant messaging system. She tapped the button on the keyboard and saw it was Bowman.

"Has Derek called you? The hostages were not at the compound, you were given false Intel. A team from Force Recon has located the hostages. Ashraf was identified to be hiding out there as well."

The news certainly perked her up and she got a second wind. She typed back quickly.

"Where?"

"Close by. The team has already been diverted and are en route."

That made sense considering they hadn't arrived back yet. Damn, she really wanted to be there when Ashraf was brought in.

"Any chance I can get in on the action?"

"Knew you would ask, and already taken care of."

As she went to respond, Staff Sgt. Hill appeared in the doorway holding up a set of keys.

"I hear you need a ride."

"How?" She smiled.

"Your friend Bowman called a few minutes ago."

Not wanting to waste any more time, she typed a quick thanks to Bowman before grabbing her phone and gun. There would be no nicer feeling than to nip this shit in the bud tonight and head home tomorrow.

Ace was trying to rein in his already short temper as he stood in a vacant building on base listening to the Colonel as he updated them on everything that happened tonight both with the mission and at the base.

Yeah, he was majorly pissed off about the mission and was looking forward to the conversation he and Bert would be having. But what had him irate was hearing what had gone down between Bert and Alex.

"So, he fucking tried to make a move on her and when she declined, he attacked her?"

"That and the fact that the agency for some reason decided at the last minute to cut the feed," the Colonel said rubbing the back of his neck. "I can't seem to wrap my head around any of this. Bert is MIA, but after this, I plan on having a word with Mical and Roland. They were found in the mess hall and they claim they don't know where Bert is either. As for Alex, she stood her ground and handled the situation. Because of her training, Bert will be seeing a plastic surgeon when he gets home. She shattered his nose."

Ace wasn't surprised to hear what the Colonel said about Alex. He needed to see her. In all the years in his career, he never knew what it felt like to go out on missions only to have someone other than his family waiting for him at home. Or in this case here at the base.

"Where is she now?" He asked the Colonel and the Colonel grinned as if knowing what his thoughts had just been.

"She's still over at base command. Staff Sgt. Hill and a couple of the others are with her."

Ace went to move but the Colonel stopped him.

"Just so you know, she did sustain some injuries during the altercation."

"How bad?"

"Nothing too bad. Some bruising on her wrists, her knuckles and hand are swollen, and possibly some bruised ribs."

Ace took a deep breath. She should have never been put in that position in the first place.

"Go and see her, I need to have a word with Mical and Roland. I'll catch up with you later."

Just then Ace's phone rang. It was the commander.

"Commander?"

"I just got a phone call from Mason; Bowman's computer was hacked. Whoever did it was sending messages to Alex telling her that they located Ashraf and that a team was already en route. Is she with you now?"

"No, she is over at base command. Do we know what team the message was referring to?"

"Your team."

Ace's grip tightened on the phone.

"Shit, someone's trying to lure her in."

"That's what Mason and I think, and she is so hell-bent on catching this asshole that she won't hesitate to go after him on her own."

"We are heading that way now."

"Call me when you get there."

Ace disconnected and explained the situation to the team as they raced across the base hoping to get to Alex in time, but the closer they got the larger the knot in Ace's stomach grew.

Alex hurried around the truck as Staff Sgt. Hill was there holding the door open for her to slide in. Once she was securely in, he ran around to the driver's side and got in. He turned the ignition and the truck's engine came roaring to life. Driving through the base was the easy part. It was the moment they drove through the gates leaving her sense of security behind her that her heart began to beat faster as she grew more apprehensive. She started to second-guess herself. Was she doing the right thing in risking her safety to join the team? Before she overthought her decision, she pushed away the negative thoughts and instead focused on the positive. Between Mason's team of kick-ass black operatives and the SEALs, there wasn't a snowball's chance in hell that Ashraf would escape this time, and she wanted a front-row seat as it all went down.

She glanced over at Hill. She was glad to see him back, but he was lacking his usual smile and laughter. She understood losing a parent was hard, and she hoped he could bounce back from his loss.

She began to feel her eyelids get droopy as the drive got longer. For some reason, if she wasn't driving or in hot pursuit, the motion of a vehicle made her sleepy. She tried to make a conversation with Hill to keep herself alert, but he wasn't in the mood to talk. She wouldn't mind a little nap before they arrived, but the problem was every time she closed her eyes, she kept seeing Ace's face. God, tonight had been a test of her will. She wasn't sure she wanted to work on other missions with any of them. She was better off not knowing what they were getting into.

With her head pressed against the window she looked at her watch. They had only been on the road for about a half-hour and she wondered exactly how far they were going. Bowman's message made it seem like it had been nearby.

It was so dark on the roads they traveled. The headlights from the truck made a path for them as they drove. Suddenly, the truck's right front tire exploded. She grabbed onto the handle as Hill tried to steady the vehicle while steering it off the road.

"Did we hit something?" She asked, getting out and looking at the damage.

Hill met her then squatted down getting a good look at the shredded tire. There was no way in hell a plug was going to fix that tire.

"I don't know. I didn't see anything on the road. There's a spare in the back, let me go get it and then I'll change it."

Alex nodded her head and Hill ran toward the back of the SUV. She looked around. They were in a desolate and unpopulated area surrounded by hillsides. A slight warm breeze blew in from the west, heightening the eerie feeling and putting her spidey senses on full alert. She reached behind her and felt the cool metal of her gun she had tucked in her waistband. She damned herself for not changing into pants before she left. At least with pants, she could've concealed another weapon on her ankle.

Hill reappeared with the spare tire and jack. She took the lug wrench from him and started to loosen the lug nuts. She was working on the last one when she felt a pinch to her neck. She looked up at Hill who stood behind her holding a syringe in his hand. His usual warm eyes that were once full of kindness had been replaced by a cold, sinful look. She tried to speak, to ask him why, but her words came out slurred. She stumbled to her feet and fell against the side of the truck as a numbing sensation started to flow through her body. As her vision started to blur, she sensed movement next to her and mustered enough energy to turn her head. Just before a fist connected with the side of her head, she heard Bert's voice, but she never could confirm a visual because as soon as she hit the ground her world went black.

Ace barged into the war room and cursed when he found it empty.

"She must have left in a hurry, she never leaves her work in disarray like this," Stitch said referring to her computer and papers strewn over the table.

Ace pulled out his phone and dialed the commander's number.

"Did you find her?" Derek asked and Ace could hear the worry in Derek's voice.

"No. She's gone."

"Fuck!"

Just then Colonel Johnson stormed into the room with Mical and Roland behind him, and going by the Colonel's expression he hadn't come to pass along good news.

"Is that Derek?" He asked Ace and Ace nodded. "Tell him to conference in through video."

Ace relayed the message and in less than a minute not only was Derek on video, but Mason, Alex's boss was visible as well.

Ace glanced over at Mical and Roland.

"What are they doing here?"

"Agent Noon and Agent Ferrero are here to enlighten us all on the current situation."

"Agents?" Ace questioned, wondering where in the hell this was going. He was under the impression they were newbies with the agency. Before anyone else could say a word, Mason interjected.

"Yes, Lt., meet Agent Mical Noon, and Agent Roland Ferrero, both with the CIA. It was just brought to my attention that both agencies recruited Alex under false pretenses, and they are here to explain why."

"How do you know about that?" Agent Noon questioned and Ace had to bite back his smile at the glare Mason gave the spy.

"It doesn't matter how I know, Agent Noon. All that matters right now is that because of the lies your agency spewed I've got a member of my team missing. Not to mention over the last week and a half you have endangered not only her but the lives of the team standing before you. If I were you, I would start explaining, and you better be quick."

Ace leaned against the table and crossed his arms while he watched Agent Noon shift on his feet before pushing his glasses up his nose. The guy was sweating, and Ace knew the poor agent didn't have a leg to stand on. Yep, he was up shit's creek without a paddle.

"Well Agent Noon, we are waiting." Derek pressed when he stalled as if he were looking for the right words to say.

"Mr. Whittmore is correct. We, the agency that is, brought in Ms. Hardesty under false claims. However, we had a good reason too." He took a breath. "We've been investigating Bert McMahon for treason, aiding and abetting, along with a slew of other charges."

"Aiding and abetting who?" Derek again questioned, and Ace could tell the commander was about to lose his shit.

"Ashraf Fayed." The gasps circulated the room, but before anyone could speak Agent Noon continued. "Over the course of many briefings Alex had with investigators after she returned home, some of her statements had raised the eyebrows with the higher brass. Those comments along with some circumstantial evidence found their way to the top and here we are now. The CIA was brought in to assist."

Ace listened to both agents as they explained how the agency started paying more attention to Bert and his trips to the middle east. They were scrutinizing his every movement as well as investigating his finances. According to Agents, four offshore bank accounts linked to Bert had been uncovered, and there was a possibility there could be others.

"It sounds like you guys had enough to bring him for questioning. Why didn't you? And how does Alex play into all of this?" Ace asked.

"You're right Lt. Commander, we could have. However, if the allegations against Bert are true, he could lead us to the ultimate catch. Ashraf himself. But, to do so we needed someone who was in tune with Ashraf. Someone who knows his history, and we needed someone to put the heat on him. Someone who would make him feel threatened. Someone who would make him reach out to Bert."

Ace shook his head in disbelief, "I'm sorry, I don't think I heard you correctly."

"I think you heard me just fine," he fired back with a bite of masculine sass.

"You might want to check that attitude of yours at the door Agent Noon. From where I stand, you are on the opposite side, so if I were you, I would continue with what I have to say," the Colonel bluntly stated.

"Alex was our only hope. We knew Ashraf was getting information from someone inside our walls and we suspected Bert, but we needed to catch him in the act."

"If your agency had this belief, why did you let Alex walk? Surely, someone could've spoken with her and brought her in the loop."

"After that last briefing with her, we knew we couldn't convince her to stay. She is a woman of passion and loyalty when it comes to her job. Bert had thrown her under the bus."

"And yet they let it happen?"

"At the time they didn't know. Over time, the agencies started connecting some dots, and those dots lead to bigger dots. We now believe Bert has been in Ashraf's back pocket for the last four or five years.

"Holy fuck!" Ace exclaimed running a hand down his face. He was disgusted right now. He didn't know who to believe anymore.

"You're stalling, Agent Noon; get to the real issue. Please tell the team about the hoax you and your agency pulled together to assure Alex's involvement in your scheme," Mason said with a hint of annoyance.

When the Agent started to explain, Ace didn't think he could get any angrier. He was seconds from losing his shit.

"You mean to tell me you staged a fucking hostage situation to get her to cooperate with you? You used her to bait a fucking terrorist and traitor? Do you realize I had men who could've been injured or killed during these missions?" Derek stated.

"We needed Bert to slip up and since we knew it would piss him off if we brought Alex in, we went with what we thought best."

"Why not just tell her? Why lead us all to believe and chase down phantom hostages?" Ace paused for a minute thinking about the two videos they had gotten. *Jesus, were those doctored as well?* He wondered. "Did you stage those videos?"

"We couldn't say anything, because Bert might not be the only one on the inside passing Intel, and, no, those videos were not ours. We were not able to find out where those originated from."

"Wait, the guy who worked for Ashraf. His name was Reynolds. Could that be Bert, being cute, and using an alias? Reynolds, as in *Bert Reynolds*."

"Shit that explains the few times you guys were seconds from being blown to pieces while looking for make-believe hostages. He's been relaying information back to Ashraf this entire time." Derek said not looking too pleased. He looked utterly disgusted which matched every other person's expression in the room.

"You didn't pick up on any of his activities since he's been here?" Derek pressed Agent Noon.

"He didn't give me any reason to suspect anything until this evening. When I overheard him on the phone with the UAV operator telling him to cut the feed, I knew something wasn't right. I stepped outside and made a call to Washington to confirm what Bert was relaying, and I was told that was not the case. However, it had been too late."

"Well, congratulations Agent. Look what it fucking got you. You not only lost track of your number one suspect since he is nowhere to be found, but now it looks like you've handed Alex over to the enemy, as I suspect whoever was in contact with her is leading her into a trap," Mason stated angrily.

"I believe you and your agency owe us a more in-depth explanation once my daughter is found, Agent Noon," Derek barked at him.

Agent Noon swallowed hard. "Yes, sir. Please know the agency is doing everything possible to find Alex."

"I don't have much faith in either agency, so I am pulling in some of my own resources. People who I can trust and believe have mine and my team's best interest.

"Understood, Sir."

Ace looked around at all the angry and pissed off expressions of everyone in the room. They all knew if Ashraf got his hands on Alex, he wouldn't let her live.

"Where do we start?"

"Don't the trucks have a tracking device?" Frost asked.

"It was disabled. I've already checked," the Colonel stated looking as disgusted as the rest of them.

"What about her cell phone? We can track it."

"That too has been disabled."

"Shit."

Derek spoke up. "Agent Noon, I will expect full cooperation from the agency and any of their partners who may be traveling through the area."

CHAPTER SIXTEEN

The stinging slap across her cheek had Alex slowly opening her eyes. Her head hurt and her mind was fuzzy.

"How much of that shit did you give her, Bert?"

Another slap. This time a little harder and she gritted her teeth.

"I gave her enough that she won't be a hindrance once she wakes up."

She lifted her heavy head and tried adjusting her eyes. Wherever she was it was hot, and the air felt thick as sweat dripped from her brow. Not to mention, the stench in the room was enough to make her gag. It smelled like a garbage landfill on a hot summer day.

Pushing back the bile forcing its way up from her stomach, her sight became a little clearer. An older Middle Eastern man crouched down in front of her.

"Salaam Alaikum," he said with a slimy grin on his face. He was saying hello in Pashto.

He had to be in his late fifties, early sixties. His styled black hair was streaked with silver throughout. The designer slacks and dress shirt he wore told her he had money. But it was his eyes that she wanted to turn away from. They were cold and uninviting. She fidgeted under his glare, but she didn't move much thanks to the restraints on her arms and legs. The hard floor she was sitting on offered her no comfort.

Her eyes darted around the room. The first thing she noticed was the lack of windows meaning limited escape routes. There was a door that led to what looked like a hallway. The only source of light was a single light bulb that hung by a wire from the ceiling in the middle of the room giving it an eerie ambience. The small table off to the side of the room with a video camera perched on a tripod didn't give her a warm and fuzzy feeling. It was set up as an interrogation room.

She looked back at the guy. He wasn't getting any information out of her.

"What do you want with me? Where am I?"

He stood up, and that was when she noticed the other men in the room. She wasn't surprised to see Bert standing off to the side. When her eyes locked on Hill, she saw nothing but evil as he glared at her. Was he a mole just like Bert? She wished she had free use of her hands because she would love to go one round with him. She assumed he was the one responsible for getting her here. She took another glance at Bert, and wished she could wrap her hands around his neck and watch his little beady eyes bulge out of his head. Shaking that thought from her head she continued to eye her opponents. She spotted another guy who stood back in the far corner. He had a hat pulled way down covering his eyes and causing a shadow to shield his face. With his arms crossed she sensed he was staring at her. There was something familiar about him.

"Hello, Alexandra."

Another male voice said in a thick accent causing her to look the other way, away from the mystery man in the corner.

"Oh god," she whispered as she took in the man who walked with purpose towards her. One look into his eyes and there was no mistaking who he was.

"I can tell you remember me."

How could she not? She would never forget the way he had looked her over the last time they ran into each other. Her skin started to crawl.

"I see you don't need any introductions to my sons," the older man said.

Sons? Oh, Jesus. Her stomach knotted and she felt as if she was going to be sick. She looked at Hill and Yaseen, and she saw the resemblance between the two. But if they were this guy's son that would mean she was looking at... Her eyes widened.

Ashraf Fayed.

She swallowed hard and licked her dry lips, wishing she had a bottle of water right now. Her breathing grew rapid and she tried pulling on the restraints, only for the metal to dig deeper into her skin. It was a knee jerk reaction. She stilled as soon as she felt her skin tearing. She was panicking and that was the worst thing she could do at a time like now. Remembering what her uncles had taught her in survival training, the first rule was to stay calm. That tasked seemed a little difficult, but she needed a clear head if she wanted any chance of getting out of this alive. But with seven men, all who were armed, the odds were stacked against her. She wasn't a quitter though, and if she had an opportunity to get her hands on any sort of weapon she could do a lot of damage. But that wasn't happening unless she was able to free herself.

As gracefully as she could, she got up onto her knees and straightened her spine. She held her head up, lifting her chin to appear confident, even though her body shook with fear. She had no idea what she was about to face, but from the vile expressions, it wasn't going to be good.

Ashraf gave her a wicked grin as he approached and stood before her. One look into his dark eyes and she knew she was in deep trouble. This man was bad news, but apparently her mouth spoke before her brain warned her not to.

"Finally, I get the pleasure of meeting you."

"That's great asshole. because I really can't say the same for you." No sooner had the last word left her mouth, the left side of her face exploded in a fire of pain. She tasted the blood as her lip busted from the blow. Damn, that had been a mistake. No use in poking the bear when she was in no position to properly defend herself.

Observing her, Ashraf looked at Hill and Yaseen and smirked. "You were right; she's a lively one." Grabbing a fist full of her hair, he wrenched her head back. Her scalp burned and she was breathing heavily, wondering what his next move was as his black evil eyes bore into hers. Too many bad thoughts had her shaking.

Releasing her hair, he unsheathed the knife from the holster secured to his belt. He brought the tip of the sharp object up to just above her chest bone and held it there as he stared into her eyes and she swore she could see into the depths of hell. With the knife hovering over her skin she started to tremble, and he laughed as he eyed her body.

"My sons have been boasting about this exceptional body of yours. I think it's only fair we get a better look." Before she could take her next breath, he sliced her tank top from her body. The top fell to the floor, leaving her exposed in just her white lace bra and shorts. He ran his thick fingers along the top of the cups to her bra making her grimace. His smile had her digging her nails into the palms of her hands. She was at their mercy and there wasn't a damn thing she could do about it. She dropped her head in defeat and closed her eyes. She was fucked.

He took a step back and ordered the two men she didn't know to release her.

The cuffs around her wrists were loosened and she was yanked to her feet. She groaned as her muscles stretched. Balancing with her feet bound was a problem until the two goons on each of her sides gripped her biceps holding her steady. She still wasn't sure how long she'd been here. She couldn't even tell if it was day or night. She looked down and noticed her watch had been removed. Of course, they had probably taken her gun and phone.

Ashraf cleared his throat redirecting her attention.

"You should be grateful for your uncle. After all, it was his phone call that saved your life two years ago. While you were outside on the phone, a couple of my men went into your house and killed your team before they blew it up."

That was no surprise to her, but she was glad to hear him admit the truth.

"You see, you thought you had everything to obliterate my organization. But what you hadn't known was that I knew you were watching the entire time. I knew the moment you stepped foot into my country."

He pulled a cigarette from his pocket and lit it. He took a puff and blew the smoke directly into her face making her cough.

"Having a link inside your government to wipe the servers so there was no trace of your evidence was a godsend. I honestly had all intentions of having Bert put a bullet in your head, but, Yaseen objected. Having to lay low the past two years cost me a lot of money, not to mention my reputation. After a year in hiding, I started rebuilding my empire again under a different name."

"When Bert told me the United States was looking into my past again, I couldn't take any chances. When word got back that they thought I was behind the hostages at the armory compound and that they were bringing you onboard it had been perfect. It was just a shame they had to create that bogus story just to get your assistance."

What was he talking about?

He looked surprised, "Oh…I see you don't know the truth yet. Your own government set you up. They want me so badly that they concocted the story about my men taking hostages the night we broke into the armory compound."

That sounded absurd. Yeah, the government was known to fib a little, but there was no way they would make a false claim about hostages.

"I don't believe you. I saw the videos."

"Yes, they were Yaseen's videos, but it was all staged. We weren't even sure if there was a hostage situation, but I just took it and ran with it. Bert, or should I say Reynolds found out the truth just yesterday."

Her eyes darted back to Bert. So it was confirmed, out of the mouth of the devil himself; Bert was the American traitor people in the criminal world spoke about.

"Once we knew you were here, we took the Intel we stole from your team and doctored it. My only mistake was not being prepared for a team of Navy SEALs. A team that's commanded by your uncle of all people. But, with Bert and Naveed's help, we were still able to take you right out from under them."

She just stared at him. This man no doubt knew everything in her life.

He grinned. "You see, all the Intel you received was either old or falsified. It was all a hoax and used as a means to get you and that SEAL team to go and investigate. I originally wanted you dead. Now, I'm grateful Bert's traps didn't harm you too much. Believe it or not, you are actually in one of the buildings your former team did surveillance on.

She thought hard wondering which one it was. From the size of this room alone, it would have been bigger than the others she and her team had scoped out. Then it hit her.

"I can see in your eyes you know which one I'm referring to. Putting a safe house on the border of a green zone was one of the best ideas I ever had."

The green zone location was the lone one she couldn't get her government to get the go-ahead from the province leader. At least that was the spiel she was given. But knowing what she knew now, that was probably a load of bullshit. The green zone was a no-fighting zone. The leader of the province didn't allow fighting or terrorists. Sure, terrorists tried taking over the village, but the villagers were prepared, and didn't back down. The valley was a gorgeous land, and the people made sure it was kept that way. The green landscape was a steep contrast compared to most areas in the region. Then it dawned on her. She was only about 60 miles northwest of Bagram.

Her head was spinning with all this information. Bert had turned on his own country. She wondered how much money he had made working on the side for Ashraf.

She glanced at Bert who stood back just watching and listening. Hearing what Ashraf had to say answered a lot of questions, like how Bert just happened to show up right after the explosion that night two years ago. He was probably the man she saw in the flashback, and he was probably the one who had made the call and not her. He was there the whole time giving the enemy a play-by-play of what the team was doing. The fucking piece of shit! She hoped she would get the opportunity to give him a little payback. But at the moment that was looking like a pipe dream.

"You know when my team finds you, they aren't going to let you live. If I had the opportunity, I'd save them some time and do it myself. You are a worthless coward," she spat at Bert and he just shrugged his shoulders.

"Powerful words," Ashraf said looking between her and Bert. "How about I help you out?" Before she could ask what he meant he pulled a gun from the waistband of his pants and shot Bert, point-blank in the head. Alex closed her eyes as Bert's body crumpled to the ground.

When she opened her eyes back up, she sucked in a big breath. *Holy shit! He actually killed him.*

"Bert was getting too comfortable. He needed to go," Ashraf said kicking Bert's legs to the side.

He stepped closer to her. Close enough she could smell his pungent cologne. "Naveed speaks highly of you. Intelligent, beautiful, loyal to your peers, friends, and family." He ran his slimy fingers down the middle of her chest until he reached her belly button. His eyes were glued to her chest where her breasts threatened to spill out of her bra.

She jerked. "Don't touch me!" She screamed then spit in his face.

He wiped his face with the back of his hand. "You are stubborn, but we can fix that with a little bit of discipline, starting right now." He swung his gun, hitting her in the temple. Then followed it up with a fierce backhand across her face.

He grabbed one of her breasts and squeezed so hard she cried out. "Get this straight you little bitch. I'll touch you whenever and wherever I feel like it. I own you now, and you'll do what I say or there will be consequences you don't want to face." His face was so close that when he spoke, she could feel the spittle spewing from his mouth and it sickened her.

Her body went limp and thank goodness for the two men holding her up or she would have crumpled to the floor. Lifting her head which was still reeling from the blows, she peered up at him through her swelling eye. She spit some blood onto the floor.

"You might as well kill me now, because nobody fucking owns me. Mark my words you bastard, I may die before the team finds me, but I can assure when they come for you, they will kill you the first chance they get."

His lips twitched. "We'll see about that. And, don't worry, I'll definitely kill you. Just not yet. We haven't had any fun." He threw his fist into her stomach, knocking the wind out of her and sending her already bruised ribs screaming for mercy.

Ashraf grabbed his knife, and she flinched, but he bent down and cut the ties around her ankles. "You need to understand how serious I am."

Alex stood still while Ashraf studied her. With her feet unbound she could at least work out the cramps in the arches of her feet and calf muscles, but her ribs and face were hurting badly.

He grabbed her jaw in a bruising grip. "You are going to get your first lesson in my form of discipline." Sticking his tongue out he licked a trail of blood from her jaw up to her temple. "Delicious. Just as sweet as I thought you'd be."

She cringed and tried to jerk out of his hold, but he moved his hand to her throat, putting enough pressure on it cut off her air to the point she was starting to see black dots in her vision. With her arms immobile her other reflexes kicked in. Lifting her leg, she kicked his knee. It was hard enough to knock him off balance causing him to release her and she started gasping for air and coughing.

Rubbing his knee, Ashraf glared at her as his nostrils flared. "You little cunt."

The strikes to her body and head left her unable to fight back. He turned towards the two men holding her.

"Get her to the table and hold her down."

Alex had no fight left in her. Between having her air cut off and being used as a punching bag she hung there gasping for air.

She was shoved face down on to the table and cried out as her ribs pressed against the hard surface. Her arms were pulled out to

195

the side and the men held them down as Yaseen walked over and held her by the back of her neck. Ashraf stood behind her and kicked her legs apart. Hill joined in the action, tying ropes around her ankles that connected to the legs of the table. She didn't want to know what they had planned for her next. Her only thought was that if it were death, hopefully it would be quick.

With no warning or time to prepare, she heard the crack of the whip right before her back lit up like the Fourth of July. She hadn't recovered from the first strike when she heard and felt the second. Agony and pain ripped through her, and unable to hold it in any longer, she let out a blood-curdling scream as she felt her skin split open. The men all laughed as Ashraf whipped her repeatedly, over, and over, calling her names. From her shoulders down to her lower back, she could feel the wetness from the blood.

Her lips quivered and the tears flowed. She was on the verge of passing out. For every shallow breath she tried to take, her ribs protested. If she didn't pass out from the pain soon, the lack of oxygen would definitely do her in.

Her legs began to shake, and she knew she couldn't hold on much longer. She wasn't sure how many times he hit her, but she imagined her back looked as if it had been filleted.

She heard the whip fall to the floor then felt a body press up against her backside. His shirt brushed against her back, tormenting her open wounds. He snaked an arm around her waist placing his hand on her stomach. Using a finger, he circled her belly button before moving to the waistband of her shorts. The feel of his hands on her sickened her. She was crying and pleading with him to just kill her.

"I can only imagine how it is going to feel fucking you." He licked the back of her neck then sunk his teeth into her bare shoulder breaking the skin and making her cry out again.

He yanked the button to her shorts, and she squeezed her eyes shut praying for death to take her now. Mentally and physically she could not endure any more kind of torture or pain.

Just as she heard the zipper of his pants being lowered, a loud explosion rocked the building. Ashraf let go of her and she fell to the floor. Everyone ran out of the room as if she never even existed.

A few seconds later the room became eerily quiet. She was curled into a protective ball with her eyes closed. She cracked open her one eye that wasn't as swollen and breathed in a sigh of relief when she saw the only person left in the room was Hill who was standing by the doorway looking out. Thinking this could be her only opportunity, she had to try and do something.

She heard gunfire which drew Hill out into the hallway. She inched her battered body closer to the legs of the table. She needed to cut the ropes around her ankles. Looking around she didn't see anything she could use. She knew there were some knives on the other table across the room, but even if she could make it over there on her own, Hill would be on her before she made it.

Think Alex!

Her eyes lit up when she remembered her necklace. They took her watch but never removed her necklace. Reaching behind her neck she unclasped the chain. She pulled on one side of the silver leaf-like trinket and it opened, producing a sharp two-inch blade.

With a lot of effort, she sawed through the thick rope until her legs were freed. Using the table as a brace, she pulled herself up. She was breathing heavily and felt like she would collapse at any given moment. Sweat dripped down her back and seeped into the open wounds bringing more agony for her. But no matter how bad she felt, her mission wasn't over.

As fast as her feet could move her without alerting Hill, she moved up behind him. She eyed two knives lying on the table just behind him. Having a gun would have been a better choice but beggars couldn't be choosers in a situation like this, so she'd take what was given to her at the present. With her training, she could incapacitate someone with a knife, but with her injuries, she'd be lucky to be quick enough to get a couple of good jabs in. She passed by Bert's dead body and thought it was too bad Yaseen had grabbed the two guns off his body.

As her fingers wrapped around the handle of the knife, she managed a small smile for the first time since she had woken up in this nightmare. It was time to fight, or at least die trying to.

CHAPTER SEVENTEEN

Six Hours Earlier

"This is ridiculous. Where the fuck could she be?" Ace said, shoving his hands into his hair as everyone in the packed room looked over intelligence reports and maps. It was all hands on deck, and everyone was doing whatever they could to get the one lead to where Alex could be.

Of course, everyone's main concern was Alex's well-being. She was tough as nails, but even the toughest have trouble adapting in captivity. Add in her being a beautiful woman, and it could be much worse. Ace closed his eyes trying to block out the images of what he imagined she could be going through. He'd seen the conditions of what men like Ashraf put women in, and the thought of Alex experiencing any of it had him seething.

Without much information to go on, they were grasping at straws. The Commander was working diligently on his end to get all the information he could. They had the full support and any resources the US government could offer them.

Everyone was spread around the room, some deep in conversation, others on the phone. Ace took a moment to sit down. Bracing his elbows on the table he rested his head in the palms of his hands.

The hardest part had been watching his Commander deal with the situation. Derek had been busting his ass just like the rest of them, but there had been moments where Ace had seen him staring off as if he had completely shut down on the spot. But, seconds later as if shaking off the thoughts, the Commander that he knew was back barking orders. Ace couldn't blame him a damn bit either. They were all anxious.

He sat there for a few more moments; the chair next to him squeaked pulling him from his thoughts. He looked over and was surprised to see Skittles sitting there. Skittles hadn't left his computer since they started searching for Alex's whereabouts.

"Anything new?" Ace asked.

"No, but a thought just occurred to me that none of us considered. Bear in mind, it's just a hunch."

Ace sat up straighter in the chair and nodded his head for him to continue.

"What about that location that Alex told us about? The one that her team never got clearance for. Now knowing Bert is involved, I started wondering if he may have been the hold up in that process. Maybe he never pressed the issue and just told Alex and her team that the government didn't approve."

"Did she mention where it was?"

"Just that it was in a valley near the base of the Hindu Kush mountain range."

Ace considered what Skittles was saying, but then he reminded him that the gorgeous but treacherous mountain range spanned roughly five hundred miles between central Afghanistan and northern Pakistan. That was another possibility; that they moved Alex across the border.

"That's a large area to cover and without coordinates, we could spend days or even weeks searching for possibly nothing," Ace admitted, sounding defeated to his own ears.

"It may be, Ace, but what are the chances that she wrote those coordinates down or some other detail about that village in those handwritten notes she said she kept and brought with her?"

Ace's eyebrows soared and he slapped Skittles on the back. "It's worth a shot. Where's her bag? She kept everything for work in her backpack."

Skittles pointed to the back of the room where Alex's bags were laying on the floor. He hurried over and dumped its contents onto the table. Everyone gathered around the table while Skittles started explaining.

There were a shit ton of notebooks, all filled with Alex's handwriting. Jesus, the way she kept notes made Ace wonder if she had a photographic memory. He handed out the notebooks instructing them to scan every page to look for any language referencing the location. It had been a godsend she had neat and readable handwriting.

Within minutes it was confirmed from a source within the agency that Skittles had been spot-on, and that Bert never requested the approval to enter the valley land.

Dino shouted that he'd found something and all conversations in the room ceased. As Dino relayed the information, Ace felt like an angel was watching over them. Skittles was right, Alex had written down information, and the hell of it was that the valley was only a hop, skip, and a jump from Bagram. The Commander was already on the phone ordering up satellite images of the area. Ace felt the hope and confidence begin to rise, but he wouldn't dare celebrate until Alex was found and safe. They had a starting point, now they just had to wait for the orders to go get her.

Two hours later and after a call between the U.S. and the Governor of the Province, they had confirmation. A young boy and his grandmother had been at the river yesterday morning and saw a man carrying a woman who matched Alex's description into a building that sat alone from the riverbanks surrounded by farmland. They had told the little boy's father who then went to the authorities.

This valley was one of the safest areas in Afghanistan due to the sky-high mountains surrounding it along with the tight security in place at its border. Being that the area was considered a Green Zone, the U.S. government didn't want to ruffle feathers, and it gave a courtesy call explaining the details and it was then the Governor's office and Afghan Police who put two and two together and told the government official about the sighting of the mystery woman by villagers.

As the sun started to set and the moon started to rise, the team gathered for one last discussion with base operations and their commander. They were now joined by their buddies from Bravo team who arrived about an hour ago and would be aiding in the rescue operation. They were just as upset and pissed when they were told about Alex's abduction. An actual working surveillance drone with thermal imaging was sent to the location and detected multiple heat signatures both inside and outside the building. All the heat signatures inside the building showed signs of active movement, so they were going on the assumption that Alex was alive.

Once all sixteen men were on board, the helicopter lifted into the night sky. Not a word was spoken as the sound of the rotors took over. Ace looked around at each of his teammates. Each one gave a slight head nod or chin lift as if saying "we got this". By god, he hoped they did. This was what they all lived, breathed, and took an oath for. They would search and overturn every rock until Alex was found.

Alex took a couple of painful shallow breaths. Hopefully, she could get through this without passing out. Eliminating Hill would garner her another weapon, and that was what she was going to need if she planned on surviving.

Just as she got into position behind Hill, gunfire erupted from another part of the building. Knowing this was her only shot she gripped the knife in her hand and reached around Hill's body surprising him. He hesitated which was his downfall. She used the quick seconds at her disposal to yank his head back and run the sharp blade across his neck, severing his jugular vein in one swift motion.

Letting go, his body dropped to the floor. She looked away from the gruesome scene, but that didn't stop the coppery metallic scent of blood from filling her nostrils. If it weren't for the adrenalin flowing through her body that kept her moving, she'd be down for the count. She was shaking and breathing heavily as she quickly tried pulling the AK-47 from under him but it was no use. The strap was wrapped around his body and she couldn't move him.

The shouting and gunfire grew louder. They were advancing to her position quickly. A knife wasn't going to hold up against the insurgence of multiple men armed with guns. Frantically, she felt around Hill's body and found another gun hidden in his waistband. She pulled the pistol out and sent a silent thank you to the heavens when she saw it had a full round of ammo.

Suddenly, Ashraf barged through the door looking disheveled. He paused, shocked as he realized his son was lying dead on the floor. Then his wild, maniacal eyes shot to her.

She was having trouble focusing. Her head throbbed so bad she was sick to her stomach. She needed a few minutes of reprieve, but she barely had seconds. She was out of time knowing the man in front of her was going to kill her.

"What have you done?" He screamed at her as he looked back at his son's body. She didn't hold an ounce of sympathy for him. They were evil people who deserved everything they got, even if that included death.

The smell of death mixed with the hot air made the scene much worse. Her body swayed just as Ashraf turned and faced her. He waved the gun in the air and began to shout at her.

"Letting you live was the biggest mistake I've ever made, and I damn well won't make that mistake twice."

She gripped the gun in her hand tighter knowing this was it. Sweat dripped down her face. She was going to have to make a move and prayed she could get an accurate shot. She was about to draw her weapon when another explosion detonated from somewhere inside the building. The blast was strong enough to cause sections of the ceiling to give way, sending chunks of concrete raining down on top of them. She got hit by a few small pieces but stayed focused on the target in front of her. Unfortunately for Ashraf, at that split second, he took his eyes off her to dodge a falling piece of concrete giving Alex the opportunity she needed, and she took full advantage of it, pulling the trigger and sending a .9-millimeter bullet into the side of Ashraf's head.

It was like watching a scene from a movie in slow motion as his head snapped sideways and his body dropped to the floor. Alex couldn't take her eyes off him, fearing he wasn't dead. It was more gunfire that shook her from her stupor just as more of the ceiling fell around her, forcing her to move further into the room. The lone light in the room started to flicker, and smoke began to drift in.

Suddenly three men burst into the room yelling something she couldn't make out because of the gunfire happening behind them. Alex didn't think twice and fired two quick shots taking out the first two guys. But when she aimed for the third guy, she feared her luck had run out. Her eyesight wasn't perfect at the moment, but she knew the man dressed in black aiming his gun at her was Yaseen. As she lifted the gun and fired, a warm sensation hit her chest sending her backward onto the floor. Quickly the warm feeling morphed into a blistering pain that tore through her body, and she screamed. Her body trembled and everything around her started to fade. As she floated on the brink of unconsciousness heavy footsteps sounded next to her.

If it was the good guys, then great. If they weren't, then all she wished for was a fast death. She couldn't fight the battle anymore. She felt so cold and started to shiver which only caused her pain to intensify. The only thing that kept her from succumbing to the darkness hovering over her was someone calling her name.

She blinked her eyes open as far as she could, which wasn't much. It was dark and smoky but the man in front of her was wearing a face mask like the ones she had seen the guys on the team wear. Maybe her eyes were playing tricks on her, but he had fascinating grey eyes.

"Who are you?" She asked, but the man ignored her and began putting pressure on the wound to her chest. She felt a sting and saw another man removing a needle from her arm. Within seconds the pain began to subside, and her body felt numb. *Was this it*, she wondered. Was this the beginning of her death? She heard the guy curse and then he told someone they needed to move.

He brushed her hair from her face. "We're going to get you out of here, honey. Your boyfriend is being a bit impatient."

Ace was there? She needed to see him to tell him that she loved him. She didn't want to die without him knowing that she loved him. Her eyes were becoming heavy and it felt as if someone was pulling her under.

She touched the man's face. "If I don't make it before I can tell Ace," her words started to slur, "please tell him…" before she could finish her sentence, her vision went black.

Bear cursed as he lifted Alex into his arms while Duke, his teammate kept pressure to the bullet wound, and they both made a swift exit toward the awaiting team and helicopter.

Ace stood by the helicopter. He and his team had cleared the area surrounding the building, now they just were waiting for Bravo team to exit the building with Alex. When Bear came over the comms saying they had found her, Ace wanted to drop to his knees and cry.

"Incoming, have the medic ready. Gunshot wound to the upper right chest, heavy blood loss," Duke said over the radio.

Ace wasn't sure he had heard it correctly, but when he saw the base medic start laying out medical supplies and Stitch jumping up to help him, Ace knew there was nothing wrong with his hearing.

His eyes stayed glued on the building in front of him that was now burning. As seconds went by, he finally saw shadows moving through the heavy smoke. As they emerged from the haze, he counted them off, one, two, three, four, five team members that had gone into the building. None of them appeared injured, which only left one person.

As Bear neared the helicopter, he knew it was Alex he was carrying while Duke applied pressure to her chest. *Oh god no!*

He jumped up into the helicopter with the rest of the team and everyone scooted back making room as Bear handed Alex off to Stitch and the medic on board.

The medic took over while both Stitch and Duke stood by to assist if needed. He heard the medic say her vitals were critical. She had lost so much blood that her body was going into shock. Duke kept pressure applied to the wound while Stitch started an IV line. The medic was looking over her body for any other major injuries as he communicated with base doctors who were assembling their team for Alex's arrival.

Ace shifted his position to where he was now by Alex's head, but out of the way as to not interfere. As his eyes moved over her mostly bare body, he was able to see the full damage done to her by those monsters. He was overcome with such emotion that it was unnerving. Seeing her lying there bloody, bruised, and swollen from head to fucking toe made him furious.

He leaned down and brushed her hair back before placing a kiss on her forehead. Her skin felt so cold. In his career, he was prepared for anything and everything thrown his way. But the scene playing out in front of him was a whole different ball game. They were all trained to keep emotions off the battlefield but sometimes it was tough, and one of those times was now and his heart was breaking. She had to live—that was all that mattered.

When his eyes slid over to Stitch, Stitch's grim expression said it all. There was a chance they could lose her.

The small waiting room at the base hospital was standing room only as everyone waited for an update on Alex's condition. Both SEAL teams filled the small space along with Colonel Johnson and some of his staff. Derek was in flight and was to arrive by mid-afternoon.

Conversation had been minimal since they brought Alex in and the doctors had carted her away. They were all getting antsy. Over the last four hours, a nurse would periodically come out just to say she was still in surgery.

Bear walked over and sat down next to Ace.

"The guys picked up some video equipment at the compound. It shows everything that went down. We also got confirmation that Bert, Ashraf and his two sons, along with a few other followers were eliminated."

Ace swallowed hard as he held Bear's gaze. He knew that Bear and his team had disappeared for a little bit shortly after Alex was admitted for surgery. Hearing that those fuckers had met their maker was positive news, but it wasn't the news he was looking for. The only real positive news he was anticipating, was hearing a doctor say that Alex was going to live.

"You'll never guess who one of Ashraf's sons was."

At this point, nothing would surprise Ace. "Who?"

"Staff Sgt. Hill."

Ace's eyes widened. "The dude that worked for the Colonel?"

"One and the same."

"Holy fuck."

Bear cleared his throat. "I know this may not be the most appropriate time to discuss this, but you need to know that your woman is a true hero. What she did to survive in the condition she was in is a fucking miracle in itself, and if I'm being honest, I don't know if I could've done what she did."

Ace could see the emotion in Bear's eyes, and it made him even more curious to know what she did because Bear was one of the least emotional men he knew.

"She killed five men. Ashraf killed Bert, but Ashraf, Hill—or Naveed as his father calls him, and Yaseen, along with two other men were her doing." Bear ran his fingers through his dirty blonde hair, seeming rather upset by having to talk about it. Hell, it was difficult for Ace just hearing details. "Jesus, Ace, they fucked her up so bad. We thought most of the blood was coming from her chest. But, her back…fuck, she took a lashing Ace. Her entire back from what we could see on the video was split open. Then along with everything else she sustained I don't know how she was able to function, much less go on the defensive like she did."

Ace could tell there was more to the story, but before he could ask the doctor walked in.

Ace along with everyone else stood and the doctor seemed thrown for a loop at the large audience.

"Well, I see the nurse wasn't exaggerating when she said Ms. Hardesty had a crew waiting for her. I'm Captain Addock."

Ace stepped forward and introduced himself. "How is Alex, Sir?"

The doctor removed his glasses and took a deep breath. Ace's legs almost gave out as he prepared for the worst.

"She's out of surgery and currently stable. She will have a long recovery ahead of her." Ace swore he heard everyone release a breath hearing she was alive, then the doctor continued, "With the severity of her injuries, it was touch and go for a while. We lost her twice on the table, but she had a will to survive. We will monitor her for a couple of hours, and if she stays stable, we'll get her on a plane to Germany where she'll probably stay a few days."

He shook the doctor's hand and the doctor said they could see her once they moved her to a room and got her settled. He did warn them that she wouldn't be awake because she was sedated, and that was fine with Ace: he just needed to see her.

Ace wasn't sure how much time has passed, but finally, they were being led back to where Alex was resting. As all sixteen team members and the Colonel made their way through the hall, they caused a lot of heads to turn.

When the nurse pointed to the last room on the right Ace thanked her. As he opened the door and saw her small body lying in bed hooked up to wires and tubes, he almost lost it right on the spot. It was Potter's whispered voice next to him that pulled him out of the dark hole he was heading down.

"She's alive. Be strong for her, man."

He stepped up next to the bed and the rest of the guys followed creating a safety barrier around her. The bruises they could see looked even worse now.

Ace looked at the guys, "I swear to god, if those sadistic bastards weren't already dead, I would hunt them down and give them a slow painful death."

"You'd have a lot of help," Stitch angrily said as he took her one hand in his.

"I'd say our girl here gives a new meaning to *fight to survive*. How in the hell she managed is another story. All that matters is that she survived and kicked ass," Irish commented and smiled.

"Like the doctor said, she's going to have a long recovery," Ace admitted looking in Stitch's direction.

Frost blew out a breath and Ace could see the tormented look on both Frost and Stitch's faces. They'd known her for most of their lives so he could only imagine how they were feeling.

"Good news is she'll have her family to help her through this. And, I don't see any of us turning our back on her. We will all be there to support her with whatever she needs. Hell, she'll have the support of every SEAL once they hear what she did. Right now, I'm more worried about how Derek is going to handle seeing her like this."

Everyone stayed by Alex's side until Derek and a few of Alex's other uncles had arrived, and only then did they leave their teammate's side so that her family could have some alone time with her.

Leaving her was hard for Ace, especially when he found out from Derek that the team was being shipped out again. It was the first time in his career he wanted to disobey a direct order. However, Derek must have read his expression because he pulled Ace aside and assured him that he and Alex's uncles would take care of her, and that he needed a clear mind to focus on his next mission.

Hearing and doing were two vastly different things, but Ace understood. Until he got through with this next mission and could get home, he would rely on Derek to help her through her recovery. Derek at least gave him a couple of minutes alone with Alex as if knowing he needed to say good-bye to her.

Once he was alone, he took her small delicate hand into his and kissed her knuckles. God, this was so hard to do. He didn't want to leave her, not now when she was going to need him. But he knew he had to.

He leaned over the bed rail and kissed her cheek and forehead. Then he gently pressed his lips against hers.

"I love you, baby."

CHAPTER EIGHTEEN

Alex leaned back in the lounge chair and tilted her face up towards the warm sunshine. With her eyes closed, she focused on the soft sound of the gentle waves lapping at the shoreline mere yards from her. She was shocked at how relaxed she felt laying here alone.

Over a month had passed since she had gone through what she considered to be to hell and back. In that time a lot had changed in her life. Besides recovering from the injuries and being whisked off to secret locations by the government every day to be mentally picked apart until she felt she had no brain cells left, she had also moved back home to be closer to her family.

She had been super lucky to snag the house that had gone up for sale right next door to her friend Tenley. It was in one of the newer communities in the area. It was a gorgeous 4,100 square foot home with five bedrooms and four and a half baths. Yeah, it was a little over the top for the ordinary person, but she wasn't ordinary. Her uncles had stopped giving her shit about how big it was when they had seen how much stuff she owned. While she rested at Derek's house, her family and friends had all driven up to Maryland and packed her rental house up and moved everything to her new home. Which reminded her once she got home and was back up to speed, she wanted to have them all over for a cook-out as a thank you for helping her.

Another huge life change was her job. She no longer worked for Mason, although she had stayed in contact with both him and Bowman and maybe did a little consulting work on the side from home, but that was something she wasn't telling her uncles. During the long plane ride from Germany, she thought back to her and Potter's conversation about her enjoying what she did. She explained her conversation with Potter to Derek and the others. To say her uncles were happy had been an understatement. They were ecstatic about her idea of forming a non-profit organization to help aid military personnel and their families. They even offered suggestions, and by the time their plane landed the Jacob Hardesty Foundation had been unofficially formed.

Unfortunately, the changes weren't all positive, as she had been falling into a deep depression. She knew the signs of PTSD and knew she had symptoms, but she chose to ignore them rather than reach out for help. She kept telling herself each day she could get through it on her own, but it only progressed. Every time she would fall asleep either day or night, she would relive those last hours of her confinement. She was so afraid that she always had someone stay the night with her. Most of the time it was Tenley, but if she had to work at the hospital, Derek or one of the other uncles would stay with her.

To make matters worse, she couldn't stop thinking about Ace and the guys. Not hearing from them had further pushed her down the depression hole. She wasn't blaming them for having shipped out as she understood they were out doing their jobs. But, call it selfishness or whatever, she was feeling needy, and her need for the last few weeks had been Ace. Having him near was an instant safety net. Her love for him was still forefront and she only hoped he was still interested when he returned.

Most of her days were spent laying around in complete silence since that was about as much as her body would tolerate. That had lasted until a week ago when she'd finally had enough and needed an escape. Something to possibly bring her out of the funk she was in. Which was why she could now hear, see, and smell the crystal blue waters of St. Thomas.

The past week had been somewhat therapeutic. She'd done a lot of soul searching and pondering of her future. She had been staying in the guest house of Dr. Caleb Matthews, a college friend of hers. Caleb helped in running his family's medical practice on the island. The two of them had met when she was enrolled at the University of Maryland. Even though he was a few years older than her, they had become great friends. His family was like royalty on the island; very wealthy with a long line of well-established doctors.

When she had called and explained to him her predicament, and the need to get away for a few days, he didn't hesitate to help. Even going as far as having his family's private jet available to come to pick her up and take her home when she was ready.

Physically she was healing and getting better each day. The bruising on her face had almost completely faded. Though not quick enough in her opinion. Her midsection was still very sore. How she walked away with only three fractured ribs still amazed her. The gunshot wound had healed nicely, though she was still sore which was expected since the bullet had torn through muscle tissue. Her back had been a different story. It had taken over a hundred stitches to close all the wounds she suffered. Two of the larger lash marks still had stitches, but Caleb told her he may be able to take them out later today. He had warned her that she would most likely have some scarring from the damage done by Ashraf.

The hardest part had been dealing with the flashbacks and nightmares. Sleeping of course had been a major issue and something she hadn't had much of since returning home. She was prescribed some sleeping aids, but she'd been afraid to take them out of fear that she wouldn't be able to wake up during one.

She took a deep breath and again could smell the saltwater air.

"Alex?"

She popped her eyes open and saw Caleb sitting on the lounge next to her. Damn, she must have been really daydreaming because she never heard him approach.

He smiled at her. Caleb was a very handsome man, and not to mention a total sweetheart. There had been a time back in college where she and he had almost started dating, but things worked out the way they were meant to be. She would have hated if they had dated and things ended badly ruining the great friendship they had.

Caleb looked at her. "How are you doing today?"

She shrugged her shoulders. "Okay, I guess."

"Just okay?"

Okay, that was lame, of course, she wasn't going to leap up and exclaim she was fantastic. Something was missing and she didn't know how to explain it.

Caleb took her hand in his. "I'm going to offer my professional medical advice. You need to talk to someone. You may be healing on the outside, but I can tell that you are wilting away on the inside. Sweetie look at you, you aren't sleeping, you've lost weight, your nightmares are getting worse, and certain things trigger panic attacks. You need help, Alex. Please let your family help you."

Alex looked down to where their hands were clasped together as she let Caleb's words sink in. She didn't want to put any burden on her family, but now she realized that she was hurting them by pushing them away when they were trying to help her. Her uncles had all dealt with PTSD at one time or another during their careers. The nightmares, flashbacks, and panic attacks from their days in the Teams weren't anything new to her. She had the best resources at her fingertips to help her get through this and she was being a stubborn fool for not utilizing them.

She squeezed Caleb's hand. "Thank you, Caleb, for everything. You're a great friend. I think I'm ready to face this head-on."

"Does that mean you're ready to leave this paradise?"

"As relaxing and peaceful as it has been, yeah, I'm ready. I need to be with my family." She leaned over and hugged him. "Thank you for being patient with me."

"How about if I take a look at your back, then I'll arrange for the plane to be ready at your disposal?"

She thanked him. She was ready for this. Thinking of all the support she had back home, she couldn't help but feel a little bit of emptiness not knowing where things stood with Ace.

Every night she fell asleep with him on her mind. She missed sneaking snuggles with him. She hadn't asked her uncle for any type of update on the team. She would wait for as long as it took to see those blue eyes of his that captivated her from the start.

Derek sat on the patio deck at Bayside Bar and Grill. It was a clear summer evening with a breeze that blew in from the ocean. The waves rolled in as the seagulls chirped and scoured the beach for dinner.

Alpha team had arrived back stateside earlier in the afternoon. After the debriefings and standard bullshit, they were all enjoying a nice cold beer together. It was sort of a tradition when the team returned home from a mission.

Everyone sat in silence for a few minutes sipping their beers and gazing out at the horizon. Derek knew that Alex was on all their minds. Since they landed in the afternoon, every one of them had asked about her. His standard answer had been that she was okay.

He knew them having to leave her in Bagram had weighed heavily on them all. He wasn't surprised to learn they had declared her an unofficial member of their team. Every one of those men would protect her from anything and anyone. Derek knew most of these guys would admit they didn't have a heart, but she had found a way into each of theirs. They were trained killers and protectors, and for them to see the aftermath of what a malicious individual had done to one of their own—especially a woman—angered them.

After he had a chance to review the video from her time in captivity, he knew she was going to come back home a different person, and he was prepared for it. The time he had gotten to spend with her he could see she was struggling emotionally. He knew from experience that she needed to talk to someone.

Her ordeal was the talk of the base and he couldn't be any prouder of her, although he wished she never had to endure the situation to begin with. She not only survived the wrath of a madman, but she also saved the lives of a lot of people.

"So, commander, how is Alex really doing?" Irish asked, his low but deep voice slicing through the nighttime air.

Derek blew out a breath and shook his head. "I won't lie. She's in a bad place right now. She has some good days, but most are bad. Tenley and I have been staying with her."

"Wait, staying with her? Is Alex here in Virginia Beach?" Ace asked, and Derek had to hide his smile at the Lt. Commander's sudden upbeat tone.

"Sure is. She's been here since we got her home."

"What about her job?"

Derek's eyes moved from Ace to Potter.

"She resigned. Apparently, she had a very moving conversation with someone. Now she has moved on to something that makes her happy and will bring even more happiness to a lot of people. I'll let her explain it to you guys."

"So, she's staying with you?" Stitch asked.

"No. She bought the house next door to Tenley. The couple who owned it were looking to make a quick sale. As soon as Tenley told Alex about it, she jumped on it and things just fell into place. Tink and the guys drove up with me and together we packed her up and moved her home."

He peered over at Ace and tipped his beer bottle in his direction. "I'm hoping now that you're back maybe you could try talking to her. From what I hear, you seem to have a way with her." He gave Ace a wry smile before lifting his beer to his lips.

Ace raised his eyebrows in question, obviously stunned, but Derek found it amusing. Did he and Alex think he wouldn't find out?

"Oh, don't look at me like that son. Are you seriously going to sit there and insult my intelligence and tell me that you don't have any feelings for my little girl?"

Derek heard the snickers from the others. He knew something was going on between Ace and Alex the day they had that video conference with him. He wasn't stupid. And honestly, he couldn't be any happier for Alex. Ace was a good man and she deserved someone like him. But that didn't mean he couldn't make the guy sweat a little.

"No, sir. I'd never do that," Ace replied looking a little unsure.

Derek grinned and tipped his bottle before taking another drink. "Good. Have you tried to call her yet?"

"I did, but it went straight to voicemail."

"Ah, she must have been on the plane already."

"Plane?"

"Yeah, she went on a trip to St. Thomas."

"Is she healthy enough to travel?"

"I wasn't in favor of it at first, but she's staying with a friend from college and he is a doctor. His whole family are doctors."

Derek slid a piece of paper over to Ace.

"What's this?"

"Meet me there in about an hour."

Derek guzzled the last drop of beer then stood up and threw some cash on the table.

"If you want something bad enough you can't be a quitter. Trust me on this. Meet me at the pier in one hour."

❦

Ace needed a few minutes alone. Using the excuse to make a phone call he walked to the other side of the patio and stood against the railing. He took a deep breath and exhaled as he looked to the sky. The stars and moon had started to reveal themselves against the backdrop of the dark blue sky.

"You okay man?"

Ace turned and saw Potter standing there wearing a look of concern.

"I'll feel a lot better when I can see her." He ran his hand through his messy hair. "After hearing what Derek said, I'm worried about her. I can't lose her."

"She'll recover Ace. She's one of us, remember? She's a natural-born fighter." He grinned then leaned against the wooden railing.

Ace had finally found the courage to view the videos of Alex's captivity. To see her fight with the determination she had to survive was unbelievable and moving. He was astounded by her will to fight and survive. Especially in the condition she was in.

"What was on the paper that Derek gave you?"

"The name of the park with the pier just down the street."

"Why?"

"I think he's bringing Alex there." He shrugged his shoulders. "We'll see. If not, I'll find out where Tenley lives from Stitch or Frost and go to Alex's house."

Suddenly, the guys started to get a little rowdy, and when they glanced over, Ace saw why.

"Holy shit, who is that gorgeous woman?" Potter asked looking towards the table with wide eyes, and Ace grinned.

"That would be Tenley."

Potter looked back Ace. "That's Alex's best friend?"

Ace had to hold back his smile at the way Potter seemed to perk up after laying eyes on the pint-sized brunette who was hugging Frost.

They both headed over to find out what was going on.

CHAPTER NINETEEN

Derek pulled into a parking lot and Alex was surprised when she realized they were at her favorite park. She loved coming here and sitting out on the long pier that stretched into the ocean.

"Why are we here?" She asked Derek as she looked out the window. Man, did she miss this place.

"I know how you loved this place, so I thought it would be a good place for us to talk. Come on let's walk." He said opening the door and getting out. She followed suit. It was warm but the breeze and evening air cooled the temperature down.

They walked to the pier and took a seat on one of the benches. He stretched his legs out and placed his arm along the back of the bench behind her. For a minute they both just sat there gazing out at the water.

"How was St. Thomas?" He asked breaking the silence.

"It was nice. I did a lot of thinking."

He looked over her. "Yeah?"

She gave him a soft smile then swallowed hard. She needed to be honest with him. He was offering an olive branch, so she needed to grab hold of that branch and let him in.

"I want to first apologize for shutting you and the rest of the family out." She looked out at the water and closed her eyes. "I know you are frustrated with me. And what bothers me the most is that I feel like I've let you down."

"Oh, honey, come here." He pulled her against him, and she burst into tears.

"All that we've all wanted from you is for you to open up."

Her voice cracked as the tears flowed freely.

"I felt like I was trapped and was suffocating. I needed an escape and I ran. I need help, and I understand that now. I don't want to go through this alone." She buried her face in his chest and cried harder, releasing the pent-up emotions she'd been holding onto for over two years.

He held her tightly. "You don't have to do this alone," he said rubbing her back.

She pulled herself back enough to look up at him. With tears running down her cheeks she locked gazes with him and was caught off guard by the emotions she saw in his eyes. The man sitting here with her now wasn't the hard, demanding Commander she knew him to be. No, she saw the man who was full of compassion and love, and trying, but having a difficult time holding back his own emotions over someone he loved. His eyes were glazed over ready to shed the tears that were building up.

She reached up and wiped the first tear from his eye before it spilled over. "Will you help me?"

Those four words from her weighed heavy on Derek's heart, and he was unable to hold back any longer. He hugged her tight while he let her cry on him. Hell, he shed a few tears himself. He took a second to send up a silent thank you to the powers above for bringing her home.

"I assume you saw the video," Alex finally asked him as she pulled away and leaned back.

"I did." He turned his head to look at her. He had watched it once and never wanted to see it again. He had seen many videos over his career, but when the victim was one close to the heart—a family member—it had the tendency to inflict another layer of emotion. Special Forces Operatives were taught how to detach their emotions from the situation, but when a man beats, whips and nearly rapes your daughter, it is difficult to put those emotions aside. It had broken him to watch what those evil bastards had done to her.

"My emotions have been all over the place. One minute I feel like I got it all under control and I'm ready to conquer the world, and the next I'm sitting in the corner of my bedroom crying or having a panic attack." She wiped another tear from her eye.

"Why didn't you call me? You know I would have been there for you. All of us would've. Hell, Tenley, and I have even been staying with you at night. None of us knew exactly what you were going thru, although we assumed, but we didn't want to push."

She shrugged her shoulders, "I thought that by admitting it, it would make me look weak."

"That's bullshit, Alex." He saw the shocked expression on her face at his abrupt comment. "Honey, you need to remember that you are back home now. You have your family and friends surrounding you. Sure, a lot of them don't know the extent of what you endured over there. Hell, they don't even know where you were. But even so, those people are here for you. It's tough, but support from friends and family are what get you through it. I'm not going to sit here and tell you that you'll eventually forget everything that happened. If I did that, I'd be lying. Shit, there are times when my past still affects me. When it happens, I just pick up the phone and call your Uncle Tink or one of the others and we talk it out."

"What if I want to talk to a professional? How does that work since missions are classified? I know there are shrinks on base for military personnel, but what about civilians like me? I don't think the government would appreciate me spilling classified information to just any doctor."

He laughed, "No, I don't think they would appreciate that at all. Would you feel more comfortable talking to a professional? Because, if you are, either me or Mason could probably talk with the base and see if one of the doctors would see you."

She let out a sigh, "To start, I think that would be best. You're not upset with that are you?"

"Not at all. I'm simply happy you're willing to confide in someone. Although I thought there may be someone in particular that you might feel more comfortable talking with."

"Like who?"

"I don't know, maybe a certain SEAL that you seemed to have caught the attention of."

He wanted to laugh when her head snapped up so fast that he thought she'd have whiplash. When her cheeks turned a little pink, he couldn't hold his chuckle in.

He smiled and winked at her. "I do have to say I'm surprised. What changed your mind? You've always shied away from dating someone in the military."

She shook her head and even snorted a laugh.

"Believe me, I surprised myself. It happened so fast; one minute I'm trying to get something to eat, and the next he saves me from making a complete ass out of myself." He gave her a sideways look. "Seriously! Ask Potter, it was so embarrassing."

He was getting ready to reply when his phone buzzed with an incoming message and he hid his smile when he saw who it was. He typed in a quick reply then stood up.

"Do you trust me?"

She scrunched her eyebrows together. "Of course, I do. Why would you even ask me that?"

He leaned down and kissed her cheek. "I only want what is best for you, and right now I want you to follow your heart. Give me a minute to deal with this." He held up his phone and then walked back toward his truck while laughing to himself. Jesus, for the last twenty-four years he tried keeping her away from boys, and here he was practically putting one right in her lap.

Ace saw Derek walking up the pathway that led to the pier and started walking towards him.

He knew Alex was here. That was confirmed from speaking with Tenley after she showed up at Bayside. Now that woman was a bouncing ball of energy and had a mouth with no filter. She was also attractive. She and Alex shared a lot of similarities. She had even landed on Potter's radar, which was shocking because Potter didn't date. He'd have to keep an eye on that situation and see how it played out. Just from watching them when they were introduced to each other, anyone with a good eye could see the pull. Not to mention Potter never left her side and even bought her a drink. She and Potter had still been talking when he left to come here.

He thought back to the information Tenley had shared with him and the team about Alex. Hearing how bad Alex's nightmares and panic attacks were not only worried him, but it broke his heart. Anyone who went through what she did was sure to have some form of PTSD. He would, however, make sure she got the help she needed and support her every step of the way.

Derek smiled as they shook hands. "She's all yours," Derek said exchanging looks with Ace and then slapping him on the back.

"How is she?"

"She's in a fragile state right now, but with some positive reinforcement in her life, I think she'll pull through. She can be stubborn, so sometimes she may need a little bit of a push. She said she's ready to talk to someone so that's positive." Ace nodded his head. "It's going to take some time for her to come to terms with everything that happened. You know how this shit works."

"You know I'm in this one hundred percent. I'm not planning on letting her go. I pretty much made that clear with her over there."

Derek's lips curled up into a smile, "If I didn't have the confidence in you, you wouldn't be standing here right now. All that I ask of you is to respect and give her the care and love she needs. She's my world, and all I want is for her to be happy. You make her happy. I'm going to make a few calls and see if I can get her in with one of the doctors on base tomorrow. Let her know I'll text her the details."

With one last handshake between the two men, Derek walked toward his truck, and Ace followed the path that led him to the woman who stole his heart.

Alex sat back and gazed out at the horizon. There were a couple of Navy ships she saw in the distance, and she placed her hand over her belly feeling that little pang of emptiness inside. She missed Ace so much. There was a brief moment right after she had been given her lashing where she didn't think she would survive the torture. She didn't have a huge family, but the family she did have she feared not ever being able to see them again, and that included Ace as well. She felt the moisture coming to her eyes as she closed them, then she took a deep breath. She looked down at her watch and wondered how long Derek would be. She was thankful for the little bit of alone time right now, but she was exhausted and just wanted to go home.

Although the thought of going home to an empty house didn't sit well with her either. Derek didn't say anything about staying over and she hadn't had a chance to ask Tenley yet. Knowing someone else was in the house helped ease her mind and fears. She wasn't looking forward to sleeping alone; at least not yet. She'd ask Derek when he returned. Maybe asking would be the first step in showing her family that she was ready to move on and accept the support they were all willing to give her.

"Alex…"

She gasped. She wasn't so much as startled by the person sneaking up behind her, it was who.

When she turned and her eyes met those baby blues she had fallen in love with, her heart skipped a beat. He stood there looking just as handsome and sexy as the first time they met. And his awfully intense eyes had the same effect on her body. Starting with her toes, she felt the heat in her body as it traveled up the rest of her body. When he smiled and opened his strong arms welcoming her, she didn't think twice as she closed the distance between them and leaped into his embrace. She looped her arms around his neck and buried her face into the crook of his neck as she inhaled his clean, masculine scent.

"You're here," she said in between sniffles and hiccups.

"I'm here, baby, and I've missed you so damn much." With one arm under her butt holding her and one hand cupping the back of her head he nuzzled the side of her head.

Ace turned and sat down on the bench, but she didn't want to let go of him. With the way her mind was lately she was afraid this was all just a figment of her imagination.

Eventually, she came to terms with herself and loosened her hold a little and leaned back. He pressed his forehead against hers and they were eye-to-eye. "Hi," he whispered.

She whispered hi back, rubbing her nose against his giving him little Eskimo kisses. "I'm not dreaming, right?"

He laughed. "No, you're definitely not dreaming."

"When did you get home?" She asked.

"A few hours ago. I tried calling you."

"I was on my way home."

"So, I hear. In fact, I've heard a lot of changes are happening."

She grinned. "Derek has a big mouth sometimes."

"But he loves you and wants what's best for you."

227

She sat up straight and palmed his cheek. His cheeks had a dusting of scruff which added to his sexiness.

"I have so much I want to say right now, but I honestly don't know where to start."

He placed a finger on her lips. "I know baby. We both have a lot to talk about, but right now I just want to hold you in my arms for a minute." She was absolutely fine with that. She laid her head against his shoulder and snuggled closer. Since waking up in the hospital four weeks ago, she finally felt at peace.

After a while, she yawned, and he chuckled.

"How about we get you home?"

"You're taking me home?"

He kissed her nose. "If that's okay. I'd like to."

"I'd like that very much."

He bent down and she thought he was going to kiss her, but instead, he lightly brushed his lips against her forehead. He then lifted her in his arms and walked towards his truck.

Shortly after Ace had gotten Alex situated in his truck, she had fallen asleep. He pulled into her driveway and stared at the monstrous house in front of him. Why in the hell did she need a house so fucking big? He peered over and was surprised when he saw her green orbs staring back at him.

When the hell did she wake up?

Unbuckling his seat belt, he leaned over and brushed his knuckles against her cheek. He was happy to see the bruising on her face was fading. The last time he saw her, both eyes were almost swollen shut and her entire face was discolored.

She gave him a sleepy smile and he could tell she was exhausted. He intended to use this time with her to pamper her and show her exactly how special she was and that he would do anything for her.

He got out of the truck and came around to her side. When she went to move to get out Ace saw the way her eyebrows scrunched together and knew she was still in pain. He reached in and lifted her against his chest, and he smiled when she went willingly. It also made him laugh remembering how she always would snuggle against him, referring to him as her personal heater and pillow, but he didn't mind it at all. He looked forward to a lot of nights and mornings cuddling with her.

"Why are you laughing?"

"Just remembering how you used to snuggle in those damn tiny racks we shared."

"That's because you're warm and snuggly." She said with a hint of humor and he grinned. Christ, what would others say if they heard her say that? SEALs weren't snuggly, they were badass.

"Let's get you into the house and get some food in you."

"Okay, but first there is something I need."

"What's that?"

"Kiss me…"

He grinned. "With pleasure." He lifted her a little higher and bent his head as she closed her eyes and lifted her chin. The moment he felt her soft, warm lips brush against his, he couldn't hold back the beast inside him. He pushed his tongue between her teeth, and she must have had the same idea because their tongues locked together. Remembering they were standing outside in front of her house he released her lips.

"Goddamn, did I miss you." He told her making her laugh, and she snuggled against his chest as he carried her inside.

He walked them into the living room just off the kitchen and sat on the couch. She switched positions so she was straddling his lap. He looked at her seriously as he ran his hands up and down her ribs. He knew she wanted to talk and so did he. He thought it was best to get the heavy shit out of the way so they could just sit back and enjoy one another for the evening.

"You know when I got a chance to talk with Derek earlier and he told me what was going on with you, it scared the shit out of me. I was so worried."

She sighed and looked down before she made eye contact again. "I scared myself. This last month hasn't been rainbows and unicorns that's for sure. There were days I didn't think I'd be able to make it." She lowered her head. "Every time I look into a mirror and see my injuries, I'm reminded of what I went through. As I told Derek, I thought asking for help would make me look weak."

Tears gathered in her eyes and he used his index finger to lift her chin so she was looking at him.

"You? Weak? I hate to tell you this sweetheart, but you are the farthest thing from weak. I can guarantee that anybody who knows your story has the utmost respect for you."

"I know that now, but try putting yourself in my place. Sure, my uncles taught me survival methods, but I don't live and breathe that every day like you do." She covered her face with her hands. "Christ, I had to kill five people. Honestly, that bothers me more than my injuries even though I know they deserved it."

Shit, he never thought about it that way. Having to kill another person could wreak havoc on anyone's mental status. She was right, it was different for her as her resources were limited compared to what he had at his disposal.

He grabbed her hands and linked his fingers with hers. "Killing another person even in self-defense can be difficult for someone to handle. Trust me, been there, done it. But, think about what you just said. You said that you 'had to' kill them. You had no choice, Alex. Consider what the outcome would've been if you hadn't handled the situation as you did."

He could tell she was processing what he was telling her and knew the moment she understood.

"You're right, I never thought about it like that. I just looked at the negativity that came from it. I'm still not proud of the way I handled myself once I got home though. Ignoring my family and friends was not cool."

He tucked a strand of hair behind her ear. "They all understand, and now you understand your days of being alone are long gone. Remember what you said the one night we were up talking?"

She chuckled, "We were up every night talking."

He smiled at the memory of all the nights they spent cuddled in bed talking. "You and I are a team now. So, as I see it, we're in this together. But you have to promise me that when I can't physically be here for you and you're having a bad day, you'll pick up the phone and call someone. I've seen too many people keep shit bottled up and end up doing something stupid."

She hugged him. "I promise as long as you promise to do the same." He nodded.

"Now, I have an important question for you," she stated.

"What's that?"

"Will you stay with me tonight?" She asked shyly. She was too adorable for her own good.

He grinned, "I planned on staying whether you wanted me to or not." She arched her eyebrow, "Confident, are you?" She teased.

He tickled her side making her laugh until she cringed bringing the seriousness of her injuries to the forefront.

"Shit. I'm sorry. That answers my next question. You're still in a lot of pain, huh?"

"It's manageable now, but my ribs are still sore." She pulled the top of her shirt down, showing him the pink puckered scar just above her breast, and he swallowed hard. A few inches lower and she wouldn't be sitting here right now.

"How about your back?"

"I got the last of the stitches out this morning. Dr. Matthews said I'll have some scarring." She slid off his lap and lifted her shirt so he could see.

Scooting forward on the sofa he ran his fingers over the angry looking pink lines gracing her back. "Do they still hurt?" He asked as he placed a kiss to each one causing her to shiver and break out in goosebumps. He smiled knowing he had that effect on her.

She turned in his arms and placed her hands on his shoulders. Looking down she scrunched up her nose.

"Sometimes, although I think it is more in my head, if that makes sense." And it did to Ace. She was experiencing phantom pains.

With his hands on her hips, his fingers caressed her sides. "We all have scars. Some have them on the inside, and some on the outside. Just remember that scars on the outside don't determine who a person is." She nodded her head.

Giving her hips one last squeeze, he stood up. "Here's the plan for tonight. Why don't you go and take a nice relaxing shower or bath, and I'll order something for us to eat?"

"Oh, I think Tenley was going to bring something from Bayside. At least that is what her text said."

Ace snorted a laugh. "I wouldn't count on it."

Alex gave him a sideways look. "Why not?"

"When I left to come and meet you, she had been detained."

"Detained?"

"Yeah, she and Potter seemed very comfortable and engrossed in conversation."

He laughed again when Alex's mouth formed an "O".

"Well then, what do you like?"

"Tenley gave me the name of the Chinese restaurant you like to order from. I'll place the order then grab a quick shower myself. Then you and I have a date to sit and relax together on the couch with a movie."

Before she could respond he bent down and gave her a quick kiss on the lips and then turned her towards the stairs, giving her ass a light tap to get her moving.

Ace watched as she slowly climbed the stairs. Once he saw she safely made it to the top he grabbed his phone and dialed the number for the Chinese restaurant and placed their order.

After a quick shower, Ace walked around the lower level of her house. Going room to room he couldn't fathom why one woman needed something so big for just herself. But then again, by the number of boxes stacked around the house not to mention her full garage, he was beginning to understand. He noticed there were a lot of boxes that were half-unpacked as if she had started to unpack one but then decided to move onto a different one. Along the walls, in different rooms, pictures and wall décor were propped up against them, obviously waiting to be hung.

He walked over to the French doors in the kitchen and flipped on the outside light and saw the in-ground pool in the backyard. As he moved along, he noticed several small picture frames on top of the breakfast bar, but it was the top one that caught his attention. The picture was taken during one of the afternoons her and the team were playing a game of soccer against some of the base guys. Whoever took the picture managed to capture a rare but memorable moment, as all nine of them were gathered together and laughing as if they didn't seem to care they were smack dab in the middle of a war where shit could hit the fan at any given moment.

"That's one of my favorite pictures."

Jerking his head up Alex stood by the entrance to the kitchen leaning against the wall watching him. She smiled. "Sorry, I didn't mean to startle you."

He was so engrossed with the photo that he never heard her enter the room. A mistake like that in the field could cost him and/or his team their lives. At least she was smart enough to know not to sneak up on him.

He ran his eyes from her toes up to her head. Her royal blue pajama shorts showed off her toned legs. She paired it with a matching blue and white striped tank top. Her long brown hair was piled up on top of her head in some sort of messy but sexy up-do. He was mesmerized by her beauty.

She joined him and wrapped her arms around his waist.

"Who took this?" He asked looking back at the picture.

"Colonel Johnson. He emailed it to me about a week ago along with some others. I had them printed right before I left for my trip." She smiled and ran her hand over the frame in his hands. "But this one stood out. I don't even remember what we were all laughing at. I've seen many pictures that my uncles took when they were deployed, and I don't ever remember seeing one like this. Look how happy we all were. You'd never be able to tell by this picture the shit storm we were going thru."

"No, you can't. Can you get me a few more copies made?" He asked as he set the picture back in its original place while Alex went to the refrigerator to grab some drinks.

"Sure. How many do you want?"

"Eight. If that's okay." He wanted to give one to each guy on the team. They would appreciate it as much as he did.

She grinned. "You got it." She handed him a bottle of water. "Do you want me to show you around the house?"

"Sure, and maybe you can explain why you have so much stuff?"

She chuckled and raised one of her eyebrows. "So, you've already snooped I see." Taking his hand she led him through the house showing him what still needed to be unpacked and where it was supposed to go, along with all the furniture in the garage that needed to be moved.

When they stepped down into a sunken room at the far end of the house that Ace hadn't gotten a chance to check out, and his jaw hit the floor when she flicked the lights on. Talk about a media room, or whatever people called them nowadays. It was a fantasy. There was something for everyone in the room to enjoy.

The two sets of French doors led out to the patio and pool area. Hanging on the wall in between the two doors was the autographed Jaguars jersey that he had given to her for her birthday. On the far side of the room was a fully stocked bar that could seat eight people. Next to the bar and just behind the massive chocolate brown sectional sofa was a pool table and an air hockey table. Ottomans matching the sofa were scattered around to use as added seating if needed. Custom-built shelving and display cases adorned the walls that held sports mementos she had picked up over the years. All that was really nice and pretty cool, but the main focal point was the massive flat-screen TV mounted on the wall straight ahead.

"I don't think I'll leave this room. What size TV is that?" He asked still trying to take everything in.

"Eighty-five inch. I had it professionally installed along with the audio." She pointed to the speakers hidden throughout the room.

They spent the rest of the evening eating dinner, catching up, and snuggling together on the couch. The action movie they were watching had just ended and Ace looked at his watch; it was just after one in the morning. Alex had dozed off about twenty minutes ago and was stretched across him. He looked down at her and

235

brushed his thumb along the dark smudges under her eyes. Hopefully, he could help ease her anxiety and she could rest easier.

He got up trying not to wake her as he lifted her in his arms. Once he got her into bed, he went back downstairs to clean up and did another trip around the house to check the windows and doors.

As he walked around the house, he realized how perfect this house was for a family. With the open floor plan, he could picture kids running around chasing each other. His chest tightened at the image he drew in his head. It was crazy, but he wanted a family with Alex.

He walked back into the bedroom and stripped down to his boxer briefs and climbed in the king bed. When he snuggled up behind Alex, she surprised him when she rolled over.

"You okay?" He asked brushing her hair from her face.

"I am now," she said rubbing her nose along his chest. "I thought you might have changed your mind and left."

Ace rolled her carefully to her back and used his elbow to prop himself up as he leaned over her. "Alex, I'm not going anywhere." He flashed his sexy smile and kissed her. It was a gentle kiss, but the passion between the two of them made his heart beat faster.

When their lips parted, he looked into her eyes. They were glistening with tears. "Why the tears?" He asked wiping them before they could spill over.

She put her left hand on his chest and the palm of her right hand against his cheek. "You," she whispered.

"Me?"

She smiled up at him. "Yes, you." She moved her hands up to his hair and ran her fingers through it reminding him he needed to get a trim tomorrow.

He shifted his body over hers using his forearms to brace himself up, making sure to keep most of his weight off her as he settled between her thighs. "I don't understand. Explain."

Alex closed her eyes and took a deep breath and he placed a hand on her cheek. She opened her eyes and locked gazes with him.

"You see there's this amazing guy I met about a month ago who took my breath away the moment I literally fell into his arms. He's a Navy SEAL, but that is a secret." Ace smiled as she continued her story. "I got to know him during the weeks we spent together on a secret mission, and to be truthful, he managed to wiggle his way into my heart. When I was taken and held captive, I kept thinking about how I never got the chance to tell him that I loved him. But then God gave me a second chance."

Ace stared down into her glistening eyes and stroked her cheek with his thumb. "What are you saying, Alex?" He knew damn well what she was going to say, but he was holding his breath until he heard the words he was longing for since the moment she stepped into his life.

"I love you, Ace. I know it seems crazy since we've only known each other for a month, but it's the truth. I love -..."

She couldn't even get the rest of her words out before he kissed her. Releasing her lips, he laid his head in the crook of her neck.

Alex felt the warm puffs of air against her neck every time he exhaled. Moments later, she felt something wet hit her skin. Ace took a couple of deep breaths and it was then she realized her man was shedding a tear. She wrapped her arms around him and ran her fingers up and down his back. His muscles jumped with each pass. He had shifted some of his weight against her causing some discomfort to her ribs, but she didn't dare say a word as they both needed this connection.

After a few minutes of silence, he raised his head and what she saw made her love for him grow even more. She wiped the remnants of tears from under his eyes. When he continued to stare into her eyes she asked, "Are you okay?"

He smiled and the wetness in his eyes made them sparkle, turning them a brighter blue.

"Sweetheart, I'm better than okay. You've just made me the happiest man." He took a deep breath. "The moment you walked into my life and I looked into those green eyes of yours, I knew you were mine, and then to think that I could have lost you." He took another deep breath and wiped his eyes again. "Fuck, Alex, I love you so much."

She felt the tear slip out of the corner of her eye and drop onto the pillow. He took his thumb and wiped the wetness from her face. "I want to make love to you right now."

Okay, now he was talking. "I have no objections."

He smirked. "Tenley told me your doctor said no strenuous activities until he gave the all-clear."

On a sigh, she said, "Leave it to Tenley to cockblock me."

Ace barked out a laugh and oh what a joyous sound that was. He was still smiling. "No, she's just being a good, concerned friend and making sure that you heal because she knows how you like to push boundaries. Am I right?" He arched one of his eyebrows making himself appear more in charge.

She rolled her eyes. "Yes, but can you at least hold me? I've missed sleeping with you and I feel safe and content in your arms."

"Absolutely."

He rolled off her onto his back and got situated then pulled her down onto his chest. She snuggled closer and smiled when she heard him take a deep breath. While soaking in the bathtub earlier she had done some thinking. Her family and friends might think they were jumping the gun, but she knew deep down this was the man she was meant to spend the rest of her life with. She wanted to ask Ace to move in with her.

She tilted her head slightly so she could see his face. "You said you live on base, right?"

"Yeah, I was going to look for a place after this last deployment. Why?"

"Well, I was thinking, what if you were to move in here? With me?"

His lips curled and his hand slid from her hip up to her ribs, stopping just under her breast. "If this is how I can fall asleep every night, with your sweet body pressed up against mine, then absolutely. How about we talk about it more tomorrow morning? Right now, you need to sleep, and I need to hold you."

"I love you, Ace."

"I love you too."

CHAPTER TWENTY

"I think I went into the wrong profession. All of you guys are running around going on secret missions and shit. I need an adventure. Well not like the one that you went on. Just something to get my adrenaline going."

Alex sat in the passenger seat of Tenley's car staring at her best friend. They were on their way to Alex's doctor's appointment. She was seeing Dr. Kaminski, and the look on Ace's face this morning when she told him should have given her a warning of what was to come.

"What on earth are you talking about? You are a head nurse in the ER department at the hospital. I've seen you in action before, and I'm quite sure that you get enough adrenaline from working there."

Tenley sighed and rolled her eyes, again. It was starting to make Alex a little nervous. Tenley's eyes seemed to roll up in her head more than they were on the road. She gave her seat belt an extra tug just to be sure she was secured.

"That's not what I'm talking about. I'm talking about doing something exciting, adventurous. You know like being somewhere or doing something that gets your heart pumping. Like zip-lining through the jungle, rock climbing or skydiving."

Alex sat back and thought about what Tenley was saying, and she was right. For the past twenty-five years they'd been friends, she'd never seen her friend do anything like she was describing.

"Have you talked to Chaz about going on a vacation and doing some of the things you just mentioned? I mean from what you've told me, the man has more money than he knows what to do with. Surely you could go somewhere and do something adventurous."

Tenley scrunched up her face and gripped the steering wheel. "Yeah, about Chaz. I'm not so sure that he's the one for me. I think that ship has sailed its course."

Alex wasn't surprised at Tenley's confession considering what Ace had told her about how cozy her and Potter had been together at Bayside. Alex wasn't a fan of Chaz. He was cocky and Alex didn't like the vibe she got from him when she had met him. But at the time her friend was happy, so she wasn't going to rock the boat with her opinion.

"A certain SEAL wouldn't have anything to do with this, would it?" She questioned her friend. Tenley could try and deny the attraction to Potter all she could, but Alex could see the tinge of pink that dusted Tenley's cheeks.

"It's your life Ten, and you have to make choices that are going to make you happy. I'll support you whatever you decide. However, I will not stand back if I see that you're unhappy and not being treated with respect. That's not a way to live."

Tenley pulled into the parking lot of the doctor's office on base and put the car in park. "Thanks for always being there for me, friend. I don't know how I would have survived all these years without you by my side."

Alex turned toward Tenley. "Listen Ten, if you're interested in Potter, I can vouch for him. He may look like a hard man on the outside, not to mention he's scary quiet, but I can honestly say he is one of the most caring guys I've met. And, from what Ace says you should feel special."

"Why is that?"

"Because according to him, Potter doesn't date or take an interest in women to spend time and get to know them."

"Good to know," Tenley replied then opened her door and got out sending a clear message that the conversation was over.

241

Alex stepped out and took a deep breath as she looked at the front doors to the building. *Here goes nothing.*

৵

Ace was hanging out by the pool with the team at Alex's house relaxing and having a beer. He'd invited them and Derek over to help move furniture, hang pictures, and unpack boxes. When Alex had given him the tour of her house last night and had explained where she wanted everything placed, an idea had formed in his head.

Knowing she would probably be mentally exhausted when she got home from her appointment, he thought it would be nice to surprise her by having everything placed where she wanted. But with the amount of shit she had, he was forced to call in reinforcements. Being it was for Alex, none of the guys had hesitated. Shit, they'd walk over hot coals and swim through a pool of sharks for her.

"How was Alex last night?" Derek asked taking a slug of his beer.

"She was exhausted. We talked for a while, had dinner, and then watched a movie."

Out of respect, Ace wanted to tell Derek what Alex had asked him last night about moving in with her, but he wasn't sure if he wanted to rock the boat.

"Spit it out, son. I can tell there's something else." Christ, he swore nothing ever got by the Commander. Ace picked up his bottle of beer and took a big gulp.

Here goes nothing....

"Alex asked me to move in with her."

Derek sat forward in his chair, cleared his throat, and Ace couldn't tell what reaction he was going to get.

"Ace, Alex is an intelligent woman. She's never made a decision without thoroughly thinking through all of the ramifications of it.

242

As I told you yesterday, you two are good for each other. She understands our line of work. If every SEAL could find a woman like her I don't believe that the divorce rate amongst SEALs would be as high as it is, and more men would be married." Ace nodded his head in agreement.

"She's it for me. I can't explain it, but I just knew it the moment I met her."

"Well, as long as she's happy, I'm happy."

Ace looked at Derek with wide eyes, making Derek laugh.

"I know it's serious because she's never introduced any other men to me. Plus, this saves me the hassle of doing a background check on you. I already know your life story." Derek reached over and shook Ace's hand. "But I'm telling you now, you fuck her over and I will make the rest of your life miserable."

A huge grin spread across his face. "Thank you, sir, but unless she leaves me, I'm not going anywhere."

Derek tapped his beer bottle against Ace's and chuckled. "Ah, speak of the devil—there are the girls now."

Ace turned toward the French doors and the expression on Alex's face made him flinch. Someone had gone and pissed her off.

Alex was confused when Tenley pulled into her driveway. At first, she did a double-take just to make sure Tenley pulled into the correct driveway. But she looked at the address on the house and sure enough, it was hers. The front of her house looked like a parking lot with all the trucks and SUVs parked there. But, one vehicle stood out from the rest. She knew the silver Tahoe was Derek's. Good thing he was here, it would save her a phone call. She had some choice words for him. The nerve of him to send her to that lunatic of a doctor.

She stormed through the house making her way to the back door with Tenley following behind her giggling. She was glad someone found her ordeal amusing. She flung the back doors open and went straight for Derek who was sitting at the patio table with Ace.

"Hey, honey. How was the appointment?" Derek said with a smile, but the smile quickly faded.

Stitch who was kicked back on one of the lounge chairs next to the pool must have seen the scowl on her face because he sat up and yanked his sunglasses off. "Oh shit, I know that look. Who done pissed you off?"

She turned toward Derek and he opened his mouth to say something, but Alex stopped him.

"I will never step foot into that egotistical, arrogant bastard's office again. I would rather sit around and talk to monkeys than be put through that torture." The way she was fired up, she'd put on one hell of a fireworks show.

"Friend, I think you scared the poor doctor so much that he already notified the guards at the gate on base and told them that you weren't allowed to come within fifty feet of his office." Tenley was doing everything possible not to laugh at Alex and that just pissed her off more. To the point that it started to make her cry, again. For the love of God, she was tired of crying. Not wanting to be the freak show of the hour, she turned around to gather her composure.

Ace could tell Alex was truly upset so he got up and pulled her into a hug and rubbed her back.

"Sweetheart, what's got you all fired up? This appointment was supposed to help you not upset you more."

Ace knew the doctor she was seeing tended to be an asshole, but for Alex to be this upset he must have said or done something extreme to make her this emotional. She tilted her head back. Her puffy red eyes and a red nose from her crying nearly did him in.

"I felt like he wouldn't listen to what I was saying, instead he tried to speak for me. You know, like putting words in my mouth and interrupting me."

Ace tightened his hold around her waist and looked at Derek. None of them were fans of Dr. Kaminski. But the other doctors on base didn't have any openings for another two weeks and her uncle wanted to get her in before she had second thoughts and changed her mind. That was the only reason she saw Dr. Kaminski.

"Are you comfortable sharing with us what you discussed with Dr. Kaminski?"

"I don't mind." She turned toward the others who had started to get up to leave. "No, stay, you don't have to leave. You all have seen me at my worst already, so I don't mind sharing with you."

If Ace was right, he was sure that his teammates' respect for her just shot off the Richter scale.

He got her settled in the chair then took a seat next to her. Ace noticed Potter had gotten up and offered his seat to Tenley then stood to the side, not taking his eyes off her. *Interesting.*

Ace took Alex's hand in his and squeezed it.

"I think what initially started us off on the wrong foot was when he asked me how I was doing emotionally and I told him that I felt emotionally constipated because I haven't given a shit about things in weeks."

A couple of the guys snickered which drew a faint smile from Alex. "See, that was what I was doing. I was trying to lighten the mood a little, but the doctor didn't seem to like my sarcasm. He told me that I was trying to mask my true emotions by trying to redirect my mind. Asshole." She said the last word under her breath but loud enough that everyone could hear her.

She took a deep breath, "Anyway, his response to everything I said was 'well from my point of view', and I just got tired of him saying that so I finally told him that I'd like to see things from his point of view but I couldn't seem to fit my head up his ass. The icing on the cake was when he told me that my anger and aggression concerned him because those were traits of someone who was suicidal. So, I told him that if I ever wanted to kill myself I would climb his ego and jump to his IQ. And let's just say that was the end to our session."

Ace was biting the inside of his cheek so hard to keep from bursting out laughing that he swore he tasted blood. Hearing her innocent voice talking, nobody would ever expect what she told the doctor to come out of her mouth. And from the glances to the other guys, neither did they.

He watched as she turned to her uncle. "I'm sorry and I know I've probably embarrassed you, but I promise that I'll do whatever to clean up the shit storm I've probably caused."

Derek threw his head back and barked out a laugh. He grabbed her hand and gave it a gentle squeeze. "Alex, if you hadn't already earned the respect of every man here, you just did. That prick of a doctor has the worst reputation, and I'm sorry for subjecting you to him. If one of the other doctors had an opening, I would have sent you to them instead.

ʕ•ᴥ•ʔ

Alex looked at Derek and broke into a fit of giggles. "Well, now we know why he had an opening."

She glanced at all of the guys, "What are you all doing here anyway? Not that I'm not happy to see you all."

Jesus, she was exhausted. Not caring in the least that Derek was sitting right there, she climbed over into Ace's lap. She curled her legs up and laid her head against his chest and closed her eyes. She

246

would never get tired of being near him. The feeling of his steel thighs under her ass and his strong arms wrapped securely around her, she was in heaven. The way things went with her appointment this morning had zapped all the energy right out of her.

"When you were giving me the tour last night you pointed out stuff that still needed to be done, and I knew it would still be a while before you were able to do most of it. So, I called the guys so we could surprise you."

Alex sat up and then remembered she had seen things on the wall when she came in. She stood up and looked at everyone.

"You guys are the best, you know that?" She told them as tears once again threatened to spill over. "I don't know how I'll ever repay you for everything you've done. Damn, I'm starting to cry again."

Irish walked over and hugged her. "Aww, sweetness, don't cry." She hugged him back, but then she heard a growl come from behind her which made her giggle.

Ace stood and pulled Alex against him. He looked at the rest of the guys giving them his best scowl. "Hands off, all of you. Go find your own woman. I know for a fact that you won't have any issues."

Tenley snorted a laugh which drew the attention to her. The look she got from Potter had her squirming in her seat.

Tenley had been sitting back watching and enjoying the friendly banter between the team. Yesterday was the first time she had gotten to meet the whole team in person. She had hung out with Stitch and Frost on several occasions, but those outings just consisted of the three of them.

One, in particular, had snagged her attention from the start. Potter was tall, dark, and dangerous, and had dark eyes that were filled with an intensity she couldn't explain. Alex was right, she had been drawn to Potter. There was something so unique about him that fascinated her. Or maybe it was because he seemed to actually pay attention to her when she was speaking, unlike her current boyfriend who lately only paid attention to her when they were in bed. Even then, the sex was all about him.

Everyone thought she was so happy and in love with Chaz, but boy did she have them all snowballed. In fact, it was the complete opposite. She was miserable and had been so for a while. Over the past month, Chaz had changed. He'd become secretive and distant. Just recently he had become verbally aggressive, and that didn't sit well with her. She wanted what her best friend had. Someone honest, caring and protective. Could she get that from the man standing beside her?

Refocusing on the present, she watched as Ace playfully reprimanded his team for flirting with Alex. When he commented on them finding their own woman and not having to have any issues with it, she hadn't realized she had snorted a laugh out loud. Now she had the attention of every person on the patio including Potter— the man who had a starring role in her dreams last night.

Clearing her throat, she opted for her witty act that had everyone fooled, "What?"

"You think that we would have problems finding a woman?" Potter asked as his eyes penetrated hers, making her want to throw caution to the wind and jump into his arms and say take me.

She stared right back at him. "Nope, completely the opposite. I'm sure any of you can have any woman you want." She waved her hand in the air, "I mean, look at you guys. You all have kick-ass bodies. Any woman in their right mind would be stupid to pass up an opportunity with you." *Like me. If I had the opportunity, I'd be on you like white on rice.*

"You guys are like gremlins. What do they do to you at BUD/S training, drop a couple of you in water so you can multiply?" She said laughingly. The others thought it was funny but when she looked up at Potter, he was in a dead stare with her. Her smile faded, and a sudden uneasy feeling washed over her. It was as if he could see through her charades. Maybe she needed to explore more of the attraction that was obviously between them. Before she could say something, Alex started talking about food and just like that, the spotlight was directed elsewhere, and she breathed a sigh of relief. She had a lot to talk to her friend about, but for now, she would just kick back and enjoy being in the company of friends.

CHAPTER TWENTY-ONE

"Where the fuck is the rest of the gear that was delivered last week?" Ace shouted over the loud music playing as he and the team did the gear inventory.

"Christ man, who in the hell yanked your dick?" Irish asked giving Ace a sideways look.

Potter chuckled. "That's the problem. Nobody, except maybe Ace's rosy palm and her five sisters. Our Lt. Commander here needs to get laid," he said giving Ace a friendly slap on the back.

"Fuck you, Potter." Ace replied shaking his head but giving his teammates a smirk.

If someone had asked his teammates, they'd say he'd been a bear to work with the past few weeks. He had so much tension built up in his body that if he didn't find some relief soon, he thought he might explode. He had been walking around with a serious case of blue balls. Since moving in with Alex four weeks ago, sleeping with her had gotten more difficult. The way she liked to cuddle at night had been testing his patience. Her frustration was growing as well, but he wasn't doing anything until she got the all-clear from the doctor.

Although sexually frustrated, he was so damn proud of her. After the fiasco she had with Dr. Kaminski, Derek introduced her to Dr. Ruskin. He was a well-respected psychologist on base. Since her first appointment with him two weeks ago, Ace had already seen a vast change in Alex's recovery rate. Her nightmares had lessened drastically, and when one did occur, she wasn't afraid to talk about it.

Another positive in her life had been when she received the approval status for the new charity organization she started in honor of her late father. The organization would aid veterans and their families with gaining medical help and expenses that the government wouldn't cover.

She had plans to open a medical clinic fully staffed with medical volunteers that would cater strictly to veterans seeking medical help or advice. The best part about it was that there would never be a waiting period to get an appointment and all treatment would be covered free of charge. She already had money coming in and people were lining up to volunteer when the clinic did open.

The planning, meetings, and paperwork had kept Alex's mind occupied which had been a tremendous help with her recovery as well.

For the most part, things had been quiet, however, Alex had received a call from Mason two weeks ago informing her that the agency was closing in on a suspect who they believed was working with Bert. The agency had been very cooperative with Alex considering the issues she could cause for them as to how they handled her situation back in Afghanistan. She had even received a hefty bonus which she used as the startup funds for her foundation.

Mason had told her that he would keep her in the loop if he heard any news but for her to keep her eyes open. Since then she had taken precautions when she'd been out in public and always carried a weapon with her.

Ace heard his phone chime with an incoming text. Pulling it from his pocket he saw it was Tenley, but what stole his breath was the picture of Alex with the words "your woman is rocking it."

And indeed she was. The pair of blue jean hip huggers fit firmly over her round ass. The black long sleeve shirt hung off her shoulders showcasing her fit upper body. And lastly, she wore a pair of black, open-toed stilettos. Her long chestnut brown hair was half up in some sort of messy but sexy up-do. Her face was free of make-up except for her eyes, which were done in a smoky palette of colors making her green eyes even more stunning.

The picture was taken at the house out by the pool, and it was obvious Alex didn't know Tenley was taking it. She appeared deep in thought and he wondered what had been on her mind.

He heard a long whistle over his shoulder and saw Diego looking at the picture.

"Damn, she is gorgeous. You taking her out tonight?"

"No, she and Tenley are going to a new club that opened recently. She mentioned the name, but I can't remember it. The owners are huge supporters of the military. They heard about Alex's Foundation through some friends and want to contribute. She met with them yesterday and they invited her to the club tonight for some show they're hosting.

"You're letting her go to a club alone looking like that? Aren't you afraid of all of the men that'll hit on her?"

Ace shook his head. He knew men would try and hit on her, but he knew Alex only had eyes for him, so it didn't bother him for her to have a girl's night out. Plus, he wasn't a fan of the club scene or any scene really where people would be packed into a building like sardines. It made him uncomfortable.

"She can handle herself. Anyways, one of the owners is former law enforcement. And from what Alex told me he runs a tight ship. So, I don't anticipate any problems."

"Well, if Alex is going out how about joining the rest of us for a beer?"

"Yeah, I could go for a beer and just chilling for a few hours. The first round is on me for me being a prick the last couple of weeks."

Diego grinned and gave Ace a fist bump before walking away.

Ace couldn't have asked for a better group of guys to serve with. He was looking forward to hanging with them over some beers for the evening.

℘

"So, Ace doesn't know you went to the doctor today?" Tenley asked over the loud music in the club.

Alex gave her friend a mischievous look then took a sip of her fruity drink and set it down on the table. "Nope. I was going to surprise him tonight. He's going out with the guys and I thought you and I could head over there after we leave here. But neither one of us are in any shape to drive," she said with a giggle as she eyed the six empty glasses on the table.

They were each on their fourth cocktail and feeling no pain.

The owners Ron, and Sal were awesome guys. Each of them personally donated five-thousand dollars to the foundation and told her that anytime she wanted to use the club to hold fundraisers that it was hers. Both men were in their mid-forties and had ties to the military, which was why, as soon as they had heard about the foundation, they got in touch with her.

Their nightclub: Club B&W was an upscale club that held headliner events one night a week. Tonight, the club was featuring a drag show and both Alex and Tenley were amazed at the talent for the evening's performance. The high-top table where they sat was near the entrance to the club.

The club itself was decorated with an upscale modern flair with clean lines made up in the color scheme of black and white, hence the name of the club. It reminded Alex of a club she went to in South Beach a couple of years ago.

Charlie the head security manager of the club approached the table smiling. After talking with Ron and Sal, Alex learned that Charlie was a police officer with the local police department. All the bouncers the club hired were all either current or former law enforcement officers. They had explained that the safety of the club's staff and patrons was the most important.

As Charlie stood at their table Alex smiled at him. He was over six feet tall with blond hair that reminded her of a surfer. "Hey, Charlie!"

Grinning, he asked, "Are you ladies enjoying yourselves this evening?"

"Very much so. Ron and Sal have outdone themselves."

"Yes, they have. We have a steady crowd the four nights we're open." He eyed their empty glasses. "When you ladies are ready to leave, do you have someone coming to pick you up, or do you need for us to call you a cab?"

Alex thought about it. If they called for an Uber, Ace would go ballistic. Decision made, she fetched her phone from her purse and sent off a text to Ace only to receive a message back within seconds. She smiled and looked at Tenley and Charlie. "Ace said he'll be here and he's bringing one of the guys so they can drive your car home," she told Tenley.

Tenley smiled. "That means we can have another drink." She looked to Charlie and batted her eyelashes at him which made him laugh.

"I'll be right back."

The show was starting to wrap up. With the alcohol flowing through her veins she was feeling really horny and couldn't wait to get to the next part of the evening. She wondered what Ace's reaction was going to be when she told him that she was officially medically cleared. Would he be gentle thinking he could still hurt her, or would he ravish her body and take her hard? She had been so wound up the past few weeks that at this point she'd settle on either. Then she remembered how yummy he looked this morning when he

254

got out of bed. The light scruff along his jaw was so sexy, and how she imagined what those prickly whiskers of his would feel like rubbing against her inner thighs. She felt her clit tingle in anticipation. She wiggled on the bar stool. *Christ, I'm so horny I almost got myself off sitting on a bar stool in a club.*

"Damn girlfriend, I would love to know what just went through your head. Your cheeks look like little gala apples," Tenley said as her eyes twinkled with amusement.

"Ahh…" That was about all Alex could say and she felt her face flush with embarrassment even more.

Tenley waved her off, "Let me guess…You're thinking about how 'little' Ace gets to take a ride in your pink canoe tonight. Am I right?" She asked raising one of her eyebrows.

Alex shook her head and laughed. "Christ Ten, how in the hell do you think of these things?"

Tenley started laughing right along with Alex. "If I'm not mistaken, I've heard some pretty good ones come from your mouth over the years."

As they were laughing Ron approached their table and pulled over another barstool to join them. "Ladies, might I say the two of you seem to be enjoying yourselves this evening."

Alex spoke up, "We are, thank you again for your hospitality. The show was phenomenal, and the club is amazing. Tenley and I were reminiscing how back in the day she and I used to sing karaoke at Bayside. But we don't have anything on the talent you had performing here tonight."

Ron gave them a warm smile. "A lot of the acts we hire are from out of state. We bring them in from Las Vegas and New York. We are at full capacity tonight."

"Wow! That's awesome."

Ron gave Alex's elbow a nudge, "You know we are getting ready to start a little karaoke session up on the stage in a few minutes. What do you say that you and your pal here," he hooked his thumb over at Tenley, "show these fine patrons what the two of you got?"

Alex's eyes widened. *Oh shit. He wants us to sing, up there on a stage in front of about three hundred people.* Tenley was bouncing up and down on the stool clapping her hands together like a child who was just told she was going to Disney World.

"Oh, come on Alex. It'll be like old times. Who gives a shit what these people think. Pleaseeee. It will be so much fun. We can do our number one song *'Dancing in The Street'.*" She stood and started shaking her hips. Alex laughed when she wobbled and almost fell over, but Ron had caught her.

Alex looked at Tenley as she pleaded with her and then smiled. "Oh, what the hell. Can I do a shot first?" She turned to ask Ron.

Ron let out a deep laugh and walked over to the bar and came back with two shots. "Hope you ladies like Tequila." He set the drinks down and spoke into a tiny microphone clipped to the front of his shirt. When he finished, he turned toward the two of them with a grin, "It's showtime".

Ace strode into the club, letting his eyes adjust to the dim lighting. He scanned the layout of the club looking for any sight of Alex or Tenley. As he glanced over to the bar just to the left of the entrance, he saw a man walking toward him. He was well-built, close to Ace's height with short brown hair. As he approached, he held out his hand. "You must be Ace?"

Ace eyed him over then shook the man's hand. A strong handshake, outspoken, and someone who looked like they held a position of authority.

"That would be me."

"I'm Ron, welcome to Club B&W. We noticed the girls had a little too much to drink so we wanted to make sure they had a safe ride home. Alex said to keep a lookout for you."

Ace breathed a little easier knowing this was one of the gentlemen who invited Alex here tonight. He introduced Potter, Frost, and Stitch. Potter came along to drive Tenley's car home, while Frost and Stitch just wanted to see the inside of the club.

"Where are the ladies anyway?" Ace asked as he scanned the club's patrons noting there was a good mix of people.

Ron laughed and pointed toward the stage as a man dressed in a tuxedo announced the next act. A duo that called themselves Lucy and Ethel. Ace snorted a laugh. He couldn't wait to hear what this sounded like. The beat of a familiar 80s dance song blasted from the speakers and drew the crowd to their feet.

"You've got to be kidding," Frost mumbled, followed by Stitch's laughter.

Ace went to ask Frost what the problem was but then he listened and all he could do was shake his head and smile.

As he listened to them sing, he was surprised at how good they sounded together, not to mention how they danced. As the song ended the crowd roared and he and the guys were clapping and cheering along with them.

As Alex and Tenley stepped down from the stage, they were swarmed by people giving them hugs and kisses on the cheek. Ace started to move toward the stage but then Ron stopped him.

"They're fine, see the big guy down there with them?" Ace looked in the direction to where Ron pointed and he noticed the large man. Christ, he looked taller than Potter with even wider shoulders.

"That's my business partner, Sal. He's bringing them back up here."

He squinted as he watched them approach. Who in the hell was with them? Ace swore the woman in tow looked just like Dolly Parton. He shook his head and tried to get another look to confirm but then caught the sight of the petite, brown-haired, full of life woman barreling towards him. How the fuck women could run in what looked like four or five-inch heels amazed him. Bracing himself for the blow he opened his arms and Alex leaped into them, wrapping her arms and legs around his body.

"What's this all about? Not that I'm complaining because I love having you in my arms," he said to her with a grin.

Her eyes twinkled with admiration as she looked over his face. "I missed you," she said with a giggle.

He nuzzled her neck. "Baby, how many drinks have you had tonight?" He watched her think about it. Seeing her scrunch up her nose made him chuckle.

"I don't know, about four, maybe five I think. Oh! And a shot of Tequila." She looked over at Ron and winked.

Ace was getting ready to respond when a bundle of blonde hair came running across the club squealing like a little girl. The woman stopped right next to Alex and grabbed her arm.

"Oh, doll face is this the hunk you've been gushing about all night? Oh, my heavens there are eight of you scrumptious men." The woman's eyes glazed over the eight SEALs.

Ace watched as 'Dolly' fanned her face with her exceptionally large hands. It couldn't be? She looked like Dolly in the face, chest, and hair but the rest of her body was more like a man's physique. And, from the deer in the headlights look on the rest of his team's faces all but confirmed that the Dolly standing in front of him was indeed a man.

Alex giggled causing Tenley to double over in laughter. "Dolly, I'd like you to meet my boyfriend Ace."

Ace set Alex down on her feet and extended his hand out. "It's nice to meet you." *I think.*

Dolly grasped Ace's hand, smiling. "Dang, sugar you've got a hell of a handshake but with arms like yours, it's to be expected. What do you do for a living? Construction?"

"Oh, he's in the Navy," Alex blurted out and Ace covered her mouth with his hand before she could reveal any more information. She was so going to pay for this. When "Dolly's" eyes lit up he knew he was screwed.

"My, my, my...I just love a man in uniform," Dolly said licking her lips and eyeing Ace like he was tonight's dinner special. "Tell me, Sailor, do you enjoy 'riding' the waves and playing with big 'torpedoes and guns'?

What the fuck? Ace was speechless as were the others. Hearing the laughter coming from Alex and Tenley, Ace had a suspicious feeling they'd been set up. He looked at Alex, narrowed his eyes, and crooked his finger in a 'come here' motion. When she obliged, he cupped the nape of her neck and brushed his thumb over her pulse point, feeling the fast, strong beat.

He bent down so his lips were touching the shell of her ear and whispered in a low but deep voice, "Baby is there something you want to tell me?"

God love her, she looked like she was busting at the seams. When another giggle bubbled up her throat, she took a step back and Dolly approached and patted his cheek. "Don't worry sweet cheeks the guns I was referring to are your arms. However, I wouldn't mind getting a peek at the weapon you're packing below." She glanced down at Ace's crotch and Ace swore that his dick deflated to the point that it was going to take an air pump to get it up and working again.

He heard the snickers coming from the guys, and when he looked at Potter with an angry expression Potter threw his head back and laughed. The fucker was actually laughing at him. *Well, we'll see who is laughing come Monday morning during PT.*

He reached out and snagged Alex around her waist and pulled her into him, knocking her off balance. He had a good hold on her so she wouldn't fall. Grasping her chin with his free hand he tipped her head back and stared into her eyes as he stroked her cheek with his knuckles. "Baby, you know that you are in so much trouble, right?" He was beaming evilly as he heard the faint gasp that escaped her lips. "I should spank your ass right now for this little act you pulled."

He watched her bright green eyes dilate and her breathing become more rapid. The look of lust and desire she was giving him made his dick come back to life. *Thank god, the damage done by Dolly wasn't permanent.*

She took her hands and placed them on his face urging him down, so he was eye level with her. She took a deep breath and released it. "I think I'd enjoy that spanking." She whispered low enough so only he could hear.

He squeezed her tighter so that she was now pressed against him. "Sweetheart, you don't want to tease me right now. I'm so close to saying screw waiting for your doctor and throw you over my shoulder, take you home and fuck you until the sun comes up."

Alex's breathing was so heavy she was practically panting. She had a feeling she had awoken the beast. Her body felt on fire. His dominant words alone had her wanting to strip both of them right here. She closed her eyes and smiled to herself. Tonight was going to be magical.

When she opened her eyes, those blue eyes held hers. She leaned forward and kissed him. It was a quick brush of her lips, "What if I told you that I'd have no complaints if you threw me over your shoulder, took me home and made love to me till the sun came up?"

Ace's nostrils flared and she heard his deep inhale. She pressed her face into the crook of his neck. He smelled so good. She kissed his neck, then his jaw, then his lips before pressing her forehead against his. "Well? What do you say, Lt. Commander?"

Alex felt the tightness in Ace's body. He swallowed hard and shook his head, "Alex, I don't want to hurt you."

She silenced him with another kiss. This time she took it further, kissing him deeply, exploring every inch of his mouth that she could reach.

"You won't hurt me. I got the green light from the doctor this morning. I wanted to surprise you tonight."

Alex watched in fascination as Ace's eyes went from baby blue to dark stormy blue. He squeezed her tighter. "I hope you're ready because you and I are leaving right now. Turn around now and say goodbye to everyone." His low dominant voice told her he wasn't asking. It was an order.

Turning quickly, she said her goodbyes and made sure that Tenley would get home safely with one of the guys. Hopefully, it was Potter. Maybe tonight they could break the ice and get to know each other a little better.

Before Alex could conjure another thought she heard Ace mumble something about taking too long and then felt her body being lifted and thrown over his shoulder. She let out a squeal and everyone laughed as he stomped out the door with her.

৯৯

Ace pulled his truck into the driveway. It was late. On their way home, they had to make a detour because Alex was hungry and craved pizza. He wanted to say the hell with food and just take her to bed, but when Alex grinned at him and reminded him that he intended to keep her satisfied until the sun came up, she would need energy. Then having to sit at the local pizza joint and hear her mewl and moan over how good the pizza tasted made his dick even harder.

Putting the truck into park he looked over toward Tenley's driveway and snickered when he saw Potter's silver truck in her driveway. Potter was a love em' and leave em' type of guy. He knew how close Tenley was with their group of friends so he knew his best friend wouldn't go down that path. Over the last couple of weeks, he had noticed the interest growing between the two. Maybe there was romance in the air for his second in command.

Romance? When the fuck did I start thinking about romance and my best friend and teammate in the same sentence? God help me.

He glanced over and saw Alex gazing at him. Even after all the food she ate it hadn't sobered her much. She was a happy, sexy little drunk that he couldn't wait to bury himself in.

He reached over and pulled her towards him across the seat. Giving her a wicked grin as he pulled her out of the truck and lifted her in a cradle position he said, "I have waited very impatiently to see you tonight. Ever since Tenley sent me that damn picture of you earlier with you wearing this sexy outfit, I've been hard as a steel pipe." He dipped his head and gave her a scorching kiss. Not holding back, he ravished her mouth before nipping her bottom lip and making her gasp. "Let's get you in the house because I believe I promised you an entire night of pleasure."

CHAPTER TWENTY-TWO

Alex blinked her eyes open as the warm sunlight filtered through the beige sheer window curtains. Hearing the shower running in the bathroom, she looked over at the clock on the bedside table and saw it was a few minutes past ten.

Knowing she needed to get up since their friends would be arriving in a few hours for the barbeque she and Ace were hosting in the afternoon, she wanted to spend a couple of minutes burrowed in the comfort of her and Ace's bed. She rolled over and snuggled into Ace's pillow, inhaling his scent. Her muscles protested but she smiled remembering just how good of a workout those muscles got last night. Glancing around the room some of the candles that were placed around their bedroom still flickered.

When Ace had carried her into their bedroom last night she felt as if she had entered her very own fairy tale. The room had been transformed into a scene you'd read about in a romance novel. The soft light that illuminated the room was from the hundred or so white candles in various shapes and sizes that were placed on every available surface. Soft ocean sounds playing through her Bluetooth speaker mixed with the flickering lights from the candles gave the atmosphere of the room a tranquil feeling. The winter white sheets and brown comforter had been turned down on the bed as an invitation to climb in, while white rose petals dotted the bottom half of the bed. The bedside table held a chilled bottle of champagne and two flute glasses, though she didn't need any more alcohol.

Thinking of how Ace held her in his arms telling her in every way possible how much he loved her brought tears back to her eyes again. She had shed so many happy tears throughout the night. He was everything she had imagined he'd be as a lover.

The moment he first slid into her wet heat was like the world shifting on its axis. Feeling the stretch from his girth had almost sent her spiraling out of control before he started moving. But as he hovered above her and gazed into her eyes, linking his fingers with hers bringing them above her head and then seeing a lone tear slip down his cheek, she knew at that moment this was the man she would love and cherish for the rest of her life. He had made good on the promise he made to her months ago in Afghanistan. He made sweet love to her. Well, at least the first round of sex that is. The next couple of times were what she would call adventurous and pleasurable. He had also kept the promise he made last night as well. He had fucked her until the sun came up.

The bathroom door opened causing her to look up and there he stood, taking her breath away. He was wearing a pair of navy-blue swim trunks paired with a well-worn grey t-shirt fitted over his torso and arms. Seeing the morning stubble along his jaw made her want to rub her cheek against it.

Ace smiled, "Sweetheart, if you keep looking at me like that, I'm going to call our friends and tell them the barbeque has been canceled and just keep you in bed all day."

Alex licked her lips. *Would that really be a bad thing?* No, but she did need to get up and get things prepared before everyone arrived.

"How about just a kiss and then we can pick things back up after our guests leave. Maybe put the hot tub to good use." She winked at him and wiggled her eyebrows.

Ace stalked over to the bed. His stride was smooth and silent, like a sleek panther stalking its prey before it pounced. Bending down he kissed her and then flipped her over and gave her bare ass a good slap.

"Ow! What was that for?" She exclaimed, rubbing her hand over her stinging butt cheek.

Ace grinned. "You should've learned your lesson last night about teasing me." Oh yeah, she remembered the spanking he gave her.

He gave her one more kiss then told her he was going to make sure the grill was cleaned and ready.

She stared at his back while he walked out of the room. Man did she love him!

Chuckling to herself thinking how bad she had it for him she reluctantly pulled herself out of bed and walked to the bathroom to get ready.

"Well, well, well…the 'just-fucked' look shows well on you." Tenley said as she strode through the back door out onto the patio.

Alex turned and smiled at her best friend, "Yeah, well I'd love to know what that wild animal was that Ace and I heard when we got home. It sounded like it was coming from your house." She grinned. "But I guess Potter was able to take care of it since we did see his truck in your driveway."

Tenley's face turned a crimson red as she put the food she was carrying down onto the table. She turned back to Alex, "Y-you heard us?"

Alex was laughing. Nothing normally embarrassed Tenley and to see her face turn that red made her laugh even harder.

Alex shook her head. "No, we didn't hear a thing, but you confirmed what I thought." At that moment, Ace walked out on the pool deck and came up from behind, wrapping his arms around her from behind.

"What's so funny, and Tenley, why does your face look like you have a really bad sunburn?"

265

Alex started giggling again and tilted her head back to look up at Ace. "It seems that we weren't the only ones 'busy' last night. Although, I believe I won the bet."

Tenley's jaw dropped. "The two of you bet that Potter and I were having sex."

Alex looked at Tenley still laughing, "Oh yeah, Ace said no way because Potter wouldn't want to ruffle any feathers in our little circle of friends, but I disagreed. I've seen the way you two look at each other when you think the other one isn't looking, and let me tell you friend…there is definitely an attraction. I knew it was just a matter of time before the two of you ended up in bed together. So, tell me, was it good?"

A huge grin spread across Tenley's face; the redness barely visible anymore. "You have no idea. He is huge, and his tongue. Oh my god, his tongue can do amazing things."

"Oh, for fuck's sake I don't need to hear this. I'm going to the store to get ice and maybe a bottle of bleach to douse the image I now have of my best friend from my brain," Ace uttered drawing laughter from the women.

Stitch walked out onto the patio as Ace gave Alex a quick kiss. He looked at Ace and then at Alex and Tenley.

"What's going on?"

Ace grabbed Stitch by the back of his shirt and pulled him toward the back door he had just walked out of.

"Trust me you don't want to know. My brain is now ingrained with an image of Potter that I never wished to know. Your best choice is to come with me to the store and let them finish their conversation."

After Ace and Stitch walked into the house Alex got herself under control and looked at her friend. She saw that Tenley was glowing and happy. A good fucking made her happy too, but this was different. Tenley looked relaxed, like the weight of the world had been lifted from her shoulders.

"Why are you staring at me?" Tenley asked getting up from the lounge chair and walking over to the table where the food was going to go.

Alex smiled at her. "So, last night. Was it a one and done, or is there a future for the two of you?"

Tenley shrugged her shoulders. "I don't know. Last night was nice. Hell, who am I kidding? Last night was off the charts. He rocked my world. I was expecting him to leave right after, but he surprised me by staying the night. Do you know how long it's been since someone cuddled with me after sex?"

Alex gave her a sympathetic smile. Apparently, this ex of hers was more of an asshole than Alex originally had thought. "Ten, I don't want to open old wounds, but how bad was it with Chaz?"

Frowning, Tenley said, "It was just sex for him. There was no romance, no connection—just hard, rough sex. As long as he got off, he was satisfied. But, Potter, man, when he pulled me into those massive arms of his after loving me, I felt complete. I know, I probably sound stupid, I mean I don't even really know the guy. Hell, he probably thinks I'm some whore who jumps into anybody's bed."

"Ten, I'm sure he doesn't think that. I understand exactly the feelings you're having, and one important thing I've discovered with the guys on the team is that they may have a reputation of being players, but deep down under their SEAL of amour, they are just men wanting a fairy tale life of their own. But finding the right woman for them is difficult. You have to remember what their job entails. All the traveling, not being able to come home and talk about their day at work, sneaking off in the middle of the night to who knows where and wondering if they will make it back home alive.

It's a commitment you have to make to stand by him and support him."

Alex watched as Tenley absorbed what she was telling her. "Let me ask you this, do you want there to be another time?"

Tenley nodded her head yes. "I'd like to see if things could work between us, but I don't know how he feels about it. We didn't discuss it. We kind of skipped the talking and proceeded to the sex part. But I guess I'll know when I see him when he gets here. Anyways, enough about my night, how did yours turn out? I would've never guessed that Ace was such a romantic. You guys stopping for dinner gave Potter and I just enough time to get your bedroom transformed."

Alex wrinkled her nose. "Yeah, I was wondering how all of it was done considering Ace didn't even know about my plans to seduce him."

"Ace sent Potter a text right after you guys left and asked him if we'd mind helping."

"You guys are so sweet. It was beautiful."

"So, tell me, did Ace totally rock your canoe?" Alex busted out laughing and started telling her all about her romantic and seductive night.

The afternoon barbeque was shaping up to be an enjoyable one. With the temperature hovering in the low 90s and sun shining brightly everyone was in the pool trying to stay cool. The whole team was there and surprisingly a few of them brought dates. Only Stitch and Skittles came stag.

Potter was the last to arrive and Alex couldn't have been any giddier when he marched right up to Tenley and kissed her in front of everyone, making it noticeably clear he was staking a claim to her.

The women who came with Frost, Dino, and Diego were nice. Irish's date, Suzette, on the other hand, was something else. She had a reputation of bagging many men, particularly SEALs as she often hung out at Bayside. She was attractive with long blond hair, blue eyes, and a kick-ass body even though her big boobs were noticeably fake, but her attitude totally sucked. According to Ace, she had a thing for Potter and had been trying for the last year to get into his pants. Potter, however, didn't want anything to do with her. As for Irish, Alex was going to have to speak with him. He could do so much better than Suzette. Since she'd arrived, all she had done was whine about how hot it was and how none of the food was 'healthy'. Irish told her that if she was hot to get into the pool, but she didn't want to because she didn't want to get her hair wet. Alex wondered if she had only accepted Irish's invite today hoping she got a chance to see Potter. If that was the case, then it backfired on her.

Tenley was sitting at the table across from Irish and Suzette and had overheard their conversation and leaned over to Alex and whispered, "Christ, by the size of her big tits she's got enough buoyancy to keep her afloat. She won't have any problem keeping her head above water."

Alex had just taken a sip of beer but couldn't hold back her laughter and she ended up spraying beer all over anyone within a foot or two. Unfortunately, the two sitting across from her didn't fare so well. Fake Barbie's face was covered in beer spray including her hair that she didn't want to get wet. *Oops...*

Wiping his face and trying to hold in his laughter, Irish peered over at Suzette who was blotting her face with a napkin and frowning. "Well, your hair is wet now so you might as well get in the pool," he told her. She gave him a nasty look and with an annoyed huff, she got up from the table and stormed inside sending Alex and Tenley into a fit of giggles.

Alex got herself under control and got up and took the seat next to Irish. She placed her hand over his on the table, "Irish, you know that I consider you family so I have to ask—what in the hell were you thinking bringing her here?"

He smirked. "Well, you're not available sweetness, so a man has to scratch his itch somewhere." She scrunched her nose up in disgust and he chuckled.

"You need a woman to settle you down."

He shook his head and pointed at her, "That's not happening."

Ace walked up behind Alex and placed a hand on her shoulder but scowled down at Irish. "Are you bothering my woman, again?"

Standing up Irish held his hands in front of him and smiled, "Nope, she came onto me. Blame her."

Alex gazed up into Ace's eyes and could see the playfulness sweeping through them. She sighed, "He's right. I did initiate contact with him first."

Ace eyed her over and grinned, "Is that so?" He pulled her up and dipped his head to whisper in her ear, "You seem overheated, I think you need to cool off."

Alex was so focused on Ace that she hadn't put two-and-two together until she felt herself being launched into the air and splashing into the chilled water. She surfaced but couldn't touch the bottom. Damn, she hated being short sometimes. Ace jumped in after her. She wrapped her legs around him and rubbed her crotch along his very noticeable erection. Hearing him groan she smiled looking into his eyes.

"You're playing with fire, sweetheart," he said taking a handful of her hair and tugging gently. It gave him full access to the side of her neck. He kissed his way up her neck to her jaw before diving into her mouth.

It was a good thing when Stitch interrupted them, or things could've gotten pretty wild right there in front of their friends.

"Hey, Alex. There is a Wanda Varney on the phone for you. Says it's regarding some property you called her about."

CHAPTER TWENTY-THREE

Alex was both excited and nervous as she drove into town. The call from her real estate agent was to let her know that the building she had her eye on to serve as the foundation's clinic and administrative offices was back on the market because the previous buyer had backed out due to lack of funding.

The building had the perfect layout for what she was looking to do, and the price was a steal which was why the agent called her today because she knew at that price the building wouldn't last long.

It was in a nice section of town and only a couple of doors down from Club B&W. Ron and Sal were the ones who had originally told her about the abandoned building.

The sun was starting to set as she parked in an open spot outside the building. Ace wasn't happy when she told him to stay at home and entertain their guests, but he eventually relented after making sure she was armed.

She got out and noticed Ron was standing in front of the club and she waved to him.

"Hey, what brings you down here today?" He leaned down and kissed her cheek and she explained about the real estate agent calling her.

"That's great. Well, I won't hold you up then. Let me know how it goes."

She said bye and walked down the sidewalk with a little skip in her step and met Wanda in front of the three-story brick building. As they both entered the building chatting up a storm, neither one had noticed the black sedan with dark tinted windows pull into the empty parking lot across the street.

ை

Alex's phone rang just as she and Wanda were finishing up touring the building. With a few layout changes and of course some cosmetic work, it would be everything she imagined it to be. She smiled when she saw it was Ace. She couldn't wait to tell him the place was hers. She excused herself for a moment.

"Hey!"

"Alex, where are you right now?" He asked hurriedly and she knew that tone. Something was wrong.

"Wanda and I are getting ready to walk out. Why? What's wrong?"

"Take Wanda and head toward the back door on the west side of the building. Potter and Stitch will meet you there. Do exactly what they say."

She felt a chill race up her spine. "Ace, what's going on? You're scaring me."

"I got a call from Ron from the Club. After you went into the building, he saw a man come from the parking lot across the street. He said the guy was acting suspicious, so he continued to watch him from inside his club. When he went straight to your vehicle and opened the back driver's side door and got in was when he called me and the police.

Alex couldn't believe this was happening. And, when had Ace and Ron exchanged numbers?

"Alex...are you there?"

She shook her head. "Yeah, sorry. Ace, where are you?" She took Wanda's arm and started leading her towards the exit Ace told her to go to.

"I'm at the Club along with the police. We didn't want to spook the guy, so all of the action is around back. They're going over a plan to take him into custody."

She reached the back door and cracked it open. She breathed in a sigh of relief seeing Potter standing there. He said something into the small mic clipped to his shirt.

"Okay, baby, Potter, and Stitch got you. Go with them and they'll keep you safe."

She wanted to ask him where he would be, but he had disconnected. She looked up at Potter.

"Let's go," was all he said, placing her behind him as if using himself as a human shield. Wanda was right behind her as Stitch brought up the rear. She noticed a few cops positioned at various locations. They walked quickly down the block. As they approached a white brick building the back door opened and Ace stood there. She did not miss a beat as she ran to him. As he squeezed her tight, she felt his heart beating in his chest.

Two hours later, the standoff was finally over, leaving Alex in a state of denial along with a list of questions that she was only going to get answers to from her former employer.

She rubbed her temples. "I don't understand. Williams was in the house with the rest of the team when it exploded. They had his DNA. I went to his funeral. Why?!"

The man who had snuck into Alex's car had been one of her former colleagues. One who she thought had perished during the attack in Afghanistan. She had so many questions, but most likely none could be answered because Williams had taken his life before the police could apprehend him.

They did find an ID on him with an alias name, but a valid address, so it gave the government a starting point to investigate.

Ace rubbed her back. "Greed can be an evil adversary."

"I know that, but out of everyone on the team, Williams had the most loyalty. Not to mention, he was my friend."

"Honey, he wasn't your friend. He played you and had all the means to eliminate you."

That was obvious since they had found a stockpile of syringes, zip ties, ropes, and several guns when they searched his car. Imaging what he had in store for her sent a shiver up her spine.

The government had a lot to investigate and a lot of questions they had to answer.

Alex just wanted to go home. The police were still processing the crime scene which included her vehicle. She had already told Ace that she didn't want the car back and for the police to do whatever they wanted with it. Not after Williams had shot himself in it.

She tilted her head and looked up at Ace.

"Can we go home now?"

"Yeah, sweetheart. Let's go."

CHAPTER TWENTY-FOUR

Three months later

Christmas day at Ace and Alex's house was total chaos. Christmas music was playing as Alex stood in the kitchen and took in the sight of her friends and family who were all gathered for the holiday.

All her uncles, as well as their families were there. Tenley, Juliette, Ace, and all the guys from the team. Even Bear and his team stopped by. Plus, Ace's family made a surprise visit. If she had to guess there were probably around fifty or so people milling around her house, but she wouldn't have changed a thing. This was what the holidays were about to her; friends and family coming together to celebrate.

Ace had surprised her last night. He had been gone for the last three weeks and wasn't sure if he'd be home for the holidays.

Ace's mom, Charlotte, and his sisters had flown into town about a week ago to spend Christmas with them even though they knew there was a good possibility that Ace wouldn't make it home. They told Alex she shouldn't be alone during the holidays. She welcomed the company admitting that it did get a little lonely when Ace was gone.

Lost in her silent thoughts she didn't hear Ace sneak up behind her until she felt his arms come around her waist. He pulled her back against him and nuzzled her behind the ear.

"Not that I'm complaining because I love your beautiful smile, but what has you beaming?"

She didn't even realize she had been smiling. She placed her hands over his and tilted her head back to look up at him. "Just admiring our family and friends and how thankful I am that all of us got to spend this day together and knowing you guys are home safe."

"Here I thought you were smiling because you were remembering the Christmas present I gave you last night." Thank god nobody was around them because Alex felt the heat in her face and knew her cheeks were probably two shades of red.

"How could I ever forget that present?"

They heard someone clear their throat behind them.

"Alex, do you have a few minutes that I could speak with you privately?" Derek asked her.

She looked at Ace hoping for a hint of what it could be, but he just shrugged his shoulders. Then the doorbell rang. "Let me get that and then I'll meet you outside."

"No, let Ace get it, you come with me." He said stopping her in her tracks. He looked to Ace, "We'll be out back on the patio."

She walked with Derek and as they stepped on to the patio, she was surprised to see her uncles and the rest of Ace's team. She smiled but all she got back were blank expressions, and then she began to worry. She wasn't sure if she could deal with any more drama.

She heard the patio door click, and when she turned, she saw someone she thought she'd never see again. "Colonel Johnson!" Alex ran over and hugged him.

"Hi, honey. I hope you don't mind. Derek invited me but he wanted to surprise you."

"Are you kidding me? This is wonderful. I'm glad you were able to make it back to the states for the holidays. You don't have to go back, do you?"

"No, I'll be in the vicinity for quite a while, so you'll probably be seeing a lot of me."

"Well, I'm happy to hear that." She started to say something else but then noticed someone else standing in the shadows beside Ace. Now she felt really nervous when even his face was blank. It was

Christmas her favorite holiday, so none of these guys better be giving her bad news.

Derek stepped forward and shook the Colonel's hand. "Glad you could make it, Mike."

"Thanks. Happy to be here, and I wouldn't miss this." He shook hands with the others while Alex looked on feeling like she was the odd man out.

As the group started to form a semi-circle around her, she nervously asked, "Derek, what's going on?"

The mystery man stepped forward and Alex's eyes almost bulged out of her head the second she recognized the freaking Secretary of the Navy standing in front of her.

"Alex, I'd like to introduce to you Craig Thornwall, SECNAV."

Alex stuck her hand out. "It is a pleasure to meet you, Sir. Not to sound rude, but why are you here?" Leave it to her not to be bashful.

He chuckled and offered her a comforting smile. "The pleasure is all mine. You seemed to have made a name for yourself young lady. I am here on behalf of the President of the United States."

Alex paled and swallowed hard. "I'm sorry, did you say the President?"

He smiled. "I did. Your actions in Afghanistan didn't go unnoticed. Because of your bravery and courageous acts, you saved the lives of many people." He pulled a square black box from behind his back and opened it revealing a beautiful medal.

"Alex, on behalf of the President of the United States and the United States Navy, I'm honored to award you the Presidential Medal of Freedom Award – the highest medal awarded to a civilian for your unquestionable selfless actions in battle that resulted in the outcome of bringing down a powerful organization and the securement of stolen weapons."

Alex held the medal in her shaking hand not sure what to say. Hell, she didn't know if she could even speak.

Derek took her hand in his.

"Alex, this is something that I'd have loved to share with everyone. But I know that you don't like the whole dog and pony show. However, everyone standing here now wanted to be present, and the timing worked out perfectly. Colonel Johnson and I were able to pull a few last-minute strings and Craig here happened to be in Norfolk today and had time to stop by."

Taking a few deep breaths, she managed to compose herself enough to finally speak.

"This is mind-blowing. Thank you." She reached out to shake the SECNAV's hand.

He surprised her when he pulled her into a gentle hug. He wasn't that tall of a man, but he still had a couple of inches on her. Patting her on the back he whispered so only she could hear. "This country along with the rest of the world owes you more than a medal. What you uncovered has saved millions of precious lives."

He stepped back and pulled an envelope out of his jacket pocket. "I almost forgot this." He handed it to her.

She opened it and found two pieces of paper. One was a payoff notice to the mortgage on the building she had purchased for her foundation, and the second was a check for $350,000 made out to the Jacob Hardesty Foundation. "What is this for?"

"That was the reward the government was offering for Ashraf. Derek said you wouldn't accept the money personally, so we put our heads together and found a way for you to still benefit from the funds. We paid off the mortgage to your building and the rest of it can be used to help people. You're doing a wonderful thing, and from what I hear you'll be getting a lot of funding in the near future."

With an apologetic look, he said, "I hate to run but I am supposed to be meeting my wife and sons in about thirty minutes."

While everyone said their goodbyes, Alex snuck off to the other side of the patio where she could take a breather. She leaned against the railing and stared down at the items in her hands. As much as she appreciated it, she hated being reminded of that time in her life. She had worked hard over the months to try and purge it from her memory.

She felt a few tears slip down her cheek and she quickly wiped them away.

"Alex?"

Hoping she didn't look that bad she took in a deep breath and turned. Ace was staring at her with a concerned expression.

She wiped her eyes again, smiled, and gave a throaty laugh. "I'm sorry. I'm not quite sure what came over me. I genuinely appreciate all of this. But you guys were right. I wouldn't have wanted all the attention. This was perfect. Sharing this with all of the important men in my life means a lot."

"So, is it really true what the SECNAV said? About the weapons being found? That's where you guys were." They stood staring at her with amusement in their eyes, but nobody said a word. "Oh shit. I'm sorry. Pretend I didn't even ask." She was waving her hand in the air and everyone laughed.

Derek grabbed her hand. "Let's just say the world is a little safer today." He winked at her.

A smile crept upon her face. "That is probably the best news and Christmas present I received today." She got up on her tiptoes and kissed his cheek.

Changing the subject Stitch asked, "What do you say we go in and start opening presents? I think the kids' patience has worn off and I'm afraid if we don't let them open their presents soon, they are going to start attacking the Christmas tree on their own. Look at them." He said, motioning toward the massive twelve-foot tree that stood in her living room and the many kids that surrounded it. "They're all sitting around the tree looking like little soldiers planning their attack."

Alex laughed and led the team inside.

Once the kids all opened their gifts, they moved into the game room leaving the adults in the living room. Everyone was engrossed in conversation. Alex looked around the room hoping to find her man. Hearing his booming laughter, she found him perched on the arm of the couch talking with Stitch and his sister Mia. Seeing him smile made her happy.

With everyone enjoying themselves and everything under control Alex walked through the kitchen toward the back patio needing to get some fresh air and some alone time. She loved her family and friends, but going on only two hours of sleep and preparing the food and getting the house ready was wearing on her and fatigue was starting to set in.

She stepped outside and was hit by a blast of frigid night-time air. Padding over to a lounge chair she sat down, curled her legs up under her, and laid her head back to look up at the sky. It was a clear night and an almost full moon cast its glowing light illuminating the sky. The only sound was the faint laughter coming from inside the house. Yes, this was exactly what she needed right now. She pulled down the throw blanket that was hanging on the back of the chair and spread it over her body.

Once settled and snug under the warmth of the blanket she looked up again studying the stars. She smiled thinking of all the good that had been brought into her life over the past year. Being back in her hometown with her family and friends. Thankful for the new friends she'd made. Fortunate for the encouragement of her friends and family as she moved forward with her new charity, and especially their support in overcoming her PTSD. And, lastly, she was blessed to have met the man of her dreams. The man who swept her off her feet the moment she fell into his arms. The man who gave her his heart and a shoulder to lean on when times were tough. The man that she loved and would continue to love for the rest of her life. On that thought, she closed her eyes and let her mind drift off.

Back in the house Ace searched for Alex. He had one more present for her. One he couldn't give her last night when they decided to exchange presents in the bedroom after he had made love to her. He had kept her up into the early morning hours ravishing her body. He knew he was being a selfish bastard but being away from her for three weeks was torture. Checking the rooms upstairs he came up empty and hurried back downstairs. Walking through the kitchen toward the game room he saw Potter standing at the French doors leading out back.

"Have you seen Alex?"

Potter chuckled and slapped Ace's back. "Damn, you haven't been home for twenty-four hours and you already lost her?"

"Fuck you," he said punching Potter's shoulder. "Seriously man, have you seen her around? I checked upstairs already. I want to give her the present I had you pick up for me this morning. Where's it at anyway?"

Laughing and rubbing his shoulder where Ace punched him, he pointed to the room off of the kitchen. "I put it in your office under the desk." Then he tipped his beer bottle in the direction of the patio. "Looks like someone needed a nap. What you'd do, keep her up all night?"

Ace gave his best friend a smug smile and didn't miss a beat. "Yeah, and you would've too if you walked in on what I did last night." Christ, when he walked into their bedroom a little after midnight and found Alex bent over in the middle of their walk-in closet picking up a pile of clothes and wearing nothing but one of his t-shirts it almost made him come in his pants.

Seeing her bare ass set his alpha-male ego off and he didn't even wait to get her back to the bed. He used his booted foot to shut the closet door, walked over, and picked her up as she squealed in delight then he took her right there in the closet against the door. Yep, Merry Fucking Christmas to him!

"Really." Potter arched one of his eyebrows. "Now you've intrigued me. Care to explain?"

"Fuck no!" Potter threw his head back and laughed at the offended look on Ace's face. Wanting to know what the laughter was about, some of the other guys joined them and Potter explained making everyone laugh and causing Ace to stomp off in the direction of his office.

With the present in hand, Ace stood on the patio. He set the box down gently next to the chair then bent down and scooped Alex up before sitting down with her on his lap. He adjusted the blanket over both of them.

He looked down as she was blinking her eyes open. She must have realized she had fallen asleep because her eyes got really wide and she sat up quickly. "Oh god, I didn't mean to doze off. I just wanted to get some fresh air."

Ace chuckled and held her down until her head rested on his shoulder. She was so adorable when she got herself worked up. "It's okay. Everyone can take care of themselves for a little while longer. Everything okay?"

"MmmHmm…" She snuggled closer to him. "You're warm."
Ace laughed.

He brushed her hair away from her face and kissed her forehead. "I have another present for you."

She sat up. "Ace, you got me enough. I don't need anything else."

"I know, and I would've given you this one last night, however, I couldn't pick it up until today."

He loved the confused look on her face. "You picked it up today? It's Christmas and all the stores are closed. Plus, you never left the house today."

He kissed her nose. "I had help from an elf—a very large elf."

He leaned over and picked up the box with a blue and gold bow on the top and set it on her lap. "You can't shake it. Just pull the top off."

Ace watched as she removed the top then gasped as she peeked inside. "Oh my god! You got me a puppy?" She was smiling from ear-to-ear and her eyes were lit up like her Christmas tree.

"I thought you might like some company when I'm gone. But he will have to share you when I'm home."

"Oh, he's gorgeous." She lifted the sleepy chocolate lab puppy out of the box and snuggled him against her chest. "How old is he?"

"Nine weeks." He reached down and scratched him behind his ears and the puppy yawned.

"We need to find an open store. He needs food, toys, a collar, and a leash. Oh! And we need to give him a name. What do you think about the name Zuma?"

"It's interesting."

"Zuma is a cartoon character on the show Paw Patrol." She held up her hand. "I know what you're going to ask. My uncles' kids watch it and when I babysit them that's all they watch. Anyways, there is a chocolate lab and his name is Zuma and he loves water. See he already has something in common with his daddy."

Ace couldn't hold his laughter in any longer. She was too cute. He put his arms around her and the puppy.

"I've already gotten everything for him that he needs, at least for tonight. It is all in my office. Derek and Juliette knew and picked up everything for me. And, as far as his name, I love it."

"Thank you, Ace, I love him." She tilted her head up and kissed him. Pulling back, she met his blue eyes that held a twinkle to them. "I love you so much. I'm so lucky to have you in my life."

"I love you too, sweetheart. You mean the world to me."

He let out a sigh. "I had this all planned out for later, but I think right now is the perfect moment. Just you, me, and the new addition to *our* family." He gestured toward the now sleeping Zuma on Alex's lap.

જી

Ace was so nervous. Looking from the dog in her lap back to her face, he took her left hand in his and brought it to his lips.

"I love you, Alex. You were a treasure that I never expected to discover in the sandbox." He gave her a crooked smile and winked. "You were a true gem considering the sandboxes that I've played in."

She laughed and he placed their entwined hands over his heart. "I want to spend the rest of my life with you. Hearing your laughter, your sassiness, and you being you. I've always told you that you were mine, and I was never letting you go. You stole my heart the moment I stepped into your sandbox. Marry me?"

Releasing her hand, he reached into the chest pocket of his shirt and withdrew a ring. A simple one carat princess cut diamond in a white gold setting.

With tears running down her face she placed her palm against his cheek and leaned in so that her lips were just over his as she whispered, "Really?"

He smiled. "Really, babe. What do you say? Will you be my wife?"

She bobbed her head up and down. "I need to hear the word sweetheart."

A big grin broke out across her face. "YES!" She shouted startling little Zuma. "I'll marry you."

Taking her hand, he slid the ring on her finger. "You've made me the happiest man." He whispered as he pulled her in for a kiss.

"Come on, sexy. Let's go introduce Zuma to everyone and announce our news."

As he reached for the door he turned around and caught her admiring her ring. He couldn't wait to make her his wife.

When they stepped into the kitchen, Tenley and the guys were standing around talking. When Alex glanced over at Tenley, Alex knew immediately she was busted.

Tenley, not one to hold back with words shot her eyes over to Ace. "What in the hell did you do?" Spoken in a stern voice she had caught the attention of pretty much everyone, and before either Ace or Alex could reply she noticed the puppy in Alex's arms.

"Oh my god. You have a puppy." She hurried over to pet it. "He or she?"

"He. His name is Zuma" Alex said giving Ace a wry smile.

"He is so freaking adorable. Wait a second. Don't try to distract me with the puppy. Why does it look like you were crying?"

"Because I was," Alex answered, keeping her answers short. She was going to make her friend work for it.

"Because he got you a puppy?"

"No." Alex looked up at Ace and smiled.

"What the hell 'friend'? Then why were you crying?" She asked as she reached for the puppy to hold him. Just as Tenley reached under his belly where Alex's left hand was, Alex knew the moment Tenley felt the ring. Her eyes snapped to Alex's, and Alex nodded her head at the silent question. Tenley's face split into a wide grin. "Holy shit! You're engaged!" She shouted and the room erupted into shouts of congratulations. Lots of back-slapping and hugs greeted the newly engaged couple. Alex handed off Zuma to Ace so she could show her ring to everyone.

Potter opened a bottle of champagne. "I think this calls for a celebration."

After everyone migrated to the game room, Alex found herself standing in front of the Christmas tree. She scanned the tree looking at all the decorations. Most of the ornaments had a meaning or story to them. Some were her father's, and some were hers she had collected through the years. She spotted the newest ornaments that Diego had given to her for her birthday. Her eye then stopped on one that had a picture of her dad on it. She unhooked it from the tree and placed it in the palm of her hand. *"Merry Christmas, dad."*

Sensing someone behind her, she turned her head and saw Ace standing there with a beer in each hand. He stepped up to her and placed a kiss on the top of her head.

"You've had one hell of a day. How are you holding up?"

She took a sip from the bottle. "I think I'm doing surprisingly good, considering. I mean how many people can say they got a puppy, a million dollars, and a fiancé for Christmas? This has been the best Christmas I've had in a long time." She wrapped her arms around his waist and rested her cheek against his chest. He placed his chin on the top of her head.

"I love you, Alex."

287

"I love you too, Ace."

Six months ago, both Ace and Alex set out on a journey. A journey where finding love was least expected, until the one afternoon where fate brought them together. Before their run-in, if anyone asked either one if they believed in love at first sight, they would've said no. They each found their future in one another. Ace found a woman who would stand by him, support him, and love him while Alex found a man who would protect her, support her, and love her. This was their home, their future.

EPILOGUE

After most of the guests had left and Ace's family had retreated to their rooms for the night, only the SEALs, Alex and Tenley remained.

The guys were sitting around the TV watching the news. Earlier it was reported a 7.8 magnitude earthquake had rocked the northern coast of Ecuador near the Colombian border.

Details were still coming in, but it was said there was major widespread damage. Fatalities had been confirmed, however their government was not releasing a number yet. Sources were estimating it could reach into the thousands.

Aid from countries across the globe was already pouring in, including the United States.

"I still can't believe that you're engaged."

"I know," Alex said to Tenley as she admired her ring. "I'm still getting over the shock of it myself."

Tenley reached over and put her hand over Alex's. "I'm really happy for you, friend. Who would've ever thought that you would be engaged to of all things, a Navy SEAL?"

Alex laughed. "Yeah, I never saw that coming."

"But I have to say, you snagged yourself a good man. I can tell he adores the hell out of you. You are one lucky woman."

Alex noted the sadness in Tenley's voice. Something was bugging her friend. For the last month and a half, Tenley had kept more to herself. She hadn't wanted to hang out as much, and she had also kept a distance from Potter, which puzzled Alex because things had seemed to be going in the right direction for the two of them.

"Tenley, I've been meaning to…" She was interrupted when Tenley's cell phone rang.

"I need to grab that. It could be the hospital. They've been short-handed the last few days and I told them to call me if they needed me."

Tenley grabbed her phone and walked out of the room. Alex didn't miss the way Potter's eyes followed Tenley out of the room.

Ten minutes later Tenley walked back into the room.

"Everything okay? You look a little frazzled." Alex asked. Potter must have seen the strained looked on Tenley's face as well because he was up and walking over to where they were standing.

Tenley grabbed her purse and coat off the bar stool. "That was the humanitarian organization I volunteer with through the hospital. They've been called in to assist with the relief for the earthquake victims. They were calling to ask if I was available to help assist."

"You're going to Ecuador? When do you leave?" Potter asked not looking happy at the news that Tenley was leaving. It seemed to Alex he wanted some alone time with Tenley.

"Tomorrow morning."

"For how long?" He questioned.

She shrugged her shoulders. "I don't know. We won't know until we assess the situation down there. They said it could be weeks."

Alex watched the back and forth between Tenley and Potter. Seeing the tension between the two pretty much confirmed there was something definitely off.

"We need to talk before you leave," Alex said grabbing Tenley by the arm, and pulling her down the hall toward the kitchen. Once in the kitchen, Alex swung Tenley around. "Okay, fess up. What's up between you and Potter?"

"Nothing. Why?" Tenley snapped looking surprised by the question.

"Because since you two started dating, you've been making progress in the relationship. And now for the last month, there is obviously friction between the two of you. Not to mention the way you avoid hanging out with us. So, stop blowing smoke up my ass and tell me what's got your panties in a twist."

Tenley shook her head and lowered her voice. "Please Alex, I don't want to talk about it. Not right now. But just so you know, nothing can happen between Potter and me. Just let it be."

Alex squinted her eyes and put her hands on her hips. "He didn't hurt you, did he?"

"God, no! I'm just going through some stuff I need to deal with, and, I can't involve anyone else. Okay?"

Alex eyed her friend. She could see Tenley was struggling. She knew that both she and Potter were right for each other. Everyone could see it, especially when Potter had all but marked his territory when other men congregated around her, and, the way Tenley looked at Potter told a completely different story than the words coming out of her mouth. Her friend had it bad for a certain Navy SEAL. Now Alex just needed to figure out what was holding her friend back and give her a little nudge.

Alex let out a sigh. "You're scaring me, friend. But for now, I will respect your wishes. When you get back from your trip, you and I are going to sit down and talk. I'm worried about you."

Tenley hung her head in defeat. "Whatever. Give me a hug. I need to get going so I can pack."

Alex hugged her friend, giving her a good squeeze. When they finally let go of each other all of the guys had come out to the kitchen. They gave Tenley a hug, and some even lectured her on her safety.

ço

When the last team member said good-bye Potter stepped up to Tenley. "Come on, I'll walk you home."

Tenley bit her bottom lip. Her nerves were at an all-time high. *Just let him walk you home.*

"Okay," she told him as she prayed nobody was watching her house. The last thing she wanted was to place him in danger.

"Be safe and call me when you can." Alex offered a wave before Tenley gave her a small smile then turned and walked out the door with Potter following.

The walk next door to Tenley's house was done in silence. At the front door, Tenley turned to face Potter.

The glare he gave her was intense. So intense that she wanted to look away, but she couldn't. She was drawn to his black eyes, and she could tell those eyes were trying to see through the imaginary shield she had put up.

She felt guilty. Guilty of a lot of things, like lying to her best friend and Potter. She cared for him so much. Who was she kidding, she was already in love with him, but she couldn't act on those feelings. She had to protect him, and anyone else for that matter. She had gotten herself into a bind and didn't have the first clue as to how to get out of it.

Potter's voice pulled her from her thoughts. "Tenley, I don't know what happened to make you pull away from me, but I'm telling you right now, I'm not ready to see our relationship end. You have some concerns floating around in that mind of yours and whatever they are, you and I are going to get to the bottom of it."

Her eyes started to tear up. "Please Potter, You don't understand."

He stepped closer to her. "Shhh, we're not getting into it now. Now is not the time to hash it out. I'm just saying that when you get back, we're gonna talk. No more bullshit and no more running."

Before she could respond he leaned in and took her face between his large hands and kissed her. Not the hard demanding kiss she was used to getting from him, but a tender and passionate one.

Getting caught up in the moment of enjoying Potter's mouth on hers, she stupidly had forgotten there could be eyes on her. That thought was like dumping a bucket of cold water on her.

Placing her hands on his chest she gave a little shove breaking the kiss. "I'm sorry. That shouldn't have happened. And, it can't happen again," she told him, looking down at her feet. She was a coward and couldn't even look him in the eye, knowing if she did, she wouldn't be able to hide the truth from him any longer.

Taking his index finger and putting it under her chin he lifted it until her brown eyes were locked on his. "Don't deny what we have Ten. I know you feel it."

She silently stood there wishing she could let him in but if she did, she would be opening the doors for evil to enter their lives. Evil had already taken something from her. A precious gift that Potter had given her that she would never be able to get back, and now that same evil didn't want to relinquish its hold on her.

He leaned in and gave her one last quick kiss on the lips, then dropped his hand as he stepped back. "Stay safe Tenley." He turned and walked away, leaving her standing there staring at his retreating back.

A lone tear slid down her cheek.

"I do feel it," she whispered to herself.

Maybe going away for a few weeks would be a blessing. It would give me some time to come up with a plan to take back my life and claim my Navy SEAL.

Read Potter and Tenley's story now!

293

BOOK LIST

The Trident Series
ACE
POTTER
FROST
IRISH
STITCH
DINO
SKITTLES
DIEGO
A Trident Wedding

The Trident Series II – BRAVO Team
JOKER *(2022)*
BEAR *(2022)*
DUKE *(2022)*
PLAYBOY *(2022)*
AUSSIE *(TBD)*
NAILS *(TBD)*
SNOW *(TBD)*
JAY BIRD *(TBD)*

ACKNOWLEDGEMENTS

Wow! I don't even know where to begin. When I set out on this wild and unexpected journey my mind was filled with a lot of doubts. But with the reassurance of many wonderful people in my life, I pushed those doubts aside and got to work.

I couldn't have accomplished this dream of mine without the support of my husband and two boys. You guys have been my rock and cheerleaders. I love you three so much!

Susan Stoker – I cannot thank you enough for instilling the confidence in myself to follow my dream. Your words of encouragement mean so much to me.

Debbie R. – Thank you for not thinking I was crazy and being so supportive when out of the blue I told you I wanted to fulfill this dream. Not to mention, listening hours and upon hours while I threw ideas at you.

Vendie S. – You are probably the most thankful person to be reading this because it means the book is finished. I can never repay you for all the re-reads you did to make this book happen.

Christy F. – Thank you for being the most amazing best friend anyone could ask for. Your unwavering support means the world to me.

Lastly, I would like to extend my gratitude to all of my peeps (you know who you are because only a handful of you knew about this secret project of mine) for all the words of encouragement. I appreciate y'all so much!

ABOUT THE AUTHOR

Jaime Lewis is a *USA TODAY* bestselling author who entered the indie author world in June 2020, with ACE, the first book in the Trident Series.

Coming from a military family she describes as very patriotic, it's no surprise that her books are known for their accurate portrayal of life in the service.

Passionate in her support of the military, veterans and first responders, Jaime volunteers with the Daytona Division of the US Naval Sea Cadet Corps, a non-profit youth leadership development program sponsored by the U.S. Navy. Together with her son, she also manages a charity organization that supports military personnel and their families, along with veterans and first responders.

Born and raised in Edgewater, Maryland, Jaime now resides in Ormond Beach, Florida with her husband and two very active boys.

Between her day job, her two boys and writing, she doesn't have a heap of spare time, but if she does, you'll find her somewhere in the outdoors. Jaime is also an avid sports fan.

Follow Jaime:
Facebook Author Page: https://www.facebook.com/jaime.lewis.58152
Facebook Jaime's Convoy: https://www.facebook.com/groups/jaimesconvoy
Goodreads: https://www.goodreads.com/author/show/17048191.Jaime_Lewis
Instagram: authorjaimelewis